Also by Carrie Merrill

Angel Blade
Book I in the Angel Blade Series

What readers have said about *Angel Blade*:

"Fast paced with rich imagery."

"Keeps you engaged and wanting to read "just one more chapter."

Daemon

Carrie Merrill

SOUL FIRE
PRESS

an imprint of
Christopher Matthews Publishing

Boston, Massachusetts

Daemon

Editors: Jeremy Soldevilla
Cover design: Neil Noah

ISBN 978-1-948146-10-7
ebook ISBN 978-1-945146-11-4

Published by
Soul Fire Press

an imprint of
CHRISTOPHER MATTHEWS PUBLISHING

http://christopher matthewspub.com
Boston

Printed in the United States of America

To my parents who tried to raise me right,
even though holy water sizzles when it touches my skin.

Acknowledgments

This book would not be possible without the endless hours of encouragement and help from my family. I would also like to thank the numerous friends and acquaintances that gave Angel Blade such a beautiful welcome. It is through all of you that I have been able to continue on this journey with Daemon.

Only with the help of Jeremy Soldevilla is this work possible. He had made every step of this process enjoyable.

A special thanks goes to the cover designer, Neil Noah. Say what you want about judging a book by its cover, and these covers really explode. I love them and the fans love them.

My stories would not get the fine tuning they need without my beta readers: Honey, Heather, Shanien, Natalie and Sunny. You guys are the best.

And a special shout out to a great woman and probably my number one fan. She has been supportive in so many aspects of my life, including my writing and my "day job." Thanks to you, Cheryl Yasuda, for your support and love. Your bravery in the face of cancer would frighten any demon.

In the Beginning . . .

Daemon is the continuation of *Angel Blade*, the dark story of Nikka Connors, who was dying of cancer until a stranger provided her with a cure, but it came at a steep cost: she had to become a seraph, an angelic being with the power to exorcise and destroy demons.

With Gideon, the stranger who introduced her into this life, she learned of the battle between Heaven and Hell and about the part she must play to fight the demon horde and destroy Abaddon, the Prince of demons.

Then she met Jason, a man with a troubled past who also brought the promise of a normal life. She could have escaped with him, but she could not run from her fate.

In the great battle with Abaddon, she saved Jason but lost Gideon when he fell into the portal to Hell, where all forms of demonkind entered into this world.

Part Three

Daemon (dee-mun, noun): (classical myth and legend) a demigod;
the guardian spirit of a place or person.

—Collins English Dictionary,
Complete and Unabridged, 12th edition

CHAPTER 1 JASON

At first he only heard the sound of rocks crumbling around him, one after another. The smell of fire and char made him open his eyes, but everything was so blurry, like he was caught just under the surface of a murky pond.

He forced his hand to move, to try and clear his eyes, and that was the moment he realized that he could do it himself. For months, he had no control of his own body. But now, his arm moved at his command. The other voice was no longer present, whispering those vile and disgusting things into his brain.

He blinked his eyes, and the murk cleared just a bit, but only for a moment. Everything around him was so dark.

But then he saw an angel. At least, that's what he thought, because there was no other way to explain the woman before him. Her face was perfect. He had seen her before in a painting or a book or something. He couldn't remember where. He only knew that he longed to look at her and never turn away.

The angel's lips moved, but she made no sound. There was only the muffled noise of a voice in water. Why couldn't he hear her?

Jason blinked again, and her face grew clearer. Then the pain of a dozen bruises pulsed and ached throughout his body.

The angel still looked at him, but her eyebrows creased together in concern. Her eyes glistened with the reflection of a blazing fire somewhere around him.

And he realized she had no hair on her bare scalp. He had definitely seen her before.

She was no angel, but she might as well have been one.

"I know you," he said; the words felt like hot tar in his throat. He could hear his own voice now. "You're real."

"Yeah," she said. Her voice was no longer lost in murky water, but clear and crisp, and it was a voice he recognized. He had heard it so many times before through his hijacked ears.

No. He was sure she was no angel now. An angel never saved his life, but this woman did. He remembered the pain of it as her hand plunged into his chest, burning white light tearing into his soul. When it happened, he thought that he was going to die. But then she freed him. She took that spirit—or whatever it was—right out of him. After that, everything was just dark smoke and haze. For weeks he had prayed to the thought of her in his memory, begging her to not let him die. And she must have heard his prayer.

"I remember you," he said. He felt his lips moving and words pouring from his mouth as though he couldn't stop himself. His head cleared just enough to hear himself say, "I think I was in love with you."

Shit. Why did he just say that?

Her hand grasped his. She was small, but definitely not a waif. Her grip was strong as she helped him to his feet.

He wasn't sure that he was quite ready to stand, but he opened his eyes again. Every sound came sharp and crisp to him as his ears cleared from the dull and muffled noise that he had first heard. He now saw the source of the smoky smell, and turned to face the crumbling walls of the monastery.

He had done this. All this destruction had come through his hands.

No. Not his. *Abaddon.* He hadn't actually done any of this, but he distinctly remembered being there when it happened and feeling helpless to stop it.

Jason glanced back to the woman that had saved him. Nikka. Yes, that was her name. She stood strong before him, her face and arms dusted with a layer of ash and blood.

CHAPTER 2 NIKKA

The brick walls fell in heavy chunks of dust and masonry all around her. The north wing of the old monastery had already collapsed, and she was sure that the remainder of the church would soon follow. There was no time left to linger around and deal with the unusual situation she now faced with Jason. It would have to wait for now.

The wound in her shoulder, where Abaddon had stabbed her, still seeped with blood. Every movement of her left arm ached into the wound. When she tried to move from her knees, a shot of pain lanced into her hip where a bruise began to form. A distinct reminder of her tumble into the trench that now gaped open around the church. Another portion of the north wing wall fell, reminding her that she needed to get moving.

She helped Jason to his feet, and he staggered for a moment before catching his balance. Despite the shadows that played between them, she could see the faint moonlight reflected in his blue eyes.

"You okay?" she asked.

He nodded, bits of debris falling from his blond hair. "I will be once we get outta here."

A large section of the north wall collapsed to the ground. The sound must have startled him because he gripped her hand tighter.

"My motorcycle is still out there in the trees," he said. "I can get us back into town."

Hearing him speak like this was a little more than unnerving to her. Not even an hour ago, he—or rather, Abaddon— was trying to kill her. And now he stood right in front of her, with his angelic blond hair and GQ model looks that had first caught her attention, and talked to her like he hadn't just tried to throw her into the trench.

The world around them began to fall in pieces of brick and mortar. She felt his hand in hers, and for a moment she wanted to believe everything would be okay. The heat of the fire that had breathed forth from the Hell pit under the downtown skyscraper still burned against her cheeks and she could almost smell the brimstone again. That pit had vomited up an alarming number of beasts, most of which she had no name for, and now these demons were let loose upon the world. As much as she would like to stop and just take an easy breath, she knew that it was not going to be possible. Not in this world.

Nikka nodded her head. "Okay," she said, trying to keep the trembling out of her voice. "I need to collect some things first."

Before he could stop her, she released his hand and rushed back into the shadows of the deteriorating church. The walls had grown black with a slick of ooze that now dripped down to the floor and pooled along the stairs. The dark beasts that Abaddon had brought with him, the same creatures that had infected her home, left this thick and sticky residue everywhere, and now it seemed to seep into every corner of the building.

She bounded up the stairs, taking two at a time and stepping over the black oil should the ooze take form and rise up to grab her legs. The floor beneath her feet creaked and groaned as she moved toward her former bedroom.

Everything that she needed should be here where she left it, including Gideon's laptop. She grabbed her backpack and stuffed the computer and a handful of clothes into the bag. The strap fit easily over her shoulder, and she moved to the door, but not before turning back for one last look at the empty room. The moonlight that shone through the single window cast over the barren bed.

There was a time not long ago that she had wished to never come back to this place, to leave forever and have a normal life again. This room once felt like a prison, but now she would give anything to have that time back.

To have one more day with Gideon.

The memory of the brimstone filled her nose again. The flash of flaming light from the depths of the Hell pit followed that odor. She could see Gideon's face again, feel his hand on her arm when they knelt together as the roar of the pit and the demons that belched forth filled the space in the basement of that building.

"You must live to destroy the rest of them," he said, but even now, his voice was so distant, like a hollow echo at the end of a long tunnel.

And then there had been fire and smoke and explosions everywhere. The ground had trembled around her and she found herself in the dark again. It was all a horrible and far too realistic memory, except the ground beneath her feet actually trembled again.

"Nikka," Jason's voice broke the silence from down the stairs and somewhere in the darkened floors below her. "Hurry. I don't think this place is gonna stay upright much longer."

She blinked back the tears that began to form in her eyes and gripped the strap of the pack before she turned and headed down the stairs.

The slits of light that shone through the windows lit their way through the corridors and to the main entryway. The cool night air brushed against the skin of her bare arms as they emerged into the driveway. The ground had since buckled, creating a crag that spanned over the overgrown gravel lot and had swallowed Gideon's car just after she had managed to escape it. Now, the crevasse looked like an empty, smiling mouth full of broken teeth in the earth, something that she was sure scientists would someday try to explain away as a powerful earthquake in the hills.

A tree had fallen in the aftermath of the quake and collapsed over the crag in the earth. Jason grabbed her hand, as though by instinct. This took her by surprise for a moment, but she let him lead her to the fallen tree, and they stepped over it together and into the brush on the other side of the crevasse. And, just as he had promised, the motorcycle stood hidden in the trees.

The ground trembled, and Nikka glanced back, ready to brace against another opening in the earth. A sound like thunder rolled through the trees as she saw the spires of the monastery collapse into the body of the building. A thick cloud of dust erupted from the falling church, concealing the remainder of the destruction from the light of the moon.

Her last remaining home had just caved in like ancient ruins—ruins of a life she would never get back.

She must have stood there looking back longer than she thought, because Jason's voice and the feel of his hand on her arm startled her.

"We need to get out of here," he said.

The cloud of dust flickered through the trees as she nodded. Without a word, she straddled the bike behind him as he started the engine, and they disappeared into the darkness of the wooded hills.

The bike hummed underneath her legs with each throttle Jason gave it. Her arms wrapped about his waist, holding him tighter along the turns. This reminded her of the first time she rode with him, back when he was just Jason to her and not the demon he had become. No matter how he felt against her torso, how he spoke to her, it was difficult to shake the memory of the evil in his eyes and his wicked smile when he had revealed the demon inside of him.

Before she realized it, they had emerged from the cover of the woods and into the edge of the city. Sirens wailed in the distance and the smell of smoke blanketed the streets. She had no doubt where this was coming from. The bike slowed as they approached the downtown area, now filled with throngs of people pressed against the barricades the police had erected around the block. The collapse of an entire building after an explosion was a little hard to ignore, and it seemed that half the city now collected around the block to see what had happened.

Jason veered down an alley, but not before Nikka glanced down the block to the pillars of smoke and dust that rose from the rubble of the building. Fire trucks had surrounded the area as well, and sprays of flame retardant erupted from hoses mounted to the tops of the trucks.

Such destruction. These people had no idea what happened here, and if she could do what she needed to do, they never would know.

The bike slowed to a stop at the base of an apartment building. Jason stepped away from the motorcycle, glancing back down the alley.

"What is it?" Nikka said, seeing the hint of anxiety in his eyes.

He grasped her hand again. "We've gotta hurry." He moved toward the entrance near the parking garage, and she didn't hesitate. Something had spooked him.

The back stairwell wound up three floors before he stepped out into the corridor. Dim lights shone over a red and gold carpet that extended the length of the building. As Jason led her down the corridor, she felt the air grow colder. The vibration tickled against her tattoos, which now began to sparkle. She planted her feet and stopped him halfway down the hall.

He glanced back at her. "What's wrong?"

It was difficult to explain to him, but she knew which door would open to his apartment. She also knew that something would be lying in wait for them there. The marks on her arms undulated with a faint blue light that drew Jason's eye.

"Something's waiting for us," she said. "It's an ambush." Then she glanced back at him. "Are you sure you absolutely need to go in there?"

His eyes had grown wide and he nodded. "I need something. If we're gonna stay hidden, I need to get in there."

The frosty air drifted from under the door, moving over her boots. "Okay, then."

He glanced around to the door of his apartment. Clouds of white appeared at his lips with every breath and Nikka knew he could feel it now. If he said he needed to go inside, then she would just have to open that door.

She reached behind her and withdrew the katana. Blue flames erupted down the length of the blade as she held it out before her and stepped around him to look at the door. The ache in her shoulder worried her enough now that she hoped that it was only a drone that waited inside the apartment. Otherwise, she may not have the strength to take it on.

"Just stay back here," she said to him and held out her palm to stop him.

The floor board creaked as she took a step toward the door. Her fingers wrapped around the doorknob, the metal like ice against her hand. She turned it and opened the door.

A light gust of air rushed from the room, accompanied by the smell of rotting meat. No light came from inside the apartment, and the darkness beyond the threshold was as thick as ink. She held the sword before her and let the blue flames act as her torch as she took a step into the black void.

"I know you're here," she called out to the demon that waited for them somewhere in the dark.

Something shifted in the shadows. Nikka's heart rate quickened and she stiffened her grip on the sword. Her eyes darted across the formless void inside the room.

A quick lash like a whip shot out from the darkness, wrapping about her ankle and yanking her into the dark room. She fell back hard and slid across the floor as the beast pulled her inside, her grip holding fast to the sword. The air rushed from her lungs when she hit the ground, but she caught her breath again as she slid further into the dark.

The cord around her ankle squeezed tighter as it pulled. She forced the sword around and swung it through the dark. It must have caught the thing around her ankle, because it suddenly loosened and she pulled her feet underneath her until she was able to get up into a crouch.

The beast lunged at her just then, and she saw it in the blue light of her sword. It was nothing she had seen before: squat and hairy, like a giant bull dog with ghostly white eyes and a mouth full of dripping teeth. A howl ripped from its throat as it came at her. She dodged to the right just as it rushed at her. The creature crashed into the far wall and the shelves that had lined it. Everything on those shelves fell down as the demon righted itself and moved toward her again.

Nikka held her sword in her right hand, since her left arm hurt too much to help hold the blade. She planted her feet, feeling every step of the demon shake against the floor boards. The monster growled and salivated as it came at her, faster and faster. It roared as it leaped toward her. The blade rose, and she twisted as she brought down the sword. The edge sliced something just as the creature rushed past her, catching her leg. She fell with the weight of it crashing against her. The demon's head careened across the room, but its body now collapsed into a heap of black oil that oozed from the neck stump.

The body of the creature had her pinned, but at least it was dead. Jason stepped to the open door, his silhouette filling the space and blocked the light.

"Nikka," he said and rushed toward her.

As he neared, the creature's body began to disintegrate into ash and settled in a heap around her legs. She shook off the ashes as she stood, her sword still in hand.

"What the hell was that?" he said and looked down at the pile of ashes in the middle of his apartment.

"Some new Hell horror," she said and re-sheathed the sword. "They know where you live. They must have sent him here to finish you off if you returned. So whatever you came here for, you'd better hurry."

CHAPTER 3 JASON

The sight of the creature Nikka had just killed still hovered like a ghost in the periphery of his vision as Jason shuffled into the dark room. Every corner of the apartment held a shadow that he could swear moved and crawled toward him. But he couldn't worry about those things right now.

He felt her eyes on him as he turned toward his bedroom and opened the dresser drawer. He found his backpack there and began to stuff it with items from his closet. A T-shirt. Jeans. A jacket.

"What are you doing?" Nikka asked. Her voice rebounded against the close walls.

"I've gotta get a few things," he said. His hand shuffled through a shoe box filled with so many things he should have thrown away years ago. But then he found the ring of keys and shoved them into the pack. This was the one thing he needed from this place, and then he could turn away forever.

But then he remembered the blood on her arms and down the front of her coat. There was one last thing to do. He ducked into the small bathroom and searched through the medicine cabinet until he found the first aid kit. He pulled it from the shelf and stepped back into the main room.

He crossed the large window in the front room that looked down toward the fallen building. The flashing blue and red lights lit up the far wall through the glass, reminding him of the destruction that had happened just a short distance down the street. He placed the first aid kit on the window sill and opened it in the light coming from the city.

"We don't have time for this," she said from the doorway.

He withdrew a roll of gauze and held it in the light before him. "Get over here."

She didn't budge, and he glanced back to where she stood. Her left arm still hung painfully at her side, but her face was tight and her eyes had narrowed.

"Get over here, please," he said. "You're right. We don't have time for this, so the longer you stand over there bleeding, the more time we waste. We need to get out of the city ASAP, and the clock is ticking."

Her tight jaw shifted before she took a step back into the apartment. "Fine. Just hurry."

She unbuttoned her coat with her good hand as she stepped toward him. The coat slipped around her shoulder, and she worked her other arm free to reveal the puncture wound. As the lights from the city fell upon the wound, Jason tried to not grimace at the sight. It must have hurt like a son of a bitch.

He wrapped the gauze around her shoulder and under her arm, all while trying to keep his eyes away from the black bra she wore just under her coat. She averted her eyes away from him, as though she didn't want to look at his face, but that made the tattoos along her neck and down her shoulder more evident. He couldn't help but notice them down her side, along her rib cage and to her hip as well. When he felt her stiffen, Jason glanced up to see her gaze on him. She had definitely seen him checking her out.

Jason cleared his throat and tied the gauze before she could say anything to him. She situated her coat again and buttoned it over her chest.

"We need to get going," she said as she walked over to the window and gazed down at the crime scene. Alternating blue and red lights illuminated her face.

He stepped up beside her. "That was a government building: the Department of Defense. Everyone is gonna think terrorist attack and there are cameras all over the city. Big Brother can see us everywhere."

"Big Brother is not our biggest problem right now."

"You and I are both on those cameras. Arriving just before it blows, and leaving right after. Big Brother is definitely a problem for us."

She looked at him, her blue eyes faint in the flashing lights through the window. As tough as she tried to be, he could see the worry and fatigue in her eyes.

"So they're going to be looking for us right now," she said.

"If they aren't, they will be soon. But it's your lucky day 'cause you have me." He flashed her a smile. It wasn't much, but maybe if he could exude enough confidence, then he could take care of them both. "We're gonna get out of town and off the grid until we can get all this under control and you tell me everything you know."

CHAPTER 4 NIKKA

Nikka held close against Jason's back as they rode down the highway on his motorcycle. It didn't take a genius to know why he kept to the backroads instead of the freeway. If anybody was looking for them, the main road would be the first place to find them.

The heavy smell of smoke still hung in the air, drifting from the rubble of the building downtown. As the wind whipped past her body, she rested her head against him. But this made it hard for her to see where they were going. Not that it mattered. Everything out here was so dark. The city was too far away now, and there were no more street lights. There was only the single light of the motorcycle that lit the way to their secret destination.

Even the night seemed to grow darker, so Nikka glanced up once to see the road had narrowed and trees surrounded them on all sides. At some point, Jason had turned onto an isolated road that had become a gravel surface and wound up the face of the mountain. There were so many foothills and peaks that surrounded the valley and the city; it was hard to tell where they were with so many trees. And it definitely wasn't the same area where she had been staying for so long in the monastery. No. The air here was much cooler, and they were far from the city at this point.

The bike slowed as the trees opened into a small clearing. There was no way she would have known that anything was actually within this space had Jason not brought them here. The woods kept everything in shadows, but she could make out the walls of a cabin in the dark. This place was well-isolated from anybody who would wander through on that desolate gravel road.

Jason killed the engine, and they were plunged into immediate silence. The buzz of the motor still hummed against her legs and made her muscles feel wobbly when she tried to stand.

"Where are we?" she asked as she removed the helmet from her head. She hoped that her voice didn't sound too shaky.

"My grandpa's cabin," he said.

Gravel crunched under his boots as Jason stepped toward the structure and worked at unlocking the front door with the keys he produced from his pack.

Hmm. A cabin in the woods. Alone with a mysterious person that she didn't trust. Yeah, this was the beginning of every B-rated horror movie out there.

The trees behind her rustled, and an animal screeched in the distance. She felt her heart shoot into her throat as she jumped at the sound.

"It's okay," he said from the porch of the cabin. "It's just a barn owl."

She looked back at him and saw a faint reflection from his eyes. For a moment she half expected to see that hellish orange glow coming from inside his skull like two embers in the dark, but it never happened.

"Hey," he said, and she could hear his smile. "I swear I'm not gonna bite. It's safe here. I promise. Just let me get the generator going, and we'll have lights. Hell, I can even get a nice cozy fire started."

Well, not many serial killers would offer a warm fire, she supposed.

She forced her feet to move and stepped toward the front entryway of the cabin. Ahead of her, Jason unlocked the door and plunged into the dark of the room. She followed close behind him and felt the stale, cold air of a place closed far too long. The odor of old wood from the space inside the cabin combined with the pine from outside made the place feel desolate and empty.

Jason's face lit up as he clicked his lighter in front of him. The small halo of light cast gentle shadows over his face. He stepped to a table just inside the door and lit a candle in a glass jar. The firelight faintly glowed against the walls, but could not penetrate into the complete darkness of the room.

"Here," he said and handed the candle to her. "This is just a little something for light while I go out and turn on the generator."

Thank heavens, she thought. She was beginning to think that this little light was all that they would have tonight. The cold glass of the jar filled her palms as he slipped past her and back out into the night.

And just like that, she was alone in this strange place. She held out the light in front of her and stepped further into the cabin. The room smelled of dust and canvas, something she remembered of her days with her grandfather when she was a child. He had been an avid fisherman, and in his attempt to teach her how to fish, he took her on many trips with him. She remembered the smell of the wet canvas bags that contained the life jackets they wore when on the river. If she searched long enough, she was sure that she would find fishing gear somewhere in this cabin.

The walls, composed of stacked logs and the joints filled with a dark mortar, were bare until she happened into the kitchen area. She nearly stumbled into a cast iron stove set against the wall. She placed the candle on the top surface of the stove and turned back to gaze at the open door.

Everything had fallen quiet. She no longer heard Jason walking around the back of the cabin. With all that had happened tonight, she thought that the silence would be welcomed. But it was only unnerving. Too many things can hide in dark and quiet places; things that she used to believe were only stories to scare children. Those weren't just fairy tales anymore.

A rhythmic chattering started from somewhere outside the cabin and a light bulb at the doorway came to life. That light, no matter how small it was, became a relief and she let out a breath that she didn't realize she had held for so long. Jason appeared at the doorway and bolted the door behind him.

"Got it," he said as he turned to her. "I wasn't sure there would be enough fuel, but grandpa was always prepared."

He stepped up to a shoddy sofa against the wall and turned on another lamp sitting on a side table. This was the first time she could see the room all at once.

The cabin was simple but efficient in its layout. A single main room with an off-shoot kitchen and another door at the end. She glanced back to the small stove and saw a hardwood counter extending under a curtained window.

"We have everything we need here, at least for a while," Jason said and stepped to the plain white sink in the kitchen. "With the power from the generator, we'll have running water." He turned the faucet on and a stream of brownish-red water sputtered from the spigot. The pipes rattled and he immediately turned off the faucet.

He winced and looked back at her, his cheeks a little red. "I guess the pipes haven't been used in a while. But there will be hot water, I promise."

Jason then nodded toward the living room area. Nikka turned to see a small television sitting on a sawed-off tree stump that someone had turned into a makeshift TV stand.

"Grandpa couldn't stay here without some TV," he said. "He had it rigged with an antenna and got one of those digital converter boxes. He just wanted to know what was going on outside when he was up here."

He walked past her and opened the door at the far end of the main room. She stepped in to see a small bedroom and a full size bed covered in homemade quilts.

"Just one bedroom. You can stay in here. I'll crash on the couch." Jason smiled and pointed to another door within the bedroom. "Bathroom. No shower, but there's an old tub if you want to get cleaned up, and I promise that if you let the water run for a bit, it'll clear up."

He stepped back from the door as she stood there and looked at the simple room. Jason grew quiet, no longer the talkative host of his empire.

Nikka glanced back at him and saw him leaning back against the far wall, his hands stuffed into the pockets of his jeans and his eyes studying the floor.

"Thank you," she said. "For this. It'll work for now."

"You don't have to thank me," he said, but never looked up to her. "I owe you. You could have—no, you should have—killed me tonight, but you didn't. You saved me. I know it sounds old fashioned, but I owe you my life. Whatever is going on, I'll never leave your side. I promise."

She licked her dry lips. "You have no idea what you are promising."

"Yes, I do, probably more than anybody. I was stuck in that body for weeks, doing and saying things that I had no control over. And the things I did to you . . . "

"That wasn't you," she said.

"But I was there, and there was nothing that I could do about it. I saw everything. But I also knew what that thing was thinking. Whatever is going on, I can help you."

"I can't ask this of you . . ."

"You don't have to. And you can't get rid of me, either," he said as he smiled.

She turned away from him and gazed once again into the dark bedroom.

"Are you hungry?" he said before she stepped into the room.

Nikka shook her head. "No. I think I just want to rest." She wasn't ready to tell him that she really just wanted to be alone, away from him, the one that looked like Gideon's killer.

She didn't glance back at him. Of course he wanted to talk more, to learn more about everything that had just happened, but she was not even close to ready to talk about that right now. She just wanted a few hours of quiet and solitude. She closed the door behind her and flicked on the lamp beside the bed.

The room fell silent other than the creaking of the floorboards as Jason walked about the cabin outside the bedroom. She settled down on the edge of the bed, her eyes falling on the empty wall in front of her. This was the first time she had the time to herself to feel the trembling in her hands. She knew she was cold, but this was also something else. It was all the adrenaline and pain of the last few hours. The image of the wall before her blurred into ripples of tears that flooded her eyes. Her shoulders shuddered as she wrapped her arms around her torso.

Everything hurt so much now, and not just the bruises and lacerations that covered her body, or even the stab wound in her shoulder. Again and again, her mind replayed the last thing she saw of Gideon as he pulled Abaddon into the pit and to his own death by fire and brimstone. And it was all for nothing. Abaddon still came for her. The demons still poured from the pit. Gideon was dead.

What else was there for her now? How could she continue on without him? It was because of him that she was able to do what she did. He brought her into this life, and as difficult as it had become, she wanted to live it with him.

But that would never happen again.

She squeezed herself tight, afraid that she might fall into a thousand pieces. The cries shuddered through her body and she leaned down over the pillow and cried, hoping that Jason could hear nothing from the bedroom.

Chapter 5 Jason

Jason just stood there after Nikka closed the door, chiding himself for sounding so stupid.

Why did this have to get so awkward?

He heard her moving around behind the door and the squeak of the mattress as she must have climbed into bed. Finally, he turned away and moved toward the dark stove. At least getting a fire started was something that he could do to keep himself busy for now.

Ever since he woke up free from the demon, he couldn't seem to get rid of the subtle trembling he felt all over his body. He didn't think he was cold, but maybe a blazing fire in the stove might help to rid himself of that constant shaking. He placed pieces of dried wood into the belly of the stove and stuffed enough old newspaper shreds between the logs before he struck the match. It took several tries before the paper caught fire and extended to the remainder of the kindling. He closed the doors to the stove and felt the slow warmth begin to extend into the room.

Jason sat back on the couch and just watched the orange glow through the glass hatch on the stove. He wasn't sure how long he had been staring because he was still too distracted from the shaking. He held out his hands before him and saw the faint tremble in his fingers.

It would go away soon. It's nothing.

He clenched his fingers and rested his elbows on his knees as he watched the fire. For a moment, he closed his eyes, the dark now inviting and quiet. He just needed to rest his brain from all of this, from the events of the last twenty four hours, from the way Nikka looked at him.

A crack sounded from inside the stove like the sound of a gunshot, and his eyes flew open. But everything around him had changed. There was no cabin. No stove. Only fire from the depths of Hell. The glow filled the room in a blaze of orange and red that brightened. The heat roared in waves so hot that he could no longer breathe.

A deep gaping hole had opened below his feet, a pit that breathed out heat and fire and brimstone. And he could only watch as it tried to consume him, helpless that he couldn't hear himself crying out for help.

The image faded as he blinked his eyes. There was no pit. No volcanic heat. There was only the old couch and the stove.

But he shuddered and closed his eyes as he brought his hands to his face. His fingers clutched together, and before he knew what he was doing, a whisper of a prayer arose in his throat.

"Please help me," he said. There was nobody else with him, and Nikka surely couldn't hear him from the other room.

He stammered for a moment, unsure of what to do next.

"I've never done this before. So if you're listening, God or whoever, I need help."

The room remained quiet, not that he had expected to see a bright light or hear a blare of trumpets. There was probably nobody listening anyway, but it seemed to ease the shaking in his hands.

"I need to help her, but I don't know what to do." He paused again just in case he heard anything. Nothing.

"Whatever I did to have that demon in me, I'm sorry. Just tell me what to do."

The only sound in the room was the crackling fire in the stove. He even listened for any sounds coming from the bedroom, but Nikka must have fallen asleep. At least she wouldn't have heard him trying to pray for the first time in his life. Nothing else answered him, not even the smallest sign that anybody listened.

"Okay," he said and placed two fingers above his head. "Peace out, God, if you're listening."

He pulled a quilted blanket from the back of the couch, shook out the dust, and lay across the couch with the old quilt draped over his legs. The orange glow of the fire and smell of the burning wood reminded him of the last time he had been up to this cabin. He was sixteen at the time, and he had come up here with his grandfather to get away from his parents for a little while. That had been a time of difficulty, just after his first arrest and less than a year after his brother's death.

Jason closed his eyes. He never wanted to think about those things ever again, but here they were, infecting his memories. That was the past. Nothing could change that, no matter how much he wanted to.

Then he remembered the moment he had awoken to the face of an angel, who looked down at him for the first time as a free man. Even when the world crumbled around them, she had helped him in the ruined church.

A scream jolted him awake. At first he thought it was a dream or that he had imagined it, but as he blinked his eyes open, he still heard the chilling end of the sound. He wasn't sure how long he had been asleep, but it felt like minutes. He tossed the blanket aside and moved to his feet. The light of the fire had diminished to a faint orange glow. He stumbled past the couch, bumping his shin in the dim light, as he rushed toward the bedroom door where he could still hear Nikka crying.

CHAPTER 6 NIKKA

The heat of the fire seemed to thread into Nikka's throat and deep into her lungs as she tried to take in a breath. The flames burned through her chest, bleeding into her flesh as though her ribs would rupture at any moment. Nikka tried to scream, but the smoke rolled over her again. The haze cleared for only a second, long enough for her to see Gideon's hand grasping onto her wrist.

Her fingers clutched around his, but he began to slip from her grip. She leaned further into the hole and tried to pull him up to the ledge. A gush of heat and smoke belched from the pit again, followed with a deep glow of orange and red like a skim of blood on the surface of a pool of milk. Gideon looked up at her, his face speckled with flecks of ash. His hazel eyes pleaded for her help, but she felt him slip again.

"I can't hold onto you," she cried through the haze.

Nikka tried to tighten her grip and her fingers pierced through the flesh of his hand as though it was made of gelatin. The skin slipped from his bones like a wet glove. She screamed as she could no longer hold him, and his bloodied and sinewy hand slipped from her grasp. The smoke swirled as he fell into the pit, the blood dripping from her fingertips.

Her throat was raw when she jolted awake, the scream still lingering on her tongue. She sat up in the bed as the last of her cries dwindled into the absolute darkness of the bedroom. The cold mountain air that filled the cabin prickled against the skin of her bare arms. Tears flowed down her cheeks and seemed to freeze around her chin.

The last vestiges of the nightmare shuddered through her body. Her shoulders trembled as she covered her mouth, hoping to stifle the cries from her throat.

The bedroom door sprang open, and Jason's silhouette filled the threshold. Candlelight glowed from the jar in his hand and cast golden hues over his scant goatee. Even in the dim light she saw his wide pupils and his lips parted.

"Nikka? Are you okay?"

In that firelight, the shadows cast across his nose and cheeks brought back the memory of the ember orbs that once rested in his eyes, the eyes of Abaddon. It was merely hours ago that the demon had tortured Gideon and then tried to kill her.

It was all too much to take in and she could no longer bear to look at him.

"No," she cried, "stay away."

"But . . ."

"GET OUT."

He took a step back for a moment, the candle wavering in his hand. "Okay, I'm—I'm sorry. I didn't mean to scare you." Then he closed the door, leaving her in the darkness once again.

The scratch in her throat made her cough and nearly choke before she could catch her breath. She drew her knees up to her chest and wrapped her arms around them. At least in her small cocoon of space, she could try to sweep away the memories that plagued her. She rested her forehead on her knees and let the tears trickle down her cheeks as she shivered in the cold.

Earlier that evening she had slipped out of her sleeveless duster coat and into one of her T-shirts. Now she wished she had brought more clothing. November in the mountains was colder than most winters in the valley. The icy chill and the aftershocks of her nightmare made her bones hurt. And now she had to worry about Jason. She hadn't intended on yelling at him, but it just came out before she could stop it. Abaddon had been so horrible, and she still fought to separate the demon from Jason when she looked at him.

But she had to face it: he was here and Gideon was gone. Without Jason, she would be utterly alone and probably wandering the city or in police custody by now. And she had demonstrated her thanks by screaming at him just now. He would be totally justified if he kicked her out of the cabin and left her to fend for herself.

No. She had to make amends before it chewed at her any more. She wiped her cheeks with the heels of her palms and gathered up the quilt, wrapping it about her body as she stood and padded toward the door. The air in the main room was not much warmer than in the bedroom, but the stove light at least illuminated Jason's small space on the sofa. He sat up when he saw her at the door.

Nikka took in a short breath. "I'm sorry."

"It's okay. I understand."

"No, it's not okay." The quilt bunched around her feet in a pile of gingham stitchery. "You have helped me so much tonight. None of this was your fault."

She stepped around the couch as Jason made room for her.

"It's gonna take a while to heal from this," he said.

Her fingers gripped the edges of the blanket closed around her shoulders. "Every time I close my eyes, I see it happen."

"Post-traumatic stress disorder."

Nikka forced a smile. "Look who's so smart."

"Hey, I worked in a library." He flashed her a smile of his own. "PTSD is very real. I saw first-hand what it can do to people."

His voice had dropped just then, and she looked at him. He chewed on the inside of his cheek for a moment before he said anything else.

"When my brother came back from Afghanistan, he had nightmares for months. He would stay up for days at a time. He said he was afraid to go to sleep, like out of that horror movie, the one with the killer that comes for you in your dreams and all the kids do everything they can so they don't fall asleep."

"I didn't know you had a brother," she said.

His head moved in a slow nod. "I was about sixteen years old at the time, but my parents were so worried. They said it was PTSD, and it was caused by the months he served as an Army ranger. I guess he had seen some really bad things that screwed him up."

Her mouth had gone dry. This was the real Jason, the one she never had the chance to know. Although the fire light made everything look golden, she could see the color drain from his face.

"It was bad," he said.

She wasn't sure she wanted to hear any more. The story of his brother wasn't likely to end on a happy note.

"The point is, PTSD is very real and I understand," he said and finally looked at her.

A shiver rocketed up her spine like a seizure. He laughed when he saw her shoulders quiver.

"Cold?" he asked and stood from the sofa. "Okay, hang out here. Let me go get some more wood and get the stove going again. It'll warm up pretty fast once I get that thing burning."

Just as he moved around the couch, she grasped his hand. "Thank you."

"Of course. I told you—you can't get rid of me. No matter what." Then he was gone and left her in the dark once again.

It wasn't long before he came in with an armful of chopped wood, trailing a scent of pine and cedar into the cabin. As soon as he had the fire blazing, the chill of the cabin began to soften and the flicker of the flames behind the glass doors of the stove provided a gentle glow into the room. Jason nestled onto the sofa beside her.

With the warmth of the fire pouring over her, she leaned back against the couch. Although she didn't want to fall asleep again, she now felt the muscles in her shoulder loosen and the ache in her bones ease.

Jason rested back against the sofa as well, just inches beside her, close enough that she could feel the body heat rise from the surface of his arm. She could even hear him breathing.

This was the moment she wanted to trust him more than anything.

"I need to tell you about why we are here," she said.

He was quiet at first. "You mean in the cabin?"

She shot him a quick look with her eyebrow cocked. "No. I mean—in this situation. I want to tell you about what I am."

His breathing halted for a moment. "A seraph? The demon said it, but I didn't know what he was talking about."

"Gideon found me, brought me into this world as you know it. You see, I was dying of leukemia, final stages."

She sensed the muscles in his arms tighten. Nikka sat up and looked at him, at the ridges that had formed in his forehead.

"Gideon came to me and offered me this life, and I took it. The transition was painful, to say the least. But I woke up like this." She exposed her arms, the curve of the black tattoos appearing like shadows over her skin. "He said I was a seraph. Part of the deal is that I can see and destroy demons. I guess I can't see all of them. Some of them are master concealers, like Abaddon. But they are everywhere, and now they know who I am."

His spine stiffened. "What does that mean?"

"It means we need to be very careful. Gideon was my teacher, and he's gone now. When the pit opened in the basement of that building, so many things came out of it; things that I've never seen before. I'm not sure that I even know how to stop them anymore."

"He was your teacher?" His eyebrow rose a little.

Nikka looked away from him and felt the lump form in her throat.

"He was more than that, wasn't he?"

She nodded. "Yeah, he was. He died in that pit for me, and now I'm not so sure that I can live up to that."

"Yes, you can. I've seen what you can do."

"Oh, such faith—" she said and leaned back against the couch.

"Just rest for now. We're safe here."

If that were only true.

She felt his breathing even out again, but with that quiet movement, she couldn't help but think about Jason's brother. She had never heard of him before this night, but she could almost see him now. Camouflage fatigues. Helmet. Assault rifle propped against his shoulder. She wanted to see him smile, but he couldn't. Not anymore.

And she knew the reason why.

He didn't survive his psychiatric trauma. Jason didn't have to say it. She could see it in his face when he talked about his brother.

He had been a soldier, trained for battle. And yet he couldn't face the tragedy of what happened in the war. How was she supposed to do this on her own?

Chapter 7 Nikka

The hinges of the door creaked from somewhere in the cabin, rust rubbing against rust. The sound was enough to stir Nikka from her sleep. She climbed out of the bed with the quilt wrapped around her body and stepped out of the bedroom, every muscle and joint aching.

The daylight poured through the kitchen windows, dust sparkling in the shaft of light like tiny fireflies. She squinted against the bright light and glanced about the room. The hangover of her deep sleep still tangled her thoughts and she didn't recognize the place at first, but then she saw Jason step across the kitchen.

"Sorry," he said. "I didn't mean to wake you."

She rubbed her hands over her eyes. "It's okay. How long have I been out?"

"About five hours. You needed the sleep. I didn't want to bother you."

The last thing she remembered was falling asleep with her head back against the couch, but she had just walked out of the bedroom. Sometime in that five hours of sleep, Jason must have carried her into the bed. Even in her sleep, he was taking care of her, and that little niggle of guilt worked its way into her thoughts. He made sure she was safe and comfortable, and all she could think of was the way he had looked when Abaddon had tried to throw her into the crevasse.

Jason shifted through the kitchen as he produced a pan and a collection of wooden spoons.

"I hope you're hungry," he said and glanced back to her. "I found some powdered eggs and what looks like maybe pancake mix."

Nikka stood and wrapped the quilt about her body again. "Where did you get that stuff?"

"Cellar."

She followed his eyes to a hatch in the floor.

"Grandpa always kept a huge food storage down there. It's bigger than it looks. I think he even planned on it being a bomb shelter at some point." Jason went back to work, opening the foil package of powdered eggs.

"He was kinda crazy; always thinking that the government was listening in on his phone calls or whatever. He built places like this so that he would have somewhere to go if he ever needed to get off the grid. I used to think this place was his hobby, but then I realized that he was totally serious about this stuff."

In the daylight, the cabin appeared larger than she had first supposed. The windows above the kitchen sink opened out to the woods that were so dense that very little light penetrated beyond the small clearing around the cabin. Most of the trees had lost their leaves, but the pines that surrounded them provided plenty of protection from the winds that could sometimes sweep across the ridge.

"Well, he picked a good place to hide if that was his intention," Nikka said.

"I think it was." Those blue eyes glanced at her and he flashed her a dimpled smile. "He became one of those doomsday preppers."

"A what?"

"You know, the prepare-for-the-end-of—the-world types. He was about storing all sorts of food and ammo. He had lots of guns in the cellar. Everything ready in case of World War III. I used to think it was insane, but it sure came in handy today." He held up the empty package of powdered eggs in victory.

Nikka smiled. "Hooray for crazy old men."

Jason's gaze returned back through the window above the sink. "Looks like a storm might be moving in. I'm gonna need to get some gas for the generator and a few other staples just in case we get stuck here for a while. There's a convenience store just down the hill. You okay here alone for a little bit today?"

"I should be." The thought of being alone in the cabin deep in the woods was a little daunting, but she wasn't about to admit it to him.

"I think it would be better if it was just me going down there. If anybody is looking for us, the two of us together would trigger all sorts of alarms."

It made sense, as much as she would rather just have him around. But with him gone, it would give her an opportunity to glance through the laptop she had brought from the church. There was a lot of information she had taken from the system at the Department of Defense before everything went so wrong.

They ate their breakfast, with Jason doing most of the talking. She didn't really listen to most of it, though. She caught the occasional reference he provided about hunting with his grandfather or reloading ammo, but her thoughts drifted elsewhere. Before she realized the time had moved so quickly, he announced that he needed to leave for just an hour or so.

She wrapped herself in the blanket and followed him out of the cabin to another out-building that she had not seen in the dark last night. Jason unlocked the chain that bound two large doors, letting them swing wide open to reveal a dusty garage. The headlights of an old pickup truck gazed out into the bright morning as though it had just been awakened from the dead. Jason plunged into the darkness of the garage and emerged with two red gas cans that he tossed into the bed of the truck.

"Why not take the bike? This piece of junk doesn't look like it has rolled down the mountain in thirty years."

"Junk?" He placed his hand over his heart as though he had been wounded. "This is a classic. And practical. It was just another one of grandpa's doomsday things. It's an old diesel. He kept it in top shape because this particular model could withstand an EMP."

"A what?"

"EMP. Electro-magnetic pulse. Something that could wipe out anything electronic for good. But not this beast." He slapped the side panel as though it were a prize stallion. "I can fill the tank as well as the gas for the generator and load it with any supplies that we need. And I'm gonna get you some warmer clothes. At least a coat. You're making me cold."

"Alright, but just be careful. You see anything weird, then get back here as soon as you can."

"10-4," he said with a smile, his dimples accentuated by the shadows of the garage.

Nikka slipped back into the cabin as she heard the rumble of the diesel engine start. Soon, the sound of the truck disappeared into the hush of the forest around their small shelter. With him gone, the cabin fell into a deep silence.

She stepped into the small bathroom and gazed at her reflection in the mirror. The glass was only about the size of a sheet of paper and covered with a thin layer of dust, but she could still see the dark circles under her eyes and the hollow of her cheeks.

Her eyes fell to the gauze wrapped around her shoulder. The center of her wound had oozed blood that had since turned brown. She unwrapped the gauze and let it fall into the sink as she gazed at the wound in the mirror. Her fingers ran over the smoothed surface of her skin that had almost completely healed overnight. Even the pain had subsided, all thanks to her seraph power of healing.

But she felt as though she had lost another 30 pounds, just like when she was dying of cancer. Her collarbones didn't protrude from under her t-shirt, though, and her shorts didn't fall from her hip bones. She wasn't sick; just so drained that it was hard to breathe or walk or not collapse into the corner and cry until her eyes hurt.

The quiet of the cabin settled around her; the first moment of true silence since everything had happened. She had thought that if she could just get away from Jason long enough, then she would feel more at peace. After all, she still continued to see the memory of his face, those two points of firelight in his eyes, when he first revealed himself as the demon to her.

She closed her eyes and turned away from the mirror. It would do her no good to keep reliving that moment, to keep seeing Jason's face there. It wasn't him; it never had been. He had only been a puppet.

Now that Jason was gone, she began to feel his absence in the stillness that crept into every corner of the cabin. There was no true peace or comfort in that silence like she had wanted. Just loneliness. Maybe she was better off with him around, and she hoped that someday she would rid herself of the memory of him as Abaddon, if that was even possible.

A shiver danced over her skin, leaving its tracks in the goosebumps that formed on her arms. She wrapped her arms around her torso and stepped out of the bathroom and back to the main room. The backpack sitting in the corner of the bathroom caught her eye. The laptop inside could have some distraction for her; at least that's what she hoped. She settled onto the sofa and powered on the computer. The opening screen remained for an annoyingly long time before it loaded to the desktop. She clicked on the icon that Gideon had downloaded from the flash drive, the same drive with all the information she had taken from the DOD computer.

She had already seen the initial folders: a collection of photos of prominent politicians and other influential members of the city that were in the demon fold, maps and blueprints to the building and documents detailing the connection between the people in the photos. But there were so many files that they had never been able to review. The first few had taken so much of their attention that she and Gideon had stopped there.

She clicked through the next files and opened more blueprints of buildings she had never seen, and they appeared to be scattered across the country in other large cities. But there was no indication as to why the blueprints were important. And there were dozens of them. Nikka scrolled through the files until she could see something different. She clicked on the icon and several pages pulled up onto the desktop.

Again, the pages were collections of newspaper articles, research papers and other documents that seemed to have no apparent connection or meaning. How in the world was she supposed to make sense of any of this? There were articles on everything from shipping lanes on the East coast to weather conditions in Death Valley at any given time of year. And there were hundreds of articles in various folders.

Somebody took the time to collect these things, though. But for what purpose?

She felt like her eyes were going to start bleeding if she continued to try and make sense of any of this stuff. But her finger hesitated over the scroll wheel of the mouse when she saw a copy of an article. For a moment she wasn't sure if it was anything worth reading, but the title made her stop.

And it was all thanks to Jason. If he had not said anything about this just before he left, she would never have taken notice.

She read the title again: Test Simulations in Transient Electromagnetic Disturbance.

Her eyes scanned the body of the article as the butterflies of excitement fluttered in her chest. The scientific jargon meant very little to her until she saw the letters she had suspected would be there: EMP. Electromagnetic Pulse. This was an entire research article with construction directions on devices that could emit EMP.

What had Jason said about it? Something about EMP causing irreversible electrical damage.

Despite the long words and formulas that she couldn't understand, she was determined to read the article. This was the only file so far that made any sense to her at the moment and she was going to find out why it was on the flash drive.

She found a pen and paper scattered among the fishing and hunting magazines on the side table and began to take notes as she read, underlining those words that she didn't quite understand. The further she read, the more it began to make sense. The one thing she was sure of: the EMP was scary as hell.

The article began to detail situations in which specific devices were used. There was no way she was going to understand the instructions on building the devices, but she was sure that the situations and the results were far more important anyway. In one scenario, a device was built and powered with a series of batteries (as far as she could tell). Apparently, these things just needed a source of power. The results were not quite what she had expected, though. These devices sounded like bombs. The diagrams made them even look like bombs. But they did nothing so obvious as an explosion.

The paper began to detail the various ways the devices were utilized and continued to emphasize the same thing. Each time the device was detonated, it resulted in irreversible damage to surrounding electrical circuits.

Nikka felt her brow furrowing and her eyes hurting as she read this. Sure, this was something that Jason had referred to, but so what? So you take this device and shut down your mom's microwave. Big deal. Why would an army of demons collect something like this in their mainframe system?

She rubbed her palms over her eyes and sighed. It didn't make sense, and maybe this article was the least important thing on this entire computer. Maybe she was interested in it because it was the only thing that sort of made some sense to her. But it didn't seem to fit in the big picture.

She glanced back at the bag and felt around until she found her cell phone. Maybe a search engine could help make more sense of this. There was no Wi-Fi for the laptop, but perhaps she could get a small signal to search something that may illuminate this EMP thing.

The signal on her phone was stronger than she would have expected. Once she typed in EMP to a Wiki page, she scrolled down to the many results. Now she began to understand the gravity of what she had just found on the flash drive. She opened the first result and read the information provided in the link.

The moths of anxiety began to swarm like bees.

The EMP was far worse than she had initially thought. The web page detailed very disturbing scenarios in which an EMP device could be used and why it was important. She soon realized the key was irreversible damage. Irreversible. Like, there was no going back once the EMP was detonated.

The author described a hypothetical situation of a large enough device loaded into a truck or attached to a rocket. If detonated in the right area, or high enough in the stratosphere, it could irreparably damage all electrical circuits in the blast zone. All circuits. Everything from cars to hydroelectric dams to airplanes. The resulting collapse of the system could be devastating, taking years or even decades to repair such widespread damage. Such a device could effectively plunge the world back into the Middle Ages if planned right.

She turned back to the laptop and the article that still shone on the screen. What this detailed could be one of the most effective terrorist events in history. This was where she needed to start. What if many of the files on this drive stemmed from this very event? Now, she couldn't get through them fast enough.

The sound of the door opening and a cold breeze startled her. She glanced back to see Jason at the door. When she saw his face, she held her breath and waited for the images of Abaddon's fire-eyes to abate before she could force a smile.

"Hey, I didn't mean to scare you," he said and closed the door behind him.

"You're back already?"

"Yeah. It's been like two and a half hours. Sorry it took so long."

All of this had consumed so much of her time that she hadn't noticed that she had spent so long at the computer. "I—I lost track of time."

"I see that." He tossed a black hoodie on her lap over the keyboard of the computer. "Found this for you. I know how much you like these things." He rubbed his hand over her bare head as though tousling invisible hair. It was playful, but it did very little to ease her fears that had begun to eat away at her gut.

"Jason," she said as he walked to the kitchen. "I need to show you something."

"Okay," he said absently.

"No. Right now. This is really important."

He turned to look at her and he lost his smile. "Okay."

"I found something that is a little—scary."

Then she began to show him the paper and watched as the color drained from his face.

CHAPTER 8 NIKKA

Jason scrolled in silence through the pages on the computer for almost half an hour before he looked up at Nikka. He said nothing for a moment, but only stared at her with that crease he sometimes got between his eyebrows.

"Okay," he said and sat back in his chair, his hands folded over his torso. "We need to talk about a few things."

This was the first time she ever really talked to him about everything that had happened to her since waking up in the hospital. Everything. One day she was dying, the next she was a supernatural force with the power of angels who wielded the sword. And not just any sword: the very one that guarded the gates of Eden. Then there were the demons: hordes of them. Things that only she could see, and she was able to remove them from people. She told him about taking the information from the defense department computer. With that, his eyebrows seemed to rise on their own.

"Whoa. You've got to let me catch my breath." He stood and paced around the kitchen. "Some of this I get. I shared a lot of thoughts with—Abaddon," he said as though the word had turned to acid in his mouth. "I knew some things about you, but nothing like this."

She understood how he felt. When Gideon had told her these things, she couldn't believe any of it either, even when she held the sword that emitted the blue fire.

"But I don't understand what any of this has to do with national defense? Why do a bunch of demons even care about our military or government or any of this?"

Nikka shook her head. "I don't know. But it's there. It's all over that flash drive. I found that they have their hands in a lot of things. But it all has to be connected for some reason; I just don't understand that reason yet."

He turned to face her again. "And even if they are, what could we possibly do about it? I mean, we are talking the Department of Defense. They could be totally entrenched in state, even national governments."

Nikka smiled. "I asked Gideon the same thing once. He said that is why I was given this power. I'm the only one that can see them. I have to try."

Jason ran a hand through his messy blonde hair. "I know, but that's what scares me."

It scared her too, but she couldn't admit that to him. That, and the fact that she had only defeated Abaddon by some miracle. Her fingers absently touched the mark on her chest, the new tattoo that she had only acquired after something intervened before Abaddon almost killed her. She could still feel the pressure of the hand on her chest when it had placed the tattoo on her skin. The Being, perhaps an angel (and she almost thought it could be God himself), had touched her and she felt the power sear into her flesh. From that moment, she had the ability to pull an upper-level demon from a human host, without killing the human. How that happened, she would probably never know. Gideon had told her she would never be able to do that, so he probably was never aware of this mark that now gave a her a unique ability that no other seraph had ever been given.

She was ready to wield this power, but one thing nagged at the back of her thoughts. Was this the only new power she had been granted?

Her fingers pulled away from the mark just as Jason glanced up to her. "So what do we do?" he asked.

She shrugged. "We wait, I guess. I need to learn more, and there's hours of information on this flash drive that I haven't even touched yet."

The next morning, Nikka woke before sunrise, thanks to the never-ending nightmares that continued to plague her. Jason had not heard her this time, and this allowed her to slip into a pair of jeans and the hoodie without him coming to check up on her. She stepped into the autumn morning, which seemed so much colder on this side of the mountain.

No birds chirped at this time of year, at least not the ones she was used to hearing in the suburbs where she grew up. An occasional twill came from the frosty branches of the pines above her, but she couldn't see the creatures that flitted from bough to bough. She pulled the hood of the sweatshirt over her bare head, which helped to ward off the cold of the morning. With each breath, she felt a prickle of frost that filled the air work its way into her lungs.

She wished she could stay here forever, in this quiet and serene place where nothing could intervene with her attempt to recover from the last week. This place remained almost untouched by man, and therefore free from the taint of Hell. There was no smell of brimstone here, like a choking cloud of decay and death. The air was cold and clear and smelled like pine trees.

Nikka closed her eyes and tried to picture this place as it might look in the springtime. There would be so many more birds then; she was sure of it. The woods were fresh, alive with new life and tree blossoms that smelled like honey. What she wouldn't give to see it in the spring.

She hoped that she would have the chance to be here then.

A bird's chorus from the tree above her head made her open her eyes and glance upward. The bird sat among the pine boughs and sang its song, a lonely two-note rhythm. She saw the black stripe on the top of its head as it glanced about the woods. The small bird continued its song, seemingly unaware of her watching it. That little creature would still sing and sit there no matter what Nikka did from this moment onward.

She turned away from the tree line and returned to the cabin, hoping that she could just enjoy the days she had left here.

Chapter 9 Jason

When he first awoke, he thought he had heard the door open. He sat up from the couch and rubbed the sleep from his eyes. He must have slept much better last night. There were no dreams of him being trapped in his own body, and he hoped that there would be less of those thoughts in the days to come.

He stood and glanced back to the bedroom to see the door gaping open. It must have been Nikka he heard. He stepped to the window to see her walking among the trees down the driveway, her head tucked into the hood of the sweatshirt she wore. He wanted to go out there with her now. Being around her made his heart lighter and his head more clear, but she needed her space too. She had a lot to worry about, especially after they had seen what was on that flash drive.

All that stuff about EMP's and delivery devices. That was some terrorist shit right there.

He turned away from the window and toward the cabinets along the far wall. Back in the days when he would come here as a little kid, he recalled that his grandfather kept a bag here. With the threats that loomed ahead, he would need it now more than ever. Sure enough, when he opened the cabinet, the duffel bag still rested on the lowest shelf. He pulled it free and carried it to the kitchen table. Grandpa used to insist on keeping that bag there in cases of emergency. He once called it his "bug-out-bag", something to grab in the event that you had to bug out of there.

The bag still had weight to it, too. He unzipped it and began to withdraw the contents: a first aid kit, dried fruit, foil-packed and freeze-dried meals that would last a hundred years, a blanket, flashlight, batteries. Everything you would need in case of an emergency. Yeah, it was old and a few things needed changing out, but it had everything they would need if they had to run out of the cabin quickly. He pulled out the outdated packages of food and the old batteries. He could easily replace these the next time he had to drive to town.

He glanced up from the table as the door opened and Nikka stepped into the cabin. Her nose had grown a little red from being out in the cool morning, but her eyes were soft and at ease.

"What's going on?" she said and unzipped her hoodie as she looked at the bag on the table.

"After what you found on the flash drive," he said, "I thought we better get a little more prepared. It's a bug-out-bag."

She smiled and let out a small laugh. "A what?"

"Bug-out-bag. It's gonna have everything we need to get through a few days in case we need to leave in a hurry. I'll even put some of our clothes in here. And cash. We'll need money." Even though she hadn't worn it since they got back to the cabin, he made a mental note to place her cool duster coat in the bag. She probably tried to ignore it, since it was still covered in ash and blood. It looked like it had been hand-made and it seemed important to her.

She stepped up to the table and glanced inside the bag. "Wow. This is a really good idea. But it's kinda freaking me out. You really think we might need this?"

"Better to have it and not need it," he said. "With the cops looking for us, and everything that's happened in the last few days, I'd feel better with this. I'll place it next to the door so it's there to grab and go."

She reached in to the bag and withdrew a packaged silver thermal blanket. "Well, it still freaks me out. I mean the thought of having to run like that—"

Creases formed between her eyes. She had looked so happy when she first came into the cabin, the last thing he wanted to do was to bring her down.

"Hey," he said and touched her hand that held the package. "It's gonna be okay."

She pulled her hand away and dropped the package into the bag. "I hope so."

Chapter 10 Nikka

Her room was still dark when she opened her eyes. She wasn't sure what made her wake up, but she still felt the cold trickle of it against her neck. This was when she realized that she didn't wake up to a nightmare. This would be a first since they had come to the cabin a week ago. Her heart wasn't racing. Her throat wasn't dry from screaming and crying.

What had changed?

The creak of the door hinges first caught her attention. A shaft of pale moonlight shone across her bed. The light was too pale to make her squint, but she could barely make out a figure that stood in the doorway.

Everything had become still and cold, much colder than normal. She held her breath, waiting for the image at the door to disappear, just like the images in her dreams, but it only stood there as if it gazed upon her.

"Jason?" she whispered, but she knew the moment she said it that the shape was someone—something—else.

The figure moved its arm and motioned to her just before it stepped away from the door and disappeared into the moonlight.

Nikka waited for a moment. It wanted her to follow, whatever it was. Good or evil, it was now out there in the main room where Jason slept, vulnerable and unaware. She had to know what it wanted or kill it before it could strike.

She stood and padded across the room and pressed herself against the frame of the doorway. Each breath that trickled past her lips fell in quick bursts. Her fingers clutched the frame as she peered into the room.

Everything was dark except the light that came from the windows. Jason slept on the sofa, his breathing slow and even. The shadows remained still despite her attempt to adjust her eyesight in the dark. Nothing else stood there and watched her; the figure had gone.

It had to be a dream, or a hallucination. Something brought on by insomnia and waking nightmares. Maybe the dreams had changed. Maybe she was going crazy.

Then something moved beyond the periphery of her vision. She turned just in time to see a hand in the dark coming at her, but it was too late for her to move. The fingers touched her chest, right over the new tattoo.

Threads of ice flowed from its fingers and paralyzed her. She tried to breathe, but the air had grown as thick as gel. The darkness disappeared in a flash of blue and white light that enveloped her like a lightning storm. The light softened to a halo of indigo that surrounded the figure before her. The frozen tendrils that emanated from its fingers abated just as it stepped back from her. Nikka found her voice as the oxygen flooded back into her lungs.

The time has come.

It had no mouth. It didn't even have a face that she could discern. But somehow she could hear it speaking to her. It had a man's voice, or at least that's what it sounded like, and everything about him felt so familiar. That was the moment she could smell the faintest hint of lavender in the light.

"Time has come for what?" she asked.

He motioned to her again, this form composed of shadow. It stepped toward the front door and opened it, but beyond the threshold of the cabin now stood a wall of shimmering light. There was no dirt road, no forest of pine trees frequented by small winter birds.

See.

As he spoke she felt the tattoo on her chest throb. She glanced down to see the mark flickering with neon purple sparkles of light, the same way her other marks came alive when she wielded her sword, but the color had changed.

She understood now why this being was so familiar. This was the angel or spirit that had granted her power over the upper-level demons. It had placed its hand upon her chest and gave her this mark. He was a messenger.

See.

He urged her toward the door again. She stepped closer, the shimmering light at the door now almost blinding. She squinted against the light and held her hand up to shade her eyes.

See.

What was there to see? She could barely see anything through the light.

"I don't know what you want—"

The light flashed brighter for a moment before it faded into something else. The cold had vanished. She gazed out of the doorway and to a vast desert at night. The warm, arid breeze drifted over the threshold, tickling at her bare toes. The clear sky revealed a blanket of stars as clear as anything she had ever seen. The twinkling of the stars blended with the lights of a city in the far distance.

"What is this?"

She turned to him, his blank and dark face still absent of any form. The angel, or whatever he was, raised his arm out the door and pointed to the desert.

Nikka looked back out to the desert and scanned the barren landscape. A second later, a streak of light erupted from the dark and raced across the night sky. At first she assumed it was a meteorite, something that her father had shone her a few times when they watched the night sky from her back yard. The streak of light left a trail of sparkling fire and then disappeared into the sky. She realized she was holding her breath when she watched the landscape go dark once again. Just as she let her breath out, a brilliant flash of light illuminated everything. It reminded her of those old videos of an atomic blast with a delayed flash. She staggered back a step as the light rippled across the night sky.

Then the light disappeared. She half expected to feel the impact blast from where she stood, or a dust storm across the desert, but there was nothing. Just the barren silence of the warm night.

"I don't understand. What am I supposed to get from this?"

The landscape faded into dark and then warped into a view of the city. She figured it was the city she had seen in the distance. Lights and people were everywhere. There was so much life until she saw the flash in the sky. It was the same flash she had just seen in the previous vision. The lights of the city flickered and then everything went dark. The taxis and delivery trucks stopped in the street. Flashing neon signs died just like every spot of light that had once filled that great city.

The scene morphed again. It was the same city; she could tell by the street and the lamp posts and building that had surrounded it. But now it was daylight and something was terribly wrong. The streets remained deserted and the buildings appeared dilapidated and empty. Windows lay on the ground in heaps of shattered glass. The cars and trucks that had died on the road were still where they had stopped, only covered in a layer of dust. Everything inside of them had been stripped. It appeared to be the same city, only abandoned and dead.

See.

What else did it want from her? She had watched everything he had shown her, but his hand still pointed out to the street.

She scanned the streets, between the cars and along the sidewalks.

That was when she saw it.

There was a body lying between the bumpers of two cars. Then another one pressed against the wrought-iron fence at the edge of the sidewalk.

She understood what he wanted her to see.

"The demons did this?"

He lowered his hand and turned an empty face toward her.

"Are you saying that this is what I have to stop?"

The being no longer spoke.

Nikka felt a nervous laugh escape her throat. "This is the EMP, isn't it? All this—" She waved her hand at the scene of the dead city. "This is what an EMP will do?"

She felt her throat tighten as she staggered back again. "How am I supposed to stop this? This is missiles and global destruction. Apocalypse. What am I supposed to do about this?"

The scene flickered again, but this time it was no longer a vast landscape of death and destruction. She looked out over a series of cars, each more dented and destroyed than the last. Two men stepped around the front of the first car, and she recognized one. He was bloodied and filthy, but it was definitely Jason sporting an assault rifle against his shoulder. The other man walked at his side. His once-white T-shirt was torn and bloodied as well, and she saw a double gun holster over his shoulders. The man stood taller than Jason and about ten years older, but he looked strong, and Jason seemed to trust him. The man's dark blonde hair was short around his ears and neck, as though he had been in the military for far too long. Through the dirt and grime that had speckled his face, she saw the piercing gaze in his eyes.

"Who is he?"

Find him.

"Who is he?" she repeated, louder, as though he would tell her. "How am I supposed to find him?"

Where you left your battle.

She woke with a start, her ribs painful from breathing so hard. The air was cold again and her room dark. Nobody stood at her door this time. She was as alone as ever. The embers of her vision began to fade, but not before she had memorized the mystery man's face, the man she was supposed to find.

Chapter 11 Nikka

ikka had run her mind's eye over every inch of the man's face—the man she was supposed to find. Somehow he could help her, but she couldn't imagine how. She wasn't sure where to even start. This was one face in a sea of millions. And according to her vision, or whatever it was, this man was there with Jason, but only after the world had fallen into devastation. This vision wasn't looking so good.

Whoever this visitor was last night, she wasn't so sure she should tell Jason about it. After all, he was just another human who had not been recruited into this like she was. The deeper they sank into this nightmare, the more she worried about the part he would have to play in it. He was just a vulnerable human. Abaddon's possession of him made that plainly clear.

In the dark of her room, she opened the laptop and perused the files that she had seen so many times before. At least it was something to do while Jason continued to sleep in the other room. Maybe something would jump out at her from the hundreds of papers and articles copied from the flash drive.

The morning light gradually appeared on the horizon after a few hours of hunching over the bright screen. She realized she had lost track of time when she heard the hinges of the bedroom door creak as the door slid open. Jason's striking blue eyes appeared on the other side of the door.

"Getting to work so early?" His voice still held the rough gravel of a long-night's sleep.

Nikka glanced up at him. "I couldn't sleep. Weird dreams."

"Why don't you close up shop for a while?"

"I can't. I'm looking for something."

"Not even for waffles?"

She heard the smile in his voice, and when she looked up at him, she saw it too. "Well, when you put it that way . . ."

The grumble came to life in the pit of her stomach when she thought of his waffles. Say what you will about Jason's cabin and his doomsday grandfather, but his breakfasts were epic. She followed him into the main room and glanced at the front door—the same place where her visitor took her last night. Nothing seemed out of place this morning.

Maybe it was a dream after all.

But it had seemed so real. She could still feel the warmth of the tattoo on her chest when it glowed in the shadow's presence.

"Hello," Jason said from the kitchen, catching her attention.

She looked at him and forced a smile.

"So which is it? Maple or chokecherry?"

"What?"

"Syrup." He held both bottles for her to see.

"Whatever you're having."

He continued to watch her as he started the waffle mix. "Everything okay? You seem a bit off this morning."

"Just a lot on my mind." This wasn't a lie, but it wasn't the entire truth either. Maybe she could tell him about her vision some other time, but she needed to figure out what it meant first.

"Can I turn on the television?" she asked and searched the couch for the remote.

"Sure. The generator's running. You should be able to get at least some local stuff."

The TV sparked to life with the push of the power button on the remote control. Nikka settled onto the couch and scrolled through a few channels until she found the local news. As expected, there was still plenty of talk about the explosion and the collapse of the government building downtown. Aerial shots of the burned-out crater flashed across the screen while the newscaster rambled on.

Jason glanced at the TV while he cooked. "It looks so much worse on television."

She wished she could agree with him, but she remembered the explosion when it happened. It was pretty much the most awful thing she had witnessed.

The reporter stood in the morning light and squinted as she held her microphone just under her chin. "Local authorities are working with the FBI as the investigation continues. There is still no word on the cause of the explosion, but arson has not been ruled out."

The camera panned right, away from the reporter and over the pile of rubble that still smoldered. Police officers cordoned off the perimeter of the scene. Scattered around the site were several men in dark blue jackets with gold FBI labels embroidered onto their backs. Wow. Everybody was getting into the investigation. This was serious.

Nikka recalled the night that Jason brought her through the city and up to this cabin. He was nervous about any cameras seeing them, and now she understood why. With so many law enforcement officials, they were certain to go looking through the footage of city cameras.

"The 23rd block is still currently closed to all traffic while investigators still search the area," the reporter continued,as the camera pulled in tight for a dramatic look at the FBI officials walking the area.

Damn. This was making her nervous.

And then she saw him. It was just a quick look, but she was sure of it.

Nikka shifted to the edge of the couch. The FBI agent that led a team of three other agents glanced toward the camera for just a moment. She had seen that face only one other time: dirty blonde hair cut neat around his ears, a strong angular jaw and steely gray eyes half closed in the sunlight.

This was the man in her vision, the one she had been instructed to find.

And he was in the place where she had left her battle, just as her visitor had said.

An FBI agent. He didn't know it yet, but he was searching for her too. And she was going to have to reveal herself to him.

"What's wrong?" Jason said. She must have been too distracted to see him standing right next to the couch. "You look like you've seen a ghost."

She couldn't look away from the television as the camera kept on this man. "Not a ghost, but maybe the next best thing. I need to tell you something."

It was finally time to tell him about the visitor from last night.

The look on his face was confusing at first; almost like he was barely listening to her as she told him about the man who came to her in the night and showed her the vision of the world being destroyed and the man, the FBI agent, who she was supposed to find. She stopped talking and hoped that he had heard everything she had said.

"So—" he stammered. "You're saying that we need to go talk to the FBI and tell them what happened."

"Well, when you say it like that, it sounds awful."

"Sorry." He said it more like a question than an apology. "But this is just a lot to take in right now. You say that someone came to you in a dream and said that you need to find this guy, and then he coincidentally appears on the news this morning. Isn't that a little convenient?"

"None of this is convenient. And it wasn't a dream. It was real, and maybe that's why it happened last night. Because maybe that visitor, or whatever he was, knew I would see the news this morning and knew that the FBI agent would be on it."

"Okay." He placed a hand on her shaking arm. "You know what—I believe you. If you say we gotta find this guy and talk to him, then let's do it. Who am I to doubt all this? Hell, I was possessed by a demon; one, I might add, that you pulled right out of my chest with your bare hands. So if you say this FBI guy is gonna be our number three, then let's go find him."

Nikka's brow furrowed as she looked at him, unsure if he was being honest with her. "Really?"

"Of course. I told you that I will be with you no matter what. Even if it means turning ourselves in. You have seen a lot more of heaven and hell than I ever want to. I'm with you on this."

He locked her into one of his blue-eyed stares for a moment until he turned away and went back to work making his famous breakfast. His unflinching faith in her almost made her feel bad, because that kind of trust can only end badly. Someone was bound to get hurt, even if there was nobody at fault.

Nikka faced the television again to see the FBI agent's face one more time before she turned it off.

Chapter 12 Nikka

Jason made Nikka rehearse it so many times before he would let her out of the truck. This almost made her want to smack him, but then he flashed his crooked smile, and it all fell apart in her head. How could she be upset when he smiled like that?

"Oh my gosh," she complained. "Fine. I'll go over it again, but this is the last time. You drop me off a block from the scene."

"And then you put on your invisibility thing," he said, his hand waving over her like he was trying to imagine a surge of magic flowing over her.

She sighed. "Yes. My invisibility thing." Jason had never personally had the pleasure of seeing her at work when she willed herself to be invisible, and he had no idea the toll it took on her strength. Of course, she never told him either. It was just one of the many things that she had discovered she could do since being told she was a seraph.

"I'll go into the blast zone and just listen; see what I can pick up from being there around the agents."

"So get in and get out. Nothing else but listen. Got it?"

"Got it," she said and moved to open the door of the truck, but he stopped her.

"I mean it, Nikka. We can't get caught. Not yet."

For a moment, she saw the concern shimmer across his face like a ghost. "I've got it."

"This is the damned FBI. We can't get caught."

"All right," she said and grasped his hand where he held onto her arm. "Just listening and learning what they have on us. You won't even notice I'm gone."

"I doubt that," he said and released her arm. "Ten minutes tops."

Nikka pushed the door open and slipped out into the cool autumn air. She pulled the hoodie over her head to ward off the chill. The morning sun should have warmed her skin more than it did, but winter was just off the horizon by the feel of the cold. She squinted down the street that teemed with the usual mid-morning traffic of the downtown district. Just a block away, she would find the yellow warning tape that cordoned off the crime scene. Even if she didn't know it was there, the collection of local news vans parked along the side street would have alerted her that something was unusual about that area today.

She stuffed her cold hands into the pockets of her hoodie and stepped down the sidewalk. Jason's eyes were on her the whole time and for some reason that made her nervous today. His excess anxiety about this reconnaissance mission seemed to rub off on her, making her jittery.

Nikka kept her eyes forward, refusing to look back at him in case he decided to call the whole thing off and scoop her up to run back into hiding. Each step brought her closer to the street corner, where she had planned to create the invisibility illusion and step into the blast zone. She hadn't shared it with Jason, but she hoped that she had the strength to hold the illusion long enough to get in and get out without being seen.

A cold wind picked up just as she stepped to the corner. She stopped and peered around the building to see the scene before she just went plodding right in. Black trucks and vans were stationed along the perimeter of the zone along the outside of the warning tape. Just within the edge of the zone, several men and women worked, presumably collecting evidence within the rubble. She hadn't seen the destruction since that night, and in the daylight it seemed like just a mountain of cement, brick and rebar. Men in hardhats worked on the east edge of the debris pile, loading sections of mortar into a dump truck piece by piece.

There were so many people here, inside and out of the perimeter. It seemed a little daunting to know where she should even start. It didn't matter. She just needed to get in there and learn something before she could begin to decide to find that FBI agent.

She glanced around her surroundings to make sure that nobody was watching, then she closed her eyes and felt in the darkness for the power that resided deep inside her soul. Finding it was like searching for the right chord on a guitar: she had to pluck it to see if it made the right sound. The fingers of her mind searched in the darkness until she found the string to pluck, and it was there, hiding in wait. She willed it to rise, imagining it rising to the surface of her skin and covering her body in a shield, telling it to protect her from any eyes.

With a sudden release, it erupted from her soul and sprang to life in a blanket of invisibility that covered her completely. She opened her eyes, feeling the drain that the power had on her. She had to move quickly now before she couldn't do it at all.

Nikka stepped across the street and ducked under the warning tape. It proved to be much more difficult traversing around the mounds of rubble than she had expected. She tried to keep to the narrow paths that had been created by the crime scene team, but it was not that easy when she had to duck out of someone's way when they came down the path. She might be invisible, but she was certainly tangible if someone ran into her.

The crime scene units seemed to be divided into teams, each collecting their particular set of evidence depending on where they stood in the blast zone. She saw an occasional FBI agent among them, guiding the inspection, but she couldn't see the man she had noticed from the TV. Stepping around the individual teams didn't help much either. They mostly just talked science jargon about the evidence, most of which didn't make sense and didn't matter to her mission today.

She tried to ward off the feelings of frustration that began to well in her gut, mostly because she couldn't give in to that feeling and keep the invisibility illusion at the same time. But it had already been at least five minutes and she had nothing. Jason was going to panic if she wasn't back to the truck in time.

Nikka glanced around the edge of the largest pile of mortar, which had to be the base of the building's foundation. Another crime scene unit worked there, and a woman in the team stood with a glass vial in her hand. She glanced back down the path and seemed to be staring straight at Nikka.

"Agent Wolfe," she called out. "I think I have something here."

"What have you got?" a man's voice spoke directly behind Nikka.

She dodged to the side of the path just in time to see the agent step past her. A half-second too late and he would have knocked her on her ass and wondered what in the world he had run into.

"It appears to be sulfur," the investigator said. "I find traces of it along here and it disappears into the center of the building."

She handed the vial to the agent. He squinted into the light as he inspected the evidence. As Nikka steadied herself, she saw that Agent Wolfe was the man she had been looking for. His short dirty blonde hair mussed a little in the cool breeze that drifted over the scene.

"Part of the explosive, maybe?" he asked.

"I don't think so," the investigator said. "There's no evidence of incineration. It looks almost like residue, but from what I can't tell yet."

"What would leave behind a sulfur residue?" he muttered to himself as the investigator turned away to continue with her work again.

I could tell you, but you wouldn't believe me. Nikka bit her lip to keep from saying anything as she watched him, standing only a few feet from her.

"Wolfe," another voice called out to him from across the blast zone. Nikka glanced at a woman with shoulder-length brown hair and big, brown eyes. She, too, wore an FBI jacket that she tucked around her slender frame as she stepped toward him. "The team found some trace evidence on the south end," she said. "What do they have here?"

"Sulfur."

Her nose wrinkled. "Sulfur? What does that indicate?"

"Not sure."

"Trace on the other side could be tire tracks. We can see if it's a match to the bike you saw on surveillance."

Wolfe still seemed distracted by the vial of sulfur in his hand. "Okay, thanks Megan. Have them get me the report ASAP."

"Of course," the woman said. "That's what partners are for."

She stepped away from him, and Nikka almost missed seeing it. The drain from the illusion had pulled so much of her energy that she could barely make use of any of her other senses. But it was there, without a doubt. This was bad. She then realized that their plan needed to be in motion much faster than she had anticipated.

Her illusion began to fray at the edges, like tissue paper in turbulent water. She had to get away before the invisibility collapsed and left her weak and exposed in the middle of the blast zone.

She stumbled away from him, wrapping her arms around her torso to help control the invisibility just a little longer, just long enough to get into a crowd of reporters or something. The illusion continued to pull at her insides, leaving an ever-growing hole in her center that threatened to swallow her. She ducked under the warning tape and plunged into the collection of spectators that had gathered along the perimeter.

In a gasp of air, like breaking through the surface of water, the illusion shattered, and she felt her body expose to the air and light around her.

"Hey," a man said behind her. "What the hell?"

She glanced at him and met his eyes. He gazed at her with amazement, knowing full well that she had just appeared before him.

"Excuse me," she said and pushed past him toward the back of the crowd.

"But—" he stammered. "Hey, did you guys see that?" His voice grew louder as she tried to distance herself from him. "That chick just appeared out of nowhere."

Nikka glanced back to him. The crowd around them now became agitated enough that she knew she had to get away from all of them soon, but she had no more energy left to bring back the illusion. The man continued to call after her, and she heard him growing louder, as though he was trying to follow her. And even if she could get away from him now, he was making enough noise to get her noticed.

She pulled away from the edge of the crowd and looked back at the perimeter of the blast zone. The man's calling had gotten Agent Wolfe's attention too, and he now stepped under the tape and gazed out over the crowd. It was only a second before his eyes met hers from under the hood of her jacket. It took that moment to realize she needed to run.

The FBI agent stepped forward first, and she didn't wait for another second. He was coming toward her. She clenched her fists and bolted into a sprint away from the scene. Her thighs burned with the last remnants of strength that she had left. The agent would be only a short distance behind her and he wasn't going to let her just go now that she was running. The moment they had locked eyes, she could sense that he was suspicious of her anyway, especially after the last thing she had heard. They had definitely seen surveillance and they were looking for Jason's bike. He undoubtedly had seen the footage of the two of them on the motorcycle as they had left the scene.

Nikka also realized that the agent would be close enough to see her get into the truck. It wouldn't take long to run the plates and find out who owned the pickup. She couldn't lead him to Jason.

She dodged around the opposite corner, away from where the truck waited for her. She needed to lose the agent just long enough to get back to the pickup and get away.

"Stop," Wolfe's voice called out behind her, echoing down the quiet alley.

Her heart nearly exploded through her ribs. She pulled herself past a dumpster and into an open door at the rear of a restaurant. She ran through the narrow kitchen of a small Chinese restaurant. The cook eyed her with surprise as she sprinted past him and into the dining area.

She oriented herself quickly and knew that the front of the restaurant opened just down the street from the truck. She could gather enough strength to will the illusion one more time, just long enough to get to Jason. Eyes from the waiting staff burned on her as she raced through to the front entrance and onto the sidewalk.

Jason's truck waited two blocks down the street from her, like a beacon that seemed so far away. She took in two quick breaths and willed the invisibility over her body once more. Beyond the pounding of her feet on the pavement, she heard the door of the restaurant open behind her. The FBI agent was there; she didn't have to look back to know that. She pushed harder, the truck growing ever closer.

Like an engine on overdrive, she pushed herself harder, feeling the engine sputtering in her chest. The illusion was slipping. She could feel it falling around the edges again.

Twenty feet. The truck was right there.

The agent behind her began running again. Had he seen something?

Ten feet.

She held her breath, knowing that one more breath would make the illusion collapse.

The cold metal of the door handle in her palm made her take a breath. She pulled the door open and leaped into the cab.

"Drive," she gasped as she felt the illusion collapse.

Jason waited for no explanation. He pushed the gas to the idling truck and the old engine blasted to life. The back wheels spun and kicked the truck forward just as she closed the door. She glanced through the window to see the confused agent standing at the edge of the block from the restaurant, looking around him for any signs of her. He hadn't noticed the truck, at least from what she could see.

Nikka lay down in the seat and gasped for air, the muscles in her arms and legs burning with exertion.

"Are you okay?" Jason asked.

"I will be. Just give me a second."

"But you're not hurt?"

"No."

She felt his hand on her shoulder. Of course he wouldn't believe her, lying next to him and wheezing with exhaustion.

"I found him," she said.

"Perfect."

"Not so fast. Things are really bad, and we are going to have to get things moving quickly."

"Why?"

There was so much more to tell him, and when she explained, she knew he understood as well. They didn't have time to wait and decide to reveal themselves to Agent Wolfe. They would have to approach it delicately, though. He would never believe them if she just came out and told him everything, especially the things she saw today . . . things that put the agent in danger now.

Chapter 13 Nikka

It wasn't going to be as easy as just walking up to the FBI agent and saying, "Hi there, I'm the one you're looking for, but that's okay because it's sorta gonna be the end of the world if you don't listen to me."

Things would be so much better if it was that easy, but that's just not how things work. Somehow Nikka had to think of a way to send Agent Wolfe a message in such a way that he wouldn't arrest her on sight and send her to a maximum security federal prison for being a domestic terrorist and blowing up a building housing a branch of the Department of Defense.

And somehow she had to also convince him of the existence of demons. That might be the hardest part of all.

If this was going to work, they had to be careful, and this had to be well-planned. Any slip up could send one or both of them to prison. Jason insisted on keeping the news playing on the TV all day just in case there was some new development. But Nikka knew that some of it was to see if the police had any leads pointing in their direction. After what she had seen at that demolition site, she knew they had to act quickly. Agent Wolfe wasn't as in charge as he thought, and he was getting in deeper than he even knew.

The first step had to be getting the agent's attention. As much as Jason hated it, she requested time to monitor the agent from afar, and that meant more undercover. Deep undercover. Invisible undercover. She had been visibly shaken after their last reconnaissance mission that left her drained for days, but this was the only way she could imagine getting close enough to the agent to be able to learn his routine. It would be in that day-to-day boring stuff that she might find a way to intercept him, take him off guard, and get him alone long enough to talk to him.

She knew she couldn't spend long each day in an attempt to follow him and learn his habits. Every time she willed herself into invisibility, if even for ten minutes, it took nearly half a day to recover.

But then she thought of the best way to get his attention, and it was so simple.

A brief letter, written in her own hand, but the paper and envelope wiped clean of fingerprints. At first, she had wanted to write it in cutout letters from a magazine or catalog, but Jason calmly suggested that was what a serial killer would do. She left it under the wiper blade of his car. Simple, just like she hoped. And Jason agreed with her on what it would say.

I can give you answers. I wish to meet with you, and only you, at Tilden's Market Café this Saturday.
Please come alone. If not, you will never know what I know.

The Girl with the Angel Tattoos

The last bit was Jason's idea, and she smiled when he came up with it. Plus, he said it implied just enough about her to link her to anything that the FBI might have on surveillance. They would have seen some of her tattoos if they had any footage from the night of the explosion.

And it was totally cool.

Saturday came, and she knew the FBI agent would be there. That was probably why she had such nerves today. It had gotten bad enough that it was hard to concentrate. She had bitten down her fingernails until they hurt when Jason grabbed her hands to prevent her from doing it any longer. She tried to pull away from him, but he held onto her tighter and pretended to watch the news as if he paid her no mind.

"Stop it," she said.

"You first."

"Okay." She rolled her eyes as he loosened his grip.

"You know that he's going to have back-up. There is no way you are actually talking to him today," he said and shot her a quick glance.

"I guess I'm kind of expecting it."

"Good. Just stay incognito and bring another letter to put on his windshield, one that states you will never show until he holds up his end."

Nikka smiled. "You're so smart."

"I know. Don't hold it against me."

"I won't," she said as she poked him in the ribs.

They left the cabin together as planned, and he drove her downtown, within a couple blocks of the café. Just like before, he would wait for her, and he warned her to be quick. In and out. No delay. There was no way that Agent Wolfe would be alone, so there was no reason for her to be more than ten minutes. Nikka nodded as he continued to prod her with his sage advice. She slipped out of the truck, pulled on her invisibility and ran to the café.

She stepped around the corner to face the marketplace across the street. At first glance, she couldn't see anything amiss, but she knew it would be right under the surface, just like Jason had warned her. She moved like a ghost toward the restaurant and gazed into the panel-glass windows. That was when she saw his face.

The agent glanced out of the window from where he sat at a table. His slate blue eyes flashed around the outside perimeter of the café, like a predator checking his domain. Nobody could come and go without him knowing it, or at least that was probably what he thought.

Nikka stepped up to the window as he looked right through her. He sat alone at his table, but according to Jason, this was only an illusion. There would probably be two more of his kind inside the restaurant and another outside the building for good measure. She looked inside the café, to the other patrons who sat around the marketplace and appeared to be normal people enjoying a lunch on one of the last sunny weekends of the year.

A mom with two kids. She couldn't be with Agent Wolfe. Two young women sitting together, but with their faces buried in their smartphones. No way.

A brunette woman sitting alone, reading the paper. Bingo. Nikka was sure that the woman was his partner, although she couldn't see her face. And she didn't really want to look at her anyway. But that had to be the same woman she saw back at the crime scene. Another FBI agent, and she remembered Wolfe calling her Megan.

One down. She didn't even need to look around the café to know there would be more of them, just like Jason had said. Nikka stepped away from the window as she felt the first twinge of disappointment grow in her knees and make her feet heavy. Even though she had expected this, she had held out a glimmer of hope that she would be wrong. This would just delay things even longer, and they were already running out of time.

She turned away from the café and felt the letter just under the front of her jacket. Well, round two would have to begin, and this game would never end until Wolfe complied with her request. As soon as she found his silver sedan in the parking lot, the same one she had tagged with a letter before, she tucked the envelope under the wiper blade and ran back to Jason just as the invisibility was beginning to take its toll on her body.

The letter was the same as the previous one, but she had underlined the part about her knowing if he had brought someone with him.

They went through the same routine the next day. Of course, Agent Wolfe showed up, only his partner was nowhere within the vicinity of the café. At least not that Nikka could tell. She walked the surrounding block until she spotted the car across the street. It was a very plain SUV, but the man sitting behind the wheel looking like he had nothing better to do was anything but plain. He was so obviously an FBI agent that she had to laugh to herself.

Well, not today. We will have to keep doing this until he learns to come alone. She left another letter at his car.

The next day, she thought he had done just that until she saw that same man that was in the SUV sitting at a table across from Wolfe.

When she saw him this time, she wanted to reach out to Wolfe and just scream at him. She giggled a little when she imagined that, but doing it as her invisible self—damn, that would be funny to see.

She left another letter for him, but she added something that even Jason didn't get to see.

Please . . . I am not dangerous, but you ARE in danger. I must talk to you, but what I need to tell you cannot be shared with others.

Hopefully he would hear the desperation in her words. He had to.

The next day, she felt the drain that the previous days had taken on her. It was much harder to will the invisibility into being, and keeping it in place was becoming much more difficult.

"You don't look well," Jason said before he let her out of the truck again.

"I'm fine."

"No you're not. But I know that you're gonna do this anyway."

She looked at him and tried to keep her eyelids from drifting closed. It would be so nice to sleep right now, but she had to keep going.

"After this one, we need to take a break for a while. You need rest."

"I'll rest when I'm dead."

"That's what I'm afraid of."

She looked at him and half expected one of his crooked smiles, but his stare was cold. He was serious this time. There was nothing funny about the way he looked at her now.

"If he brings someone again, that's it. I'm calling this off. We need to come up with a different plan."

"Have a little faith," she said and slipped out of the truck.

She willed the invisibility over her body and stepped out to the café again. The air had grown very cold, and she knew that a dusting of snow would not be out of the ordinary today. The weather had brought fewer people out to lunch, but the marketplace was still busy with the regulars who frequented the café from the local businesses in the downtown district. As she approached the restaurant, though, something had dramatically changed from her several other visits this way.

Agent Wolfe stood outside the café, hands in the pockets of his jeans. He no longer wore the usual black suit and tie that seemed to be the staple of his wardrobe. Not today. He had donned a fleece jacket and shuffled in his stance as he glanced around the vicinity of the restaurant. Nikka stopped and watched him. He couldn't hold his feet still, but they were in a constant state of motion. Agent Wolfe was nervous.

Nervous. Probably because he was finally alone.

She glanced around the marketplace. No lone FBI agent sitting in an SUV or at a table looking out of the café. No sign of his partner either. He was truly alone.

The sight of all this almost made her invisibility falter for a moment. She moved quickly around the back of the restaurant and let the veil fall from her body. The weight of it lifting from her made her take a deep breath. Each puff of air escaped her lips in little white clouds.

He was alone. And she was here, ready to talk to him. She almost believed that this moment would never happen. So when it was finally here, she felt her hands shaking and her feet were like two blocks of stone cemented to the pavement.

It was now or never. There may not be another moment where she could do this, and he was the only one that could help them.

She took in a deep breath and clenched her fists. First, one foot and then the other. This was so much harder than she had first imagined. She stepped around the corner and approached him from behind the building. He was right there, close enough she could smell the laundry detergent on his clothes.

The words felt like cotton in her throat, but she would have to speak his name eventually. It had to be done, and let the consequences fall where they might.

"Agent Wolfe," she spoke. She had meant it to sound firm and resilient, but it only came out as a whisper.

He turned around, startled, and his eyes met hers under the edge of her hood. He seemed to hold his breath for a moment as he glanced at her jacket and cargo pants. Jason had warned her that he would think she had a weapon on her; that he would be jumpy.

"It's you, isn't it?" he said. "The Girl with the Angel Tattoos. Clever."

She kept her distance from him, ready to run at any moment if she sensed that she had been wrong about him being alone this time.

"Yes."

"So," he started and stepped closer to her, but she backed away from him. He held up his hands and revealed his empty palms. "Hey, I showed you mine. Show me yours."

He nodded to her hands, which she realized she had tucked into the pockets of her hoodie. The cold had pierced into her fingers, but she pulled her hands free and held them out to him.

"I'm not armed," she said. Well, that wasn't entirely true. There was the sword—

"Do you mind if I make sure?" he said and cocked an eyebrow. That somehow made him look sort of cute and a little innocent.

Nikka bit her lip and nodded. He approached her, his hands out, and began patting his palms against her jacket. His touch moved down around her hips as she looked away from him. She had never had to go through a pat-down before, and it was a little embarrassing, even if nobody else was looking.

"Okay," he said and took a step back. "Let's go inside where it's warm. Have some coffee. Tell me what it is that you think you need to tell me."

"No." The word came so suddenly that she wasn't sure she had said it. "Right here is fine."

"Do you have something against coffee?" he said with a grin. It was then that she realized that he reminded her of Jason, just fifteen years older. Like Jason's older brother.

But she didn't have time for all of that. "It's very important that you listen to me. You're in danger."

"Yeah, I kind of got that from your letter. What do you mean by danger?"

"I can't explain it here."

He rolled his eyes and turned away from her. "I don't have time for this."

"Please," she said and grasped his arm. He stopped and looked back at her. "There are spies all around us. They know what happened at that building. They know why it fell."

"But so do you," he said, pointing his finger at her. "I know you were there too." He stepped in so close to her now that she could smell his mint mouthwash.

He was becoming frustrated, but there was only so much she could actually tell him. After all, if she told the truth, he would just walk away and never listen to her again or try to arrest her on the spot.

She felt herself nodding. "Yes. I was there."

"Then give me something I can use."

"Okay," she said as her mind began to search for anything that would help.

And then it happened. It was a long-shot, though. But it would work if he was willing to just go along with it. This "thing" would convince even her if she had seen it. Hell, it did convince her back when she was new to all of this.

"Tomorrow," she said. "Meet me here again, same time." His face softened a bit. "But I need you to trust me. I'll show you something that will explain everything, and then you can use it however you want."

The look in his eye told her that he was willing to listen, even though he didn't actually say anything at that moment. He only watched her for a second as if ruminating over what she said.

"Fine. But I am going to double check everything, and if it all turns into bullshit, then I am arresting you for obstruction. If you don't show up tomorrow, I will find you and your boyfriend. Trust me on that."

The cold only made his words bite harder. So he had seen them both on surveillance. They definitely knew about Jason. She nodded her head and watched him turn away from her.

Now it had to happen. Her plan had to work and Jason wasn't going to like it.

CHAPTER 14 JASON

nce Nikka had relayed her plan, Jason definitely didn't like it. This was so risky, but at the same time, it made sense, especially the way she said it. There was no way he was just going to go with it, though, until he thought things over.

He stepped out of the cabin into the cool evening air. Everything she had just told him still screamed in his head. All this demon stuff was beginning to sound so normal, so everyday; and that's what worried him the most. Nikka had lived with her powers for a while now, but he had lived with the demon inside of him for months. He never wanted to see another one again, even if it was in the body of another person.

He paced in circles in the driveway. This thing she had asked him to do could be a little too much.

But it was the only thing she had ever truly asked of him. How could he deny her this? And she was right: it was the only thing that could get Agent Wolfe to understand. It was either this, or go to a federal prison for a very long time when the agent decides to arrest them both.

He had promised to help her, to always be there for her. He'd even prayed to some Higher Being to find a way for him to help her. Maybe this was his answer. But it wasn't what he had expected.

And he would have to do this alone. At least if she was there, he wouldn't be so worried; but he had to do this without her. That's the only way this would work.

Damn it. This was getting difficult.

He stuffed his hands into his pockets and glanced back at the cabin, through the windows that glowed with the lights of the kitchen where he had left her. She stood against the counter, her bare head hung down, and her shoulders looking small under her T-shirt. He could see the edge of the dark tattoos along her neck before they disappeared under the neckline of her shirt.

Looking at her now, he would never tell her that he couldn't help her. She was his world now and he would do anything for her, even if she still looked at him like he was evil. Maybe someday, if he had done his penance, she would see him differently. But for now, he would help her through this because he was her ally, her friend. And they both needed this.

Chapter 15 Nikka

Everything had gone as planned so far. Nikka first relayed it to Jason, the same plan that she had thought of on the spot when she had talked to Agent Wolfe.

At first, he just stayed quiet and walked out of the cabin into the cold fall air to think about it. She used to worry whenever he just disappeared for several minutes, but it was his way of thinking and not reacting too quickly to a situation. When he had come back inside, he agreed, and everything would be set in motion.

The first part was easier than she had expected, but it had taken most of the night to finish. By morning, Nikka was too anxious to sleep or eat. And now it was up to Agent Wolfe to believe her, or to arrest both of them. By the end of the day, things were going to be very different.

Cold morning wind blew down the mountain and pulled in milky gray clouds from the west that cast a dull light on everything. Vibrant oranges and yellows that once hung in the trees fell away to shades of black and brown, leaving a slush of fallen leaves and ice across the cracked parking lot of the café.

Jason had dropped her off several blocks away and left her, just as they had planned last night. So far, everything had happened just as it was supposed to, and much to his concern, Jason's part had worked out perfectly.

The FBI agent stood at the corner, his hands tucked into the pockets of his jacket and his face pulled into the collar like a turtle against the wind.

Her gut swarmed with bees as she neared him. She hoped this would work. It had to.

"Agent Wolfe," she said from under her hoodie.

He turned, the tip of his nose red from the cold. The curves around his mouth creased into chilled folds as he smiled. "You know, I half expected you to bail on me today."

"Well, here I am, as promised."

"So, what do you have to show me?"

She cleared her throat. There was no problem with it, but it seemed the best thing to do while she tried to think of the easiest way to approach him with her proposition.

"I need to take you there."

He lost his smile. "You said you were going to show me something . . ."

"And I will. But I need to take you to it."

"I'm not going anywhere with you. My trust only goes so far."

"I understand." She held out her hand to him. "So you can do the driving. I'll go with you and just give you directions."

He thought about it for a moment as he continued to watch her. It seemed like forever before he said anything.

"Just you? Nobody else with you? Nobody else follows us?"

"Just me." She held out her hands to show him how small and harmless she was. If he only knew . . .

"And where would we be going?"

Nikka pointed to the mountain range behind the café. "Up the hill a bit."

She saw his hand brush against his hip. Of course, she knew that was where he kept his gun. After watching him for several days, she had learned enough about him to know some of his habits.

He took in a deep breath and let it out. "Fine."

The agent turned away from her and stepped toward the black SUV parked along the curb. The doors unlocked with a click of his remote, and he climbed into the driver's seat. She slid across the beige leather seat on the passenger side and smelled the fragrance of a new car. No empty coffee cups. No envelopes or stray papers for him to move for her to take her place. Either he was a clean-freak or he hardly ever used this car.

He remained quiet as he started the engine and pulled out onto the road. Nikka buckled her seatbelt and watched straight ahead. Her fingers trembled as she curled her hands into fists. Her next planned move made her so anxious that she was sure her heart would pound right out of her chest. It was something she only did with people she knew, and the only people she knew lately were Jason and . . . and Gideon.

She pulled the hood back from her head.

Although she didn't look at him, she could feel the furtive glances that he flicked toward her. She was well aware that her appearance was a little unusual. A woman with a shaved head decorated in tattoos was not a common thing to see in this town.

"So," he said. "Is it a gang thing?" His glance shot toward the tattoos on her head.

"No."

"Okay," he said with a hint of sarcasm.

"I'll explain it later. Right now, it just won't make sense. No hair because I had cancer."

She could feel the silence coming off of him. "Sorry."

"It's okay. Leukemia. I'm cured now."

He was nodding when she glanced at him. His shoulders had softened and he now drove with just one hand. Something about telling a person you had cancer makes them trust you a little more, she thought. It must be true.

"You seem to know my name," he said and glanced at her again. "But I don't know yours."

That told her more than he realized. The FBI had still not identified who they saw on surveillance. Her name felt caught in her throat, though. It was so difficult to say, especially knowing that he was trying to get as much information from her as possible. But by the end of the day, they would be quite familiar with each other.

"It's Nikka."

He nodded, and she could see him processing it, storing it for later use.

The clouds thickened as they approached the base of the mountain. She guided him up the winding dirt road, through the tunnel of trees, on the way to the cabin. Maybe he couldn't feel it, but Nikka definitely could. She sensed the prickle of nerves begin at her neck and work its way down to her forearms, where her hair stood on end. Soon, he would see what waited in the cabin and he would understand. It didn't make it much easier for her, though, knowing that she would have to show him. This was not something that was easy for anyone to handle.

The forest road cleared just enough to see the edge of the cabin. Agent Wolfe slowed the SUV with both hands clutched to the steering wheel. Maybe he could feel that buzz in the air now, too.

"This is it," she said.

The vehicle rolled to a stop at a comfortable distance from the main door. Wolfe sat in silence, his keen eyes scanning the woods around the clearing. Nikka knew what he was looking for, and there was no way of reassuring him that there was nothing out here to worry about. But he could feel it, that sense of something being off. Something wrong. He would never understand where it was coming from until he saw what she had prepared for him. It would always feel that way up to the moment that she took care of things.

Her hand moved to the door handle, but the agent's hand shot out and grabbed her arm. "Not yet."

His grip was firm, almost too strong, as he wrapped his fingers around her forearm. "What is it?" she asked.

"How do I know I can trust you?"

"It's called faith. You just have to believe in it."

"That's not very reassuring."

His fingers slipped from her arm, but she hesitated for a moment. Any sudden movements could make him more anxious and might collapse this whole thing. She reached deliberately to the handle and pushed the door open in a wide, slow arc. He watched out the window at the woods behind her, his eyes darting to the spaces around the garage and behind the cabin.

Nikka heard the click of the latch and heard his door open as well. She didn't glance back to him as she stepped up to the front door and held it open for the agent to gaze inside. Wolfe peered around her, his hand resting on the gun in the holster under his jacket.

"My friend is here to meet you," Nikka said to him.

She nodded as the signal for Jason to step into the frame of the door. Just as she had discussed with him, he held his hands out for Agent Wolfe to see. She noticed the moment of recognition move across the agent's face when he saw Jason. Of course, he recognized him from the surveillance footage that he had viewed.

Wolfe stopped, his fingers reaching around the lapel of his open jacket, ready to pull the gun at any moment.

"It's okay," Nikka said, her hands held out before her as well. "This is Jason. We both wanted to be here. To be completely open. He's with me."

The agent remained still, his pupils as black as an owl's and his fingers still hovering over the gun.

"Agent Wolfe, please come in, and I'll show you what I brought you here to see."

"Andy."

Nikka's eyebrows curved together.

"Andy. You can call me Andy," he said as his hand relaxed.

"Okay, Andy," she said and shot a glance at Jason, who moved aside. "I promise, this will be quick."

Wolfe stepped into the cabin, but kept his distance from them as they showed him inside. Nikka walked to the hatch in the kitchen floor and pulled back the rug. The moment she did this, she could feel the chill spilling from the seam in the door, like ribbons of dry ice reaching from the cellar. And it was not only here. The entire cabin had felt different. It felt wrong.

She bit the inside of her lip and hoped to avoid cringing as her fingers felt the cold ring of the latch. The door lifted with a little effort, and the rush of frosty air lapped over her legs like spilled ice water. The gaping darkness below pulsed with black energy. She knew it wasn't just because she was aware of what was down there.

Agent Wolfe could feel it too. His hand slipped from the gun holster as he stared at the hole, taking careful steps toward the kitchen. The same energy that flowed over her body and made the hair on her arms stand up had now brushed over his skin and buzzed along his spine. He stared down into the cellar as though he couldn't look away.

"I'll go first," Nikka said. "You're here just as an observer. You need to remember that. Whatever you see, just stay by Jason's side."

"What's down there?"

She could hear the slightest tremble in his voice. "Evil."

Nikka pulled the hood over her bare head, her eyes darkening into shadows, and stepped down the steep way into the cellar. The space under the cabin wasn't usually this dark and cold, but the thing that now infected the cellar made it so today. She descended down the steps like submerging herself in black, murky water. The daylight from the kitchen cast down on her in a single beam that didn't scatter from the stairs like normal light would. Instead, a single white light shone on the only exit from this dark place.

She turned away from the light and let her eyes adjust to the shadows the best they could. Wolfe and Jason descended after her, the agent taking each step with hesitation, his eyes darting into the darkness around the stairs. Jason turned on the LED lantern in his hand as he followed Wolfe.

Nikka stepped aside and let Wolfe into the darkness. The lantern light now illuminated their faces in ghostly shadows and blue light. His eyes were wide as he glanced into the dark, undoubtedly feeling the strength of the dark energy from the cellar creep into his nerves.

She reached her hand to his and grasped his palm. It had become damp and didn't have the strength of grip that he had used on her arm when she got out of the SUV.

"Remember. Stay by Jason's side. You're here to see. Nothing else. I'll take care of everything."

His eyebrows knit together, increasing the shadows across his forehead.

Nikka turned away and stepped around the first storage shelves and into the main space of the cellar. Jason followed behind her, keeping Wolfe close beside him. When the blue-white light of Jason's lantern fell upon the center of the room, everything went silent and the cellar felt like a deep freezer, crisp and hard against her skin.

The time had come. Everything would change after this.

It had to.

Chapter 16 Nikka

The light first illuminated the legs of a chair and then fell upon the black shoes of the person tied to it. As soon as the light cast across her body, the woman began to struggle against her bonds. Jason had bound her well: duct tape tied her shins, abdomen and shoulders to the chair. Her hands were tethered together behind the back of the chair and a single strip of silver tape covered her mouth. Dark brown hair fell across her left eye that squinted against the fresh light that covered her.

Wolfe stepped back and the hand that had been hovering over his gun now un-holstered it and pointed it at Jason. He backed against the wall of the cellar, his breath rushing out in thin white clouds.

"What the hell is this?" The gun trembled in his hand.

Nikka held up her hands, the palms facing toward him. "Andy, please wait a moment. I know how this looks."

Of course she did. She expected this reaction. The woman in the chair began to scream behind the tape covering her mouth. Tears flowed down her red eyes as she continued to fight against the binds. The creature put on quite a show as it looked just like his FBI partner, Megan, and elicited the very reaction she had expected from him. But she had to get him to realize.

"Step away from her." Beadlets of sweat now formed on Andy's brow. He shifted the barrel of the gun back and forth between Nikka and Jason.

"Andy. Agent Wolfe. This is not your partner," she said.

The woman cried out again, her voice muffled behind the tape.

"Untie her now."

"This woman was once your partner. But now she's not what she seems."

"What are you talking about?" He now placed both hands on the gun.

Jason stood still, his arms and legs stiff as he looked at Nikka. His eyes had grown wide and she knew what he thought: show him. Now.

Nikka still held her hands up to Wolfe. "I won't hurt her. I don't have to."

She turned toward the woman, whose soft brown eyes now looked at her with fear and pleading. The tears stained her face and beaded against the tape on her mouth. She reached to the edge of the tape and pulled it from her mouth. Tears and spit slicked across the surface of the tape as she yanked it free.

"Please," Megan cried. "Don't hurt me. Please."

Oh, she was good. Very good.

Nikka leaned in and gazed into her eyes. And there it was, the same thing she saw the day she snuck into the crime scene and discovered Agent Wolfe. She saw it when his partner first showed up on the scene and distracted him from the sulfur evidence on the rubble. It was there, slithering just below the mask of humanity.

"Tell me your name," Nikka said.

The woman cried. "Agent Megan Cavanaugh."

Nikka smiled. "I said, tell me your name."

"Megan Cavanaugh." She cried and glanced at Wolfe. "Please. Andy, help me."

"Tell me your real name." Her voice grew louder.

"What more do you want from her?" Andy yelled from the back wall.

"She knows what I want," Nikka said and stepped back. "Looks like I will have to pull out the big guns."

As the woman continued to weep and squint into the lantern light, Nikka watched her without hesitation. She reached to the zipper of her hoodie and pulled it down. The jacket slipped from her head and body, revealing the intricate tattoos that arced around her head and down her arms.

In that moment, the temperature dropped again as the ink on her body began to sparkle in fine points of light. The woman immediately stopped her weeping and stared forward, her eyes turning a deep black that filled every corner of the orb. Agent Wolfe grew quiet as he watched the scene unfold.

"I said, what is your name." Nikka's voice remained steady and forceful.

The woman stared forward and cocked her head to the side, the oil wells that filled her eyes swallowed any reflected light. Her lips spread open in a smile and a murky, black fluid dripped from the corner of her mouth and stained her teeth.

"The seraph," she hissed. "I should have known."

"What the hell?" Wolfe said, the gun still pointing at Nikka, but the barrel now trembled in the light.

"What the hell, indeed," the woman said, emphasizing each syllable, and her glance shot toward him. The smile fell from her lips. "What the hell, Andy? You let them put me down here." Her lips turned down in a mockery of a pout. "You let them get to me."

"I demand your name," Nikka said, drawing the demon's attention from Wolfe. "You know about me. You know I can destroy you whether or not I have your name."

The black eyes watched her, the room fell into deep silence. "Well, then. Let's put on a good show. After all, you brought the audience."

The lantern light flickered as the woman's head dropped back, her eyes staring up to the ceiling. The black fluid poured from the corners of her mouth and eyes. Then the light went out, plunging them into darkness. The ground at their feet began to tremble and quake. Items on the storage shelves fell to the floor as the rafters shook and rained dust to the bare ground. The lantern flickered on once again, but the woman now stood in the center of the room, the chair in broken pieces at her feet. Her feet hovered a few inches off the floor as she stared down at Nikka, her brown hair falling like wet seaweed across her pale face.

In the few minutes since it revealed itself, the demon had already left the body in tatters. The woman's lips now cracked, and the skin across her cheek-bones began to peel back in bloody layers. The black eyes stared at Nikka below the strands of hair that hung across her face.

"Your name," Nikka demanded again. The whites of her eyes began to hum until a soft light glowed in harmony with the sparkling of lights along the tattoos.

The woman twitched as though struggling against another invisible bond. She grimaced as she looked upon Nikka. The demon had very little strength against Nikka despite this demonstration of power. The woman arched back and opened her mouth in a primal, angry scream that poured from her throat like a swarm of bees. Her feet still hovered above the ground as her body spun about as if on an axis that shot straight through her center.

The creature's voice shook against the rafters again as the woman collapsed and fell to the floor. The lantern light stopped flickering and all became quiet again. The woman slumped over her knees, her hair hanging over her face and spilling across the floor. She remained still, lifeless.

Nobody moved as Nikka stared at the body on the floor.

CHAPTER 17 JASON

Wolfe took a single step forward, but Jason reached out his hand to stop him.

"Wh—what's happening to her?" the agent asked, his voice trembling.

Jason placed a finger against his lips to quiet him. The agent, his eyes wide, nodded and stepped back beside him.

He felt Wolfe tense and hold his breath as he watched this sudden change in behavior. Jason hadn't been fooled when Cavanaugh tried to give him her big brown-eye weepy stare when he had found her just before she got into her car. Just one blow to the back of her head disoriented her enough that he was able to stuff her into his truck and get her to the cabin before she awoke. It took everything in his power not to look at her face as he had tied her to the chair in the cellar.

And now she lay on the cellar floor, slumped over and lifeless.

He tried to keep the trembling in his hands under control, but the lantern light still quivered in the dark of the space beneath the cabin. Yeah, this same kind of possession had happened to him once, but he had never been witness to this in somebody else.

"Tell Agent Wolfe your name," Nikka said again

The woman remained still and slumped, not even moving her rib cage to breathe. The light fell upon the pale skin of her hands that rested limply against the cold floor.

"I will give you to the count of three." Nikka took a wider stance as she watched the woman. "One—"

The woman didn't move. Didn't twitch.

"Two—"

Jason's breathing quickened. He didn't want to see the demon's face again and what it did to the woman it now possessed.

"Three—"

Before the word fell from her lips, the woman leaped upward like a gazelle, her fingers at Nikka's throat. They fell back against the wall as the creature's claws dug into the skin of her neck.

Jason held Wolfe back against the wall, but he wanted to jump into the fray and help Nikka. Even from where they stood, he could smell the sulfur from the creature's breath, seeping from behind the woman's blackened teeth.

The creature lunged at Nikka with such anger and fury that she almost lost her footing. It howled with a piercing cry.

Nikka kicked back against the wall as her hands clutched at the woman's jacket. She tore open the top few buttons of her white shirt, now stained with black ooze that fell from her cracked lips. Nikka spun around, the creature in her grasp and pressed the woman back against the wall. She freed a single hand and reached behind her shoulder. She unsheathed the sword from behind her back, the weapon that always lived there and remained unseen until she touched it.

The katana danced in a whorl of blue flames as she unsheathed it and held it at her side. The creature's black eyes darted to the edge of the sword as it remained dangerously close.

"One last chance before you die. Your name."

The grimace on its face deepened into a scream of agony as it fought against Nikka's will. The woman's throat cried out in a gurgle of hate and anger. She fought against the word that began to well up from the depths of her chest.

"Asmodeus," the creature said through clenched teeth.

Without hesitation, Nikka released the woman, plunged her hand into her bare chest and felt the squirm of the creature that dwelled inside of her. It writhed and screamed against her clutch, but she had it firmly in her grasp as she pulled.

The beast clung with its many claws and tentacles to anything it could hold on to as Nikka pulled it from the woman's body. The scream arose from

Megan's throat, some of it human, as the beast broke free. The woman collapsed at the moment the demon fought and screeched in Nikka's hand, its true form now exposed.

Its tail whipped around and crashed into the back shelves, smacking hard into the cement wall of the cellar. The shelves collapsed around them and Jason shoved Wolfe back and out of the way, but he stood his ground, ready to help Nikka at any moment. This was the first time he had seen the un-possessed creature since she had pulled the demon from his body. It screamed and howled with a sound so awful that he cringed away from the sight of the beast.

Glass claws raked at Nikka, but she held the creature away from her body as it fought her. She heaved it against the wall and stepped back fast enough to draw her sword through the air before it could find its footing and lunge at her again. The blade struck into its shoulder and through its oily black neck, severing its head as it moved through the air at her.

The head crashed against the toppled shelves as the body skidded to a stop at her feet. A final hiss escaped its throat and then everything fell quiet again.

Black blood dripped from the tip of her sword as she held it in the position of its final death blow, her legs locked in a power stance. The blood sizzled as it dropped into the compacted dirt floor.

Jason released a long-held breath and looked up at her, at the tattoos that now dimmed and turned black. The blue flames continued to lick at the edge of the sword. She breathed hard and she turned her eyes toward him. She had a fierce energy that still resided in her gaze, powerful and alive. He had never seen her look like that before. He smiled at her and he saw the slightest curve of a grin form on her lips.

The body and head of the demon disintegrated into dust just as she straightened and turned her gaze to Agent Wolfe.

"Its name was Asmodeus. That was a demon," she said and sheathed the katana into invisibility again.

Chapter 18 Nikka

Agent Wolfe stared out the kitchen window, sipping at the cup of coffee Jason had made for him. He hadn't said a word for almost half an hour, but Nikka wasn't ready to interrupt him quite yet, even though she was sure the coffee had grown cold by now. She watched as he stood there, gazing out the window at the still pine trees just beyond the propane storage tanks that edged the cabin property.

It takes a while to get used to the fact that demons walk this earth. Maybe it takes even longer when you see it possess someone you know, or at least think you know. Perhaps there is a point at which you wonder how long that thing has infected the person and how much of that her is just the demon. It was possible that Agent Wolfe was thinking these things all at once while his partner lay resting in the bedroom.

Nikka remembered the first time she had seen an exorcism. It was awful. The stains of it still dripped from the inside walls of her memory and they would never scrub away. But she didn't actually know that person; not the way Andy knew Agent Cavanaugh.

Wolfe placed the cup down on the table and half-turned back to her. "Tell me everything."

She glanced at Jason, who stood at her side. Together they pulled the chairs up to the table and encouraged Wolfe to do the same. But he only turned to face them, his arms crossed over his chest. The color had finally returned to his face.

"That was the demon Asmodeus," Nikka started. "He was a drone."

"Drone?"

"Yeah, soldiers sent out to do the dirty work. There are three basic levels of demon hierarchy, but I'm sure there are many subtle layers within that structure. Drones are exactly how it sounds. They possess human bodies, scout out the locations, give feedback to the higher-ups."

Wolfe pulled a chair around, straddled it and sat backwards with his arms resting on the back. "And who are the higher-ups?"

"Lieutenants. Generals."

The agent glanced at Jason. "And you've seen these too?"

A half-smile appeared on Jason's lips. "You could say that."

"He had been possessed by a general," Nikka interjected, "Abaddon, the one who was sent to find and kill me."

"And you—killed it instead?" Wolfe raised his eyebrows as though he didn't know what else to call it.

She nodded. "I did."

"What do they want from us?"

Nikka felt her tongue go dry. That was such a big question. "Right now, they're trying to end humanity. That building that went down—I was there that night and so was he." She ticked her head toward Jason. "It's been a front for demon activity for a long time, using the Department of Defense as a cover. I was there when a portal opened in the sub-basement and thousands of demons came out. My friend . . ." She stopped and felt the lump form in her throat. "Gideon. He closed it. But it caused a backfire or something and it exploded."

She looked away and felt Jason's hand close over hers.

"So this portal is closed now? No more demons coming out?" Wolfe asked.

Nikka met his eyes again. "Not from that one."

"That's not very reassuring." He cleared his throat and pulled his hands to the side of his chair. "I get the whole demon thing. Possession. Exorcism. I get it. But, I don't get you. You're not exactly normal, either."

"No, she's not," Jason said and leaned on his elbows. "She's so much more."

Nikka smiled at him. "When I said I had cancer, that was very true. Gideon, my mentor, found me and offered me this life. He cured me. I was chosen to be the seraph, a human given the powers of angels to fight the demons on earth. There is only one on earth at a time, and when I die, another will take my place."

Wolfe shook his head and ran his fingers through his hair as a sarcastic laugh escaped his throat. "This is some major Bible stuff. Seraph? As in like seraphim? What next? Are there little cherubs running around this place too? Chubby little baby angels?"

"This is serious," Nikka said and stood. She reached behind her shoulder and withdrew the sword. It fazed from invisibility and the blue flame began to slither around the blade.

Wolfe immediately froze and watched her place the sword on the table. As soon as she released it, the fire vanished, leaving a plain katana with a black bone handle.

"That was given to me when I woke up naked in the basement of the hospital I had lived in for months. These marks," she said and lifted her arm to the light, revealing the tattoos across her skin, "were given to me by some higher power. God. Angels. Aliens. I really don't know. All I know is that when I woke up, I was in a hell of a lot of pain, but I was strong and healthy, and that sword was by my side. And I woke up with the power to exorcise demons. Gideon is gone, and I no longer have the ability to learn certain things about all of this. I'm just trying to figure it out as I go. But what I do know, is that the demon horde that came out of the portal downtown is gearing up for something very bad, and I was told that you needed to help us."

Wolfe held his hands out in surrender. "Okay. Fine. But what do you mean you were told about me?"

She bit her lip. This was where things would get a little fuzzy. She wasn't sure how to explain it except to just say it outright. "I had a dream, or a vision. I don't know what it was. But I saw you in the aftermath of everything and I needed to find you."

His eyebrow cocked again and he smiled. "A dream?"

"You're going to question that after everything you've seen today?" she said and crossed her arms over her chest. "I saw you in my dream, and then I saw you on TV at the explosion site. When I went down there, I knew it was true. Your partner was possessed. She was there for a reason, keeping track of you. I'm sure it was only a matter of time before they got into you too."

The smile slipped from his lips and his cheeks grew pale again, the same chalk white that he had right after he saw Nikka pull the demon from his partner.

"Fair enough," he said and glanced between her and Jason. "So, what is it that you think I can do for you? I'm no seraph." He phrased the word carefully.

"I'm not exactly sure, but I found something on a database that I pulled from the mainframe in that building."

"You hacked into the Department of Defense? This is just going from bad to worse," he said as he shook his head.

"It was being run by demons. Let's keep some perspective, okay?" She sat back down at the table. "I found something that I need you to see. Do you know anything about EMP's?"

His eyes darkened as she said the word and he seemed to stop breathing. "What did you find?"

"I'll show you."

She brought her laptop to the table and opened the files she had reviewed, everything about the EMP device and the documents she had downloaded from the DOD flash drive. Wolfe remained silent as he perused the computer. Jason and Nikka stepped away from the table and gave him his space, but she waited in a place where she could watch him.

Wolfe read each entry, his attention fixed on the laptop. Finally, as the light outside the cabin began to dim, Wolfe sat back in the chair, his eyes still watching the computer screen.

Nikka stood from the sofa where she had watched him with Jason at her side. She stepped around the table and pulled up a chair next to him.

"I think I know why you need me," he said.

She watched him, the glow of the computer screen sending colors of blue and white against his face.

"The things in these files are very concerning," he continued. "And I can get more information from the FBI database about this EMP project. If this is true, it means that there is involvement from every level of government. An EMP of this kind could take down the national power grid. And I'm betting this is not the only device out there."

He looked away from the computer and gazed at her.

"Demons have done this. They start with just a few drones. They infect enough people until they find a way in and I saw them all over that DOD building. I'd bet money they've infiltrated the FBI. Once they're in, they can manipulate people to do things, build these kinds of devices."

"As soon as they have a fully functioning device, they just deploy it over US soil and boom," Wolfe said, his hands splaying out. "Apocalypse."

"They don't have to possess every human being on the planet to destroy us. They just create the right conditions, and we'll do the rest ourselves," Jason said from behind them.

Agent Wolfe glanced back at the computer. "A device like this will put us back into the Middle Ages. No electricity. No power of any kind. That means no running water. No food delivery. No gasoline. It won't take long for society to collapse into chaos."

"And then they take over," Nikka said, her voice dropping to a near-whisper.

Chapter 19 Jason

Jason opened the door to the bedroom and peered at the bed. Since the demon had left her body, Megan's skin began to heal from the dry cracking it had created. She was no longer sleeping, but she lay there in the faint afternoon light, her eyes open and tears streaming down her face.

Yeah. He knew the feeling.

"Hey there," he said and held up a warm cup of tea that he had made. "I just thought you might want some."

She didn't look at him or say anything. She only sniffed and wiped her hand across her cheek.

He walked into the room and stepped over to the nightstand where he placed the cup. Agent Wolfe had wanted to bring it himself, but Jason intervened and offered to come instead. Of course he didn't know this woman, but he was the only one who understood what she had just gone through.

"The shaking takes a few days to go away," he said and kneeled down so that he could look at her. "But the memories take a little longer."

She closed her eyes. "I don't even know what's happening."

"Well," he said and sat back against the wall, "for starters, you were possessed by a demon. Everything that you did or said when it was there, that wasn't you. You're free now."

"I couldn't stop it. It made me do things—"

"I know. But you need to always remember that the demon did those things."

She opened her eyes again. "Why did this happen?"

He cleared his throat and began to tell her about the last few days, about Nikka and meeting Agent Wolfe. He didn't want to reveal too much about Nikka yet, but he let Megan know just enough to explain the events in the cellar. By the end, it looked like she was ready to throw up. She sat up in the bed and looked down at her own hands that were still shaking.

"And do you remove demons as well?" she said as she looked at her fingers.

He smiled and shook his head. "I'm more of a sidekick, really. But I can identify with what you're going through."

Cavanaugh looked up at him. "This happened to you too, didn't it?"

"Yes," he said with a nod. "And she saved me. It gets better, I promise. It just takes some time."

"I—it—told Andy so many lies," she said, and the tears threatened to flood her eyes again. "I don't know how he'll ever forgive me."

"I think that takes time, too. He knows it wasn't you. He knows everything now."

Jason looked at her, an FBI agent, broken into this crying mess. He had to believe that Wolfe would forgive her for everything that had happened during her possession. There was always a way back.

There had to be.

CHAPTER 20 NIKKA

Wolfe closed the passenger door of the SUV after he made sure Agent Cavanaugh was buckled into her seat. She had barely opened her eyes when he carried her from the bed and into the car. He walked around to the driver's side door where Nikka waited for him.

"Is she going to be okay?" he asked and glanced back at Cavanaugh.

"It takes a few days, like a hangover. But she'll be fine," Nikka said.

He plunged his hands into the pockets of his jacket, but Nikka knew his hands weren't that cold. He wanted to say something, but she could feel his hesitation.

"Still having trouble with all of this?" she asked.

A small laugh erupted from his throat. "You could say that. You know, I never would have suspected that she was possessed with—well, with a demon. How am I to know? What about me? What's to prevent them from getting me?"

"They can't just jump from person to person. It's not like the flu."

Jason stepped beside Nikka and glanced at Cavanaugh as well. "It wasn't sudden for me. It started as thoughts, voices. At first I thought I was just depressed or manic or something. I was having awful dreams and then one day I awoke and realized I had no control over my actions. I was just a passenger, looking out the window while something else took control of the wheel. But it all took several days. Once Nikka took it out, I was free and back at the wheel. This time, I will know it when I feel it happening."

"Religious relics help," Nikka said. "Crosses. Icons. Anything. They can at least provide some measure of protection. Holy water doesn't do much to protect, but it can help you identify one when you're suspicious. Try and get them to drink or splash a little on the skin. It'll burn."

Wolfe shook his head in disbelief. "Crosses and holy water. It's like I'm in a horror movie." He pulled open the driver's side door and climbed into the SUV. "I'm going to take her home, but I'll be back tomorrow. We need to get into the regional FBI office in town. I bet I could find more info on that device and where it's being kept. If you were able to get that bit from the DOD mainframe, I'm positive there's more where that came from, and I can access it from my office."

"And how do you propose we do that?" Jason asked as he cocked his head to the side.

"I'm still an FBI agent. Nobody knows that I'm here with you. I can just get in and out."

"And what if they do know? What if there are more of them like her?" Jason said and signaled to Cavanaugh, who slept quietly in the passenger seat. "They won't let you out once you're in."

"I could go with him," Nikka said. "I can see them when he can't. And they say I'm pretty good with a sword." A smile appeared across her lips.

Jason shot her a concerned look, but stayed quiet, even though she knew what rattled around in his mind just then.

"Sounds like we've got a plan." Wolfe started the engine. "I'll be back tomorrow morning."

"Keep her out of sight until then." Nikka nodded to his partner. "If they see that she's no longer possessed, they'll suspect that I've gotten to you. You won't be safe."

He nodded and Nikka watched as the SUV departed from the cabin and disappeared around the bend of the road.

"I don't like this," Jason said as he handed over the hoodie to Nikka.

She accepted it with a sigh. "I know. But what other choice do we have?"

"Let him do it himself."

"I can't do that." She pulled the hoodie on, letting the hood fall over her back. "Wolfe has access to the FBI database. We can get in and find the information we need and get back out again."

"Why do you have to go with him?"

"You know why," she said as she sidled up to him. At this angle he always felt so tall to her.

Getting into the FBI regional office wasn't going to be the hard part. It was getting out again with the hacked intel that was going to be tough. "I need to see for myself how many demons have infiltrated his region. I'm the only one that can see them. I can't let him go in blind."

He clutched his fingers around the lapels of her jacket and pulled her closer. She could smell the scent of the soap on his hands. "I still don't like it."

The heat from under his T-shirt rippled in small waves from his torso. Moments like this reminded her of those days when she first met him, when she thought he was the real Jason. She clutched her fingers into tight fists when she realized she wanted to wrap her arms around him like she used to. It seemed like a century ago when she felt comfortable pressed against him as she rode behind him on the motorcycle or sat beside him in the library. But he held her at arm's length now, only grasping at her jacket.

"In and out. If we can find the information on the EMP device, we may be able to stop them from using it. This little excursion would be worth it then."

"Please be careful," he said, just above a whisper, and released the edges of her jacket. She could sense the unease in his voice, that twinge of desperation he got when everything felt so out of control.

When she turned from him she still felt his eyes on her back, just as he always did when she walked away. She climbed into the passenger seat of the SUV as Agent Wolfe started the engine. Nikka glanced back at the cabin one last time before the vehicle started off and saw Jason leaning against the door frame. It was growing harder and harder to leave him behind now, and she wasn't sure why. He had to know that this was necessary, and it wasn't going to be easy. She met his gaze just before the SUV turned away, and in that moment she saw the storm of worry in his sharp, blue eyes. It was then that she realized she had stopped seeing the images of fire behind those eyes long ago. When, she wasn't sure, but Abaddon's smile had faded from her memories, and she had only been seeing the true Jason for a while now.

And then the cabin was gone in a rush of pine trees that moved swiftly past the passenger window as the SUV drove away from her hideaway.

Nikka felt the tension in her shoulders ease just a little as she sat back.

"Everything okay?" Wolfe said as he drove the windy mountain road. "Your boyfriend seems a little on edge today."

"He's not my boyfriend."

A small laugh erupted from his throat. "Yeah, whatever."

"Focus, please," she said and glared at him. "Are you ready for this?"

"As ready as I can be, considering this is probably the end of my career."

Nikka looked away from him and down at her black boots. "I'm sorry about that."

"It is what it is. I guess I'm still a little shell-shocked about this whole thing. After what I saw yesterday, I'm glad you found me."

"Yeah, well, seeing your first demon has a way of putting things into perspective."

"That's true," he said as he undid the top button of his white shirt and exposed the silver crucifix dangling from a chain at his neck. "Will this do?"

Nikka shrugged. "It sure won't hurt."

He placed both hands on the steering wheel again and glanced at her. She could tell he wanted to say something, but it only hung in the air between them. When she glanced at him, his eyes darted away from her and back to the road.

"What is it?" she asked.

"It's just, well, you're just a kid. And your boyfr—, I mean your friend is not much older than you. Is there anybody else helping you guys?"

That made the pit in her gut gape open like a bleeding wound. She chewed on her lip as she looked away, hoping he wouldn't see the emptiness that haunted her eyes. "No. It's just us."

"But you mentioned someone else. A mentor. You called him Gideon."

"It's just us," she said again and felt her voice drop. "Gideon's dead."

The crackle of the dirt road under the tires was deafening in the silence between them. She heard him swallow.

"When the portal closed, when the explosion occurred," Wolfe said carefully. "That's when it happened, isn't it? You said he closed the portal, that he was gone. He died in that explosion."

Tears threatened to cloud her vision. This was definitely something she didn't want to talk about, especially with the FBI agent.

"Yeah."

"I'm sorry," he said. "I had no idea. Our investigation hasn't uncovered any remains yet."

"There won't be any. It was a gateway to Hell, and he went through. You won't find anything."

"Again, I'm sorry. I just worry about you two kids. This is an awful lot for you guys to take on your own."

"We'll be fine," she said. She heard him take in a slow breath and grow silent. As much as she didn't want to talk about all this, though, she realized that nobody else in the world knew the truth about what was just under the surface of this reality. Agent Wolfe was the only other individual on the entire planet that could understand their predicament.

"Thank you for listening to us," she said in a near-whisper.

He nodded. "I just wish there was more I could do."

"If we can find the info on this EMP, then you will have done more than enough."

"I hope that's true."

The SUV rounded the turn to enter the highway and headed straight into the city. Nikka wasn't sure where the FBI regional office was located but she knew it had to be somewhere in the downtown district and not far from the DOD building that had fallen. Sure enough, he exited off the highway and into the busiest part of the city, under the shadows of towering skyscrapers and arcing street lights. He slowed as he neared the underground parking garage of a dark gray building. Wolfe produced his entrance badge, swiped it through the pad at the gate, and the cross bar lifted.

The shade and cold of the garage surrounded them as he pulled into the parking structure and stopped at a space near the stairwell. As soon as the engine stopped, everything fell into a dead silence. Nikka very well knew that it was still daylight outside, but all light seemed to be swallowed away and replaced with harsh, artificial bulbs that buzzed and hummed with angry power. Every car that waited in the garage felt like sleeping monsters, waiting for something to alert and feed them.

Nikka stepped out of the SUV as Wolfe came around to her side, pulling his black suit jacket over his crisp white linen shirt. With his black tie and clean haircut, he looked every bit like the agent he was supposed to be. He clipped his badge to the lapel of his jacket and glanced at the elevator doors.

"My office is on the third floor," he said and straightened his tie. "We can access the mainframe from my computer. I've only got one problem."

"What's that?"

"I don't know how to get you up there with me. Someone might get suspicious if they see you."

"Not if they're expecting me," she said and closed her eyes.

She willed the power in her bones and tissues to rise to the surface, just like she did every time she needed to be invisible or when she had learned to interpret Latin in the library. She had done this particular trick only a couple of other times before. It had been exhausting, but it was well worth the try. The energy sizzled just at the surface of her skin, like threads of static electricity that danced across the hairs of her forearms. It twisted and sparked until she could mold it to her liking.

Her thoughts moved the energy over her hair, lips and face. It glided across her clothes as she bent them with her will.

When she opened her eyes again, she looked at him through the eyes of someone he recognized. Dark brown hair fell to her shoulders, her body dressed in a dark blue pantsuit. She had placed every detail of Agent Cavanaugh over her body like a costume.

"How did you do that?" he asked.

She smiled, the same curve of her mouth that Agent Cavanaugh had. "Practice. Lots of practice."

His eyebrows rose as he looked over every inch of her face and clothes. "It's amazing. I had no idea you could do that."

"Oh, there's a lot more where this came from. Now stop staring and let's go."

Chapter 21 Nikka

Wolfe walked out of the elevator with Nikka following behind him. She kept pace with him, a confident stroll through the large open lobby. Panels of windows allowed light down across the black tile floor. Two staircases opened on both sides of the lobby, rising up to the second and third floors and arcing over the elevator bank. A wide entry desk faced the lobby, attended by two security guards. Wolfe walked around the edge of the desk and nodded to the guards in greeting.

Nikka followed his lead and nodded as well. The guards must have recognized them because they nodded in return and allowed them to pass to the left stairway. She glanced at their faces fast enough to see that neither of them were possessed, at least not with drones. She turned her eyes back down and stepped onto the stairway behind Wolfe. Other agents passed them on the stairs, but she couldn't watch everyone while trying to keep the image of Agent Cavanaugh over her body.

The stairway opened to the third floor landing, where Wolfe's step quickened as he entered the hallway. He glanced back behind Nikka and searched the corridor around them. Then he stopped at the first office door overlooking the lobby and worked at the lock with the key he produced from his pocket. The lock clicked and he moved into the office, pulling her swiftly in with him.

Wolfe wasted no time sliding around the desk and accessing his computer. For the moment, Nikka felt the camouflage fall from her body. She gasped as she felt her knees quiver. The fatigue had begun to creep into her muscles, but she was too nervous to feel it until now.

"Are you okay?" he asked, his eyes lit from the computer screen.

She leaned back against the door and took a breath. "I'll be fine. Holding onto that kind of power for that long can be a little tiring."

"Just sit down or something. It looks like you're going to pass out."

"I'll be fine."

She rubbed the back of her neck and stepped around the desk as Wolfe continued to click at the keyboard. Although the office was still dark, she could see that it was a large space. And to have this location over the lobby probably meant that he was one of the higher ranking agents. She didn't know much about the FBI except what she saw on TV, but having a couple of leather chairs in the office under the large window had to mean something.

"Okay, I'm in," he said. "I was able to get through the initial firewalls—" It seemed like he was mostly talking to himself, like he needed the encouragement to keep going.

Nikka stepped around to the window, pleated in closed vertical blinds that kept out most of the light flowing in from the lobby. She pulled one of the panels aside and peered down to the rows of windows showing light in the atrium.

"I think I found something," he said. "There's a file hidden in the central server. It's linked to the Department of Defense. And it looks like Homeland Security is linked too."

She glanced back to him. "Is that what we need?"

"I can't tell yet."

She turned back to the window and watched the flow of new agents moving in through the main doors. Throngs of men and women dressed in black suits came through the entry doors as though a cavalcade of buses had stopped outside the building. Some collected in groups in the lobby, talking like old friends. Others moved to the stairs or the elevator bank. As she watched them, she felt the air get sucked from her lungs as though the ground had dropped out from under her feet.

These men and women, the agents of the FBI, wherever they had just come from, they all were just puppets played by demons. Under their faces, below the human mask, writhed drones like reptiles stuck in their shells. She glanced from face to face, but they were all infected. There must have been over a hundred of them down there, and only a few human souls remained among the crowd of FBI agents that had just come through the doors.

"Wolfe," she said.

"I think this is it," he said.

"Agent Wolfe—" she said again.

"Project Wormwood," he said as he read the screen. "That's what they are calling it. Everything is in here." He plugged a flash drive into the computer and began transferring the file.

"ANDY!" she said forcefully.

He finally looked over the edge of his computer screen.

"We have a big problem," she said and backed away from the window. He must have seen the lack of color in her face when he stood from the desk.

"What is it?"

"We need to go. Now."

"They're here, aren't they?"

Nikka only nodded and stepped to the office door. She opened it just a crack and peered into the corridor. Agents appeared on the landing of the stairway.

"We have to get out of here," she whispered to him.

"The file transfer isn't ready yet."

The agents entered the corridor.

"Wolfe," she said and pushed the door closed as the agents neared the office. She locked the door and stepped back as she watched it, hearing the footsteps moved closer.

"Got it," he said and pulled the flash drive free. He clicked out of the files and shut down the computer just as a knock sounded on his door.

"Agent Wolfe," the man spoke from the corridor. "It's Special Agent Cameron. Can we speak?"

Nikka glanced at him, but he only stared at the door with his mouth agape. She flashed him a "say something" look.

"Uh, now . . . is not a good time."

"It is very important. It is about the investigation downtown. Some new information has come up," the man spoke.

"Okay," Wolfe said and looked at Nikka. "Just shoot me an email and I will get on it right away."

"I'm afraid we need to deal with it now."

The door suddenly crashed inward as the man on the other side kicked it. Two men in dark suits, drones hidden behind their human faces stormed through the threshold. They must have only expected Wolfe, because she noticed the look of awful recognition on their faces when they saw her.

The muscles in her shoulders flexed as she reached behind her back and pulled the katana from its hidden scabbard. The first agent reached for the gun in the holster under his jacket. Nikka willed her power down her right arm and felt the collection form in her hand until the light intensified in her palm. She pulled back and threw the ball of light toward him. It sang through the air like a fast pitch, striking him in the center of his chest. The man staggered backward as the light pierced through his body. The light caught the demon and pulled it from his body, pinning it to the back wall of the corridor. The agent's body collapsed to the ground, his hand still on his gun.

The second agent darted through the door just as the light zinged past his head. His face twisted into an angry grimace. He lunged toward her before she could move, but a gunshot screamed into the small space of the office. The agent fell to the floor, crying out as he grasped the bleeding hole in his leg.

Nikka's ears rang with the report of the gunshot as she looked up at Wolfe, the gun still in his steady hand. Beads of sweat had formed on his forehead.

Thanking him needed to wait. The sound of the gunshot would have alerted everybody in the building. She pulled the demon from the agent at her feet and dispatched it with her sword. Wolfe remained close behind her as they emerged into the corridor and she beheaded the first demon pinned to the wall.

"Emergency exit this way," Wolfe said as he stepped past her.

She ran down the back hall with him as the sound of a hundred people rushed onto the landing by his office. Bullets peppered the walls around them. Wolfe pulled her into the fire escape stairwell as flecks of drywall rained down on them from the shower of gunfire.

The sounds of shouting and footsteps echoed down the stairwell behind the heavy fire door that closed after Nikka dodged into the exit. She followed Wolfe, two steps at a time, as they descended down through each level. The crashing open of the fire door ricocheted down the stairwell, but Nikka didn't dare glance back up for fear she would lose her footing and tumble down the stairs and land on Wolfe. She managed to sheath the blade just as the agent lunged for a door on a single landing. They ran through it and into the dim artificial light of the basement parking garage.

Wolfe seemed to know where he was going as he turned right and ran down a second row of parked SUV's that all appeared to look just like his. Nikka followed him closely, knowing she would get lost if he disappeared from her line of sight.

He found his vehicle, and they climbed in just as the fire escape door opened. Agents poured from the door like ants letting loose from a hill. Wolfe stepped hard on the gas, and the SUV shot forward and down the row toward the garage exit.

Nikka fumbled for her seatbelt as the SUV careened around the corner and through the exit gate that had begun to lower. Clearly, the rest of the building had been alerted to their presence, but the alarm came seconds too late. The gate nicked the top of the vehicle, but they emerged onto the street without any further damage to the car. Wolfe raced down the street, through two red lights, while Nikka found the buckle for her seatbelt. Her fingers clutched around the upper strap as the car weaved in and out of traffic.

She didn't have to look through the back window to know that they were being followed. She could see Wolfe's eyes darting to the rearview mirror as he swerved through the lines of cars and busy intersections despite the absence of a green traffic light. The SUV veered through another intersection and turned right, heading to the entry ramp for the freeway. A car squealed, and tires smoked as the driver braked hard to miss the SUV that careened toward the ramp. Nikka closed her eyes and held her breath just before the car would have smacked right into the rear of the SUV, but she never felt the impact. The SUV continued its forward momentum, even accelerated hard, before she opened her eyes again.

As fast as the traffic signs were moving past them, the SUV had to be going about 80 as Wolfe started on the freeway ramp. His eyes still glanced through the rearview mirror and Nikka felt the SUV accelerate even more. The other agents—or demons—were still behind them. They didn't care about the chaos and carnage left in their wake as they chased her now. They were just desperate to catch her and Wolfe, no matter the cost.

The SUV merged onto the freeway, which began to get thick with the afternoon commuter traffic. Wolfe weaved into the center lane and then pushed hard on the accelerator as he wound through the stream of cars. A truck pulling a camper trailer merged into the lane and Wolfe swerved onto the left shoulder to miss it. Nikka closed her eyes again and bit her lip, trying not to scream. The SUV jostled as it navigated the gravel shoulder and then the road smoothed out again.

"You can exorcise demons," Wolfe said with a half grin as Nikka opened her eyes again, "but you can't handle a little high speed chase?"

"Only in a Vin Diesel movie," she said, trying to force a smile as she continued to grasp onto the seatbelt with white knuckles.

Wolfe lost his smile. "Well, hang on tight. Vin ain't seen nothing yet."

He slammed on the brakes and swerved into the right lanes of traffic. Car horns blared and tires screeched as the SUV darted across three lanes, into the road divide and into an exit ramp just before it was too late. Nikka was sure that the SUV must have caught some air as it accelerated off the road and into the median. The vehicle almost tilted as Wolfe corrected the wheels and then caught the pavement of the ramp just in time to speed into another part of the city.

He glanced into the mirror again, but this time his eyes lost that concentrated hawk-like stare. She waited for him to say something, but she could see the smile start at the edges of his mouth.

"We lost them?" she asked.

"For now," he said. "But we're taking the long way back home just in case."

She relaxed the grip she had on the seatbelt and felt the ache in her knuckles. This little trip into the city was enough for a thousand lifetimes as far as she was concerned. She just wanted to get back to the cabin and away from any more demons.

Chapter 22 Nikka

The SUV wound up the mountain road until the cabin came into view. Despite the cold wind, the midday light flickered through the bare trees and fell on the roof of the cabin like a beacon. Before the vehicle came to a full stop, Nikka had the car door open just as she saw Jason emerge from the front door.

The creases in his forehead seemed to have been etched into place like they had been there for a thousand years. She now understood what it was like for sailors to crave dry land as she stepped from the SUV and wrapped her arms around Jason. At first he stiffened, but then she felt him melt into her.

"I never want to ride with him again," she said, feeling Jason's arms around her as well. Her limbs trembled with the adrenaline of the last hour and her fingers still hurt from holding so tight to her seatbelt.

"Everything go okay?" Jason said.

Nikka pulled away from him. "I think we got what we needed."

"But everything is okay, right? You didn't get hurt?"

She gently slapped his upper arm. "Give me a little credit."

"Nobody got hurt," Wolfe said as he emerged from the SUV. "Easy in and out."

Nikka turned to him with a glare. "Right. Easy." Jason didn't need to know about the bullets whistling past her ears and the multiple near-miss car accidents.

Wolfe held the flash drive up for Jason to see. "Shall we find out what the fuss is all about?"

They returned to the cabin and started up the laptop. Wolfe navigated several folders through the flash drive until he opened the file that had interested him at the FBI building.

"Here it is," he said as Nikka settled beside him at the table. Jason looked over his shoulder.

"Project Wormwood. There is a lot of data attached to this file," he said.

"Wormwood?" Nikka muttered. "Why do I know that word?"

Wolfe opened a series of related files onto the main screen. One appeared to be a collection of schematic drawings and instructional manuals. They didn't make any sense to her, but Wolfe scanned the schematics with genuine interest. She glanced over the drawings as the name of the project continued to nag at her.

"What is that?" Jason asked.

"Everything that you two were worried about," Wolfe said and opened more files. "According to this, there is more than one EMP device out there, all built through the Department of Defense. This Project Wormwood is the entire plan. It looks like there are five of them. There are schematics and instructions for each of them in here, and it looks like they're massive. Not like the little homemade things that can crash a plane or something."

"What do you mean? People can make these at home?" Nikka said as she felt nausea for the first time today.

"Well, the FBI has known about these things for years. It started right about the time of World War II when researchers started to learn about the capabilities of an EMP. And then things got really scary in the 80's. That's when the FBI, Armed Forces, Department of Defense—you name it—got involved, because Russia began to show signs of real capability with these things."

"I read about that," Nikka said. "There was something about Russia developing weapons that could carry an EMP device over a long range."

"Right," Wolfe said. "Like on a rocket, for example. The U.S. was concerned that they had the capability to launch something that could detonate over American soil and wipe out the entire grid."

"So, is that the device?" Jason said, indicating the schematics on the screen.

Wolfe forced a laugh. "This looks to be something like it, but it appears to be homegrown. Years ago, the FBI, CIA, NSA were all alerted to the possibility of an emergence of EMP devices. Everybody was so focused on terrorists using these things, that it distracted everyone from the truth that they were being built right here. This device," he said, pointing to the drawing, "is large enough that it would just be attached to a launching platform in a remote location. It could be fired and it would detonate in the atmosphere anywhere in the central U.S., wiping out the entire electrical grid."

"Wait a second," Jason said. "I know that there are fail safes out there. I've re-built old engines and learned about the differences in electrical systems. Not all of them would be shot if this were to happen."

"But most would," Wolfe said and glanced back at him. "That's the crux of it all. EMP's wouldn't matter if the electrical infrastructure had been taken care of, but it hasn't. I've seen lots of federal reports about the severe weakness of the electrical grid. Being in the Bureau for all these years, I was aware of a lot of Senate hearings and other meetings that would happen to address this problem, but it was always ignored."

Wolfe opened a file filled with various reports, one from several years ago. It looked to be the minutes of an official hearing.

"It's all here. I was in D.C. for this hearing." Nikka glanced down at the statement from a Representative from Massachussetts.

Rep. Ed Markey: The electrical grid's vulnerability to cyber and other attacks is one of the single greatest threats to our national security.

"I remember listening to this hearing at the time. They described how the electrical grid is so old, outdated, with so many customizations, many of which are not made any more. An EMP would rupture transformers nationwide. There are no spares to replace widespread damage. Hell, it already takes an average of three years to obtain a single new large transformer. Imagine if thousands of them went out all at once. It would take years, maybe even decades to get the grid back on line. And it's not only transformers that take a hit. There are thousands upon thousands of individual sensory control switches that run everything from streetlights to dams and generators to the engine in your car, and every single one of these sensors dies in the face of an EMP. When the explosion happens, nothing electrical is spared unless it's shielded or can run without these sensors. So, we now live in a society of extreme electrical vulnerability because a bunch of D.C. politicians didn't want to deal with this."

Nikka sat back and gazed at the screen, to the final words of the representative from Massachussetts. "They couldn't; not really."

Wolfe's brow furrowed. "All they had to do was listen to him."

"But they weren't going to. Not ever," Nikka said and looked at him. "Not if this is what they wanted."

"Why would they want this?" he said.

"You saw the same thing I did today. Your bureau office was overrun by drones. The building downtown was filled with them too. These demons have found a way into those protected government agencies. So why would they not seek to infiltrate higher than that? This Markey guy was probably not possessed, but those who were listening, those who could have made a difference, chose not to. Why? Because this was the plan all along."

Wolfe looked back at the computer. He clicked through more files and paged through hundreds of photos—pictures that looked like they were taken for ID's and badges. All were from some government agency.

Nikka stood and paced the room, glancing at a stack of books along the far shelf that had collected dust since Jason's grandfather first built the place. Her eyes moved along all the spines until she came to one that she had hoped was there. She pulled the black leather-bound volume and dusted off the cover.

"I remember where I heard that name before," she said as Jason looked back at her.

She paged through the book, the thin white pages crinkling under her fingers. "I remember hearing it when I was a kid in Bible school."

"What are you talking about?" Jason said.

She found the right section in the *Book of Revelations*. "'And the third angel sounded, and there fell a great star from Heaven, burning as it were a lamp, and it fell upon the third part of the rivers, and upon the fountains of waters; And the name of the star is called Wormwood; and the third part of the waters became wormwood; and many men died of the waters because they were made bitter.'"

The room fell silent as she looked up from the book. "They are trying to bring about the Apocalypse. This is part of *Revelations* that talks about Judgement Day, Armageddon, all that scary stuff that we have always believed would never really happen to us."

"Seas boiling, sky's falling. Fire and brimstone," Wolfe muttered.

"Wait a minute," Jason interrupted. "One EMP can't do all of that."

"I've seen the earth open up and thousands of demons pour out from that gash in the ground," Nikka said. "I've seen the fire and brimstone. This is just another step in that direction."

"If that's true," Jason said, his voice seemed to drop a little, "then there is nothing we can do to stop it."

"Well, maybe I can delay it," Wolfe said as he clicked through the files of the computer and pointed to a single schematic. "Maybe I can at least stop this particular device."

"How?" Jason asked.

"I think I know where they're planning to launch it, if these reports are accurate. I can still get there with Cavanaugh's and my credentials. It looks like there's an army base in Nevada that seems like a good lead, and it's going to be somewhere out in the desert. Remote. Way off the grid. According to this, there's still some construction left on it so the device is not ready yet. Maybe I can find and destroy it before it even comes to this."

"Okay," Nikka said and closed the book. "Let's go."

"No. I said I can do it."

"You can't take on these demons alone."

"Maybe, but I can get around these government places with my bureau credentials, much easier without you two. Cavanaugh's coming with me, so I won't be alone. And what do you know about dismantling something like this?"

Nikka shrugged. "Nothing."

"Exactly," he said, "but I have some contacts that could help."

"No," Nikka said, shaking her head and looking away from him. "This is my mess, not yours. I have to do this."

Wolfe leaned in toward her. "No, it's not. You said it yourself, you were supposed to find me. This is why. This is for me to handle."

"But you won't know who to trust."

"That may be true, but after what I saw today, I am starting to get the idea of how to tell the difference. Look, you two are just a couple of kids. No offense."

"Much taken," Jason interjected, his arms now folded across his chest and his shoulders stiff.

"I can't put you in that kind of danger. The world needs you to stop the demons here, distract them while I slip in and destroy that EMP. If you go with me, they'll follow us there and they'll know what we're doing."

Nikka bit her lip. She wanted to fight him on this because she knew she could help him, but he had a good point. After all, she was supposed to enlist his help, Agent Andy Wolfe's help. Maybe this was why, and maybe that was all she needed to do.

"Fine," she said. "But you need to keep in contact."

He disconnected the flash drive and pocketed it. "And you two need to keep each other safe. I figure I should get out of town soon. After that little mess we caused at the bureau, I don't suppose I can stay much longer anyway. At least with Megan, she's someone I can trust now, thanks to you."

Nikka forced a smile, but she felt a painful twinge as he walked away from her and stepped out of the cabin. She hadn't known him long, but he had become an ally, almost family, in that brief moment. Somewhere in her brain she had probably thought he would be with them for much longer, guiding them through this world until they could get on their feet again and put all this behind them. But as he walked away, she knew that this would never be much better. She and Jason would always be hiding and alone while people like Wolfe needed to leave. More than anything, she wanted to tell him not to go, but that was only her selfish side thinking.

Jason walked with him as Nikka stood shivering on the step of the cabin. Wolfe glanced back at Jason, leaned in and whispered something in his ear, then turned to climb into the car. Jason glanced back briefly at her, but averted his gaze as the car's engine revved. Wolfe pulled away from the cabin with a single wave to her before he drove down the road, like a big brother leaving for war; a war from which he may never return.

Chapter 23 Nikka

The last of the dust settled, and they could no longer see Wolfe's SUV. Jason turned back toward the cabin.

"What did he say to you?" Nikka asked.

Jason hesitated for a moment and then slipped past her into the cabin. "Nothing. Just to be careful."

She probably didn't know him that well, but she could tell he was lying. Whatever it was, he wasn't going to tell her now and prodding him about it was not bound to get the results she wanted. Feeling a little aggravated, she shook her head and then followed him back into the cabin. That feeling subsided after a few minutes until she was able to just let it go.

She glanced about the cabin, which felt lighter and clearer than it had ever been since they first got there. As worried as she was about Andy and Megan, he took some of the burden that she had carried for too long. What were they to do now? For the first time in so long, she didn't know. Maybe it was time to just take a moment and breathe. But what if that was all it took for everything to fall apart? You let your guard down for one minute, and everything collapses out from under you.

Jason turned back to her and flashed her his smile, the same one that barely revealed the faint dimples just under the goatee. "Come on. Let's just watch a movie or something. There's nothing else for us to do now."

She nodded. "All right." *Just relax. Sure. Easier said than done.*

The first few days after Agent Wolfe left felt no different, as if she was just waiting for something to happen. No calls from Wolfe, but that wasn't necessarily a bad thing. She hadn't expected to hear from him so soon anyway. It took everything in her power to not put on her jacket and boots and go after him to help.

Jason tried to distract her with board games and movies, but it wasn't until the third night after Andy left that she was able to sleep through the night for the first time in weeks. A full night. No bad dreams or apocalyptic visions. She woke up to the light of a cold morning, to the smell of coffee and bacon cooking on the wood stove in the kitchen.

Nikka stepped out of the bedroom and the smell grew stronger. She rubbed the gritty bits of sleep from her eyes as she looked up to see Jason at the stove, his old sweater hanging over his broad shoulders. His flax hair had seemed a bit longer than she had last noticed. Why hadn't she even seen that his hair was long enough that he could pull it back into a tie? The guilt of her lack of attention now gnawed at her insides. Had she also forgotten to thank him for everything he had done to help her too?

"I thought I was going to have to check your pulse," he said and turned to smile at her. His voice interrupted her negative thoughts. "Looks like you slept well."

"Yeah, I did." She padded over to the kitchen table and pulled out the chair with the worn vinyl seat padding.

"Merry Christmas," he said.

Everything had felt great since waking up, but this had taken her aback. Great. Just another thing to add to the list of things she hadn't even noticed. She had lost track of time since they came to the cabin. He turned back to her and smiled as he ticked his head for her to look behind her. She glanced back to the main room and saw a small potted tree on the sofa table. It was no more than a foot tall and it probably wasn't a real tree, but it sat there just waiting for any little decoration.

She couldn't turn away from that small symbol. Christmas was a time for family and gifts and singing. At least, that's how it was when she was growing up. With everything that had been happening, she had not thought about any of these things in so long. The last Christmas she celebrated, she was a normal teenage girl in her senior year of high school. She had been with her parents then, living in a suburban cul-de-sac where every house was decorated with multi-colored lights and inflatable lawn ornaments in order to compete with each other for the most festive family. At this time last year, she had not yet learned that her cancer had returned. That wasn't to happen for at least a month later.

Had she known then that things would be so different, she would have said more to her parents, the people that now had no idea she even existed. She would have spent more time with them around their Christmas tree, all decorated in tones of blue and green with fake poinsettias adorned in glitter. She could still smell the cinnamon and citrus of the scented candles her mother burned around the home during the holiday. Gosh, she hated that smell. But now she wanted it again. It just wasn't Christmas without it.

Now there sat that tiny tree on the table. No smells to go with it. No awful holiday music playing in the stereo.

"I drove into the market at the base of the mountain this morning. Got a few things and saw that. It just seemed like something we needed right now."

She couldn't look away from the small plant. "I didn't know it was Christmas."

"Neither did I, but there were decorations everywhere and most of the stores were closed this morning. The checker told me."

Nikka turned away from the plant as Jason placed a plate of bacon and eggs in front of her. "So, Merry Christmas," he said.

"Thanks; you too," she said, trying to sound sincere, but the holiday was something that she definitely didn't feel right now. It was a little hard to be all happy and sing carols given what she knew was happening in the real world.

He sat across the table from her. "I know. I get it."

She looked up at him. "What?"

"Not much for holiday spirit."

"It just doesn't feel like a holiday. I had no idea it was even December."

"I know. This place can be a little isolating." He took a bite of his eggs. "Maybe we can plan a little time out of here. Maybe go to town or something."

"Probably not a good idea."

He chewed some more, but she could tell he wanted to push this subject more.

"We could try a little bar or something in one of the towns at the bottom of the road."

"We're still wanted by the police and by all the other things out there. We're better off just staying here."

He nodded, but she could feel that she still didn't have him convinced.

"Thanks for breakfast," she said, even though she hadn't tasted any of it. She just moved the scrambled eggs around on her plate. "Thanks for everything."

He looked up at her, the light striking the blue of his eyes as he smiled. "You're welcome. Always."

The weather remained cold, but very little snow had fallen. Living among the pine trees around the cabin, she would have thought that the snow should have been three feet deep by now. There was never much snow growing up around the city, so she was used to not seeing much this time of year, but she had hoped that the mountain would have more snow. Even though she longed to see the white stuff, the lack of it made for easier training.

She had slacked significantly on her training since everything had turned upside down. Something deep inside her tried tell her that she didn't need to train and practice like she used to now that she understood her power so much better, but there was nothing like getting outside and going through the motions. Perhaps it was the routine that Gideon had taught her, but she wanted to feel the blood flowing through her muscles again.

Nikka worked in the open space behind the cabin, under the boughs of the pine trees, with her sword in hand. Each step felt like a dance, with the heat of the blue flames tickling against her skin as the sword moved through the air in glides around her body. She imagined the trees changing into equipment around the gym of the church where she had first learned. The ground would be covered in foam pads and the entire far wall was lined with bow staffs. But this was just a small clearing in the forest and there were no walls.

And there was no Gideon, standing before her with his bow staff and sparring every blow she advanced at him.

Then she felt Jason's eyes on her, watching the battle dance over the forest floor. She paused and glanced back to him, where he stood with his jacket closed up to his throat.

"Sorry," he said. "I just wanted to watch."

"It's okay," she said and let the sword come down to her side. The blue fire ebbed and swirled around the blade.

"It's beautiful," he said.

She glanced down to the sword. "I guess so."

"Not just the sword. All of it," he said and turned away, leaving her in the clearing as she watched the space in the trees where he had left.

Her fingers clutched the hilt of the sword and placed it back in the scabbard against her back. Her gaze wandered back to the clearing where he had just stood. She wanted to say something to him, but he had just turned and walked away. Jason was being cautious. She could sense that, and he had been so good to her. Without him, she's not sure what she would have done after Gideon died.

Without him, she was all alone.

❧ ✦ ❧

The days had blended into weeks, and it must have been deep into January. Daylight was brief, and the night came swiftly these days, leaving the cabin feeling smaller all the time. The evening began to close on a clear night, casting orange and blue hues behind the black etches of the pine boughs around the cabin. Jason stood to face the wood stove and bent to pick up another log for the fire, but then he stopped.

He turned toward her and she glanced up from the edge of the book she read. Her feet were curled up underneath her from her place on the couch. The book wasn't really something that she wanted to read, and the words drifted out of her mind as soon as she read them.

"This place is driving me crazy." He turned to face her.

She smiled as she watched his eyes roll. "Okay."

"We need to go do something."

"Like what?" she placed the book down on the couch.

"I don't know. Something fun." His eyes focused on her and he smiled. "Let's go to town."

"How many times are we gonna have this discussion?"

"Get up." He grabbed her hands and pulled her from the couch. "We're going out."

"Come on," she sighed. "Don't be ridiculous."

"Get dressed." Nikka resisted until he pulled her in closer. "I'm asking you out. Are you going to reject me?" The dimples under his facial hair seemed cuter than usual.

"Are you serious?"

"As serious as canc—" He stopped himself before he said the word. "Well, you know."

Nikka took in a deep breath and let it out slowly as she turned away from the couch. "Fine. Give me ten minutes."

As she walked away, she felt a little smile form at the corner of her lip. She would never tell him this, but she really needed to get out of the cabin, and she had secretly hoped for weeks now that he would try to convince her again to leave for a while.

Nikka pulled off the old sweatshirt and rummaged through her few things to find a suitable V-neck white T-shirt and some faded jeans that she could slide into. The only thing that she had trouble deciding on was which hoodie to put on over all this and hide her bald head if she was going to be seen in public. She picked the gray one with black stripes and slipped it over her head. The nagging feeling that always seemed to arise anytime she was about to go out with anybody prickled at her skin. That same negative self-deprication: *I look awful.* She tried to dismiss it, but eventually found herself in front of the bathroom mirror, gazing at her stark appearance.

She knew that looking into a mirror was a bad idea, because she always saw the circles under her eyes and high cheekbones. The lack of hair on her head never usually bothered her, but now it did. And it was all thanks to Jason, who had to imply that this was going to be a date. Her thin fingers ran over her bare head as she looked at herself.

When she first lost her hair during chemotherapy, it was a depressing time, but she eventually came to terms with that. But since she changed, the hair never grew back, and now she only had the appearance of tribal tattoos etched into the skin along her temples. When she first met Jason, she had disguised her appearance with a blonde wig. But now he asked her on a real date and he had seen her in all her bald realness. She understood that it was ridiculous to worry about it. After all, they had been living together in this cabin every day for almost three months and she never once covered herself with a wig.

But it bothered her now.

She pulled the hoodie over her head, letting the shadows fall across her eyes.

There. Now nobody would have to be subjected to it.

When she emerged from her room, he smiled widely and pulled his coat over his shoulders. "Ready?"

She shrugged, feeling the weight of his eyes more than ever before. "I guess."

Chapter 24 Jason

They climbed into the cold truck and the engine threatened to stall on them, but Jason fired it into full functionality, and they rode down the mountain as the darkness closed in.

He couldn't help but smile as he drove the road. Everything was going as planned. Nikka had finally said yes, although he had hoped this would have happened a couple of weeks ago. He had this planned for a while now, but just needed to convince her that it was time to step outside for one night.

The drive into the base town was quiet for most of the way. For a moment, he thought that she might be a little upset as she just watched out the window and didn't say much to him. He maneuvered the truck through the quiet town, toward the bar and grill he had found on his last trip here for supplies. It wasn't much, but it had to be better than the freeze dried food from the cellar they had been eating for weeks. The grill didn't look like anything fancy; it smelled great from the street and that's all he needed for now. Even the sign proclaiming the "best burgers in the USA" had convinced him, but he was pretty sure that every small town had a place with a sign just like that.

It had been so long since he had gone on a date, he felt a little rusty. As soon as he parked the truck, he stepped from the driver's door and around the other side to open her door, but she had already opened it and stepped out onto the parking lot.

Damn. Minus one for being a gentleman. Well, second chances may be better.

He stepped beside her and held out his arm. "Is this okay?"

She must have seen the deflated look on his face, and she smiled under her hoodie.

"Of course." She took his arm and allowed him to walk her into the restaurant.

The interior was as expected: dark lighting with a bar in the front and pool tables in the back. The air was thick with the smell of fried food and cold beer. Stained glass lamps with beer company labels hung over the tables at the far wall in front of a small karaoke stage. A jukebox played somewhere in the background, and a single couple danced in the space before the stage. Nikka tucked the hood even further around her face as they entered, and she followed Jason to the back table and settled in across from him. He pulled off his coat, draped it over the back of his chair and leaned across the table.

"Can I take your hoodie?" he asked.

She shook her head. "No, thanks. I'm gonna keep it on."

He hesitated for a moment, ready to accept her hoodie, but then he sat back in his chair when she declined. Why did this have to feel so awkward?

She glanced away from him as she picked at her nails again, something he had noticed now that she did a lot when she was anxious. And that meant she was feeling nervous around him. This wasn't going well.

He followed her gaze toward a dancing couple on the main floor. The couple was much older than the two of them, and he supposed that they were probably an old married couple who came here every Friday night to dance. That's just how they looked, her head on his shoulder and his arm about her waist. They were so familiar with one another that they almost seemed to move in sequence, anticipating each other.

The waitress stepped up to the table, her pen and pad in hand. "Welcome to Shutter's. Having a good night?"

"An excellent night," Jason said, forcing a smile.

"Can I get you something to drink?"

Jason glanced at Nikka, to let her order something first. "Um," she stammered, "whatever he's having."

"All right," he said with a grin. *Let's make this good.* "Two strawberry banana shakes." He really could go for a beer, but he wasn't about to whip out his ID when he was a wanted man, and Nikka was under age anyway. A shake would have to do.

"Excellent choice. Our shakes are the best."

"And we'll have two bacon burgers with a large order of fries. Let's start there."

After he had said it, he now hoped that Nikka wasn't the type to suddenly get self-conscious about what she was going to eat. There was nothing worse for a date than to eat while the girl just looks at her food, afraid to add any more calories to their already-starving bodies.

But Nikka looked at him, her eyes brightening.

"It sounds so good," she whispered.

"I know, right? I've been dying to eat here for so long. I would kill for a good burger," he said. And that might be true if the cook didn't hurry things along a little.

Nikka started picking at her fingernails again, but Jason reached over the table and placed a hand over hers and blocked her from damaging her nails. "It's okay. You don't need to be nervous."

Her shoulders relaxed a little bit and she leaned over the table.

"Sorry."

"Well, when was the last time you really just got to hang out with someone for fun? Like in a restaurant or at a theater or anywhere?"

She shrugged again. "I don't even remember. It was before I had my diagnosis."

His hand lingered over hers, but his fingers curled around her palm. "You haven't really talked to me about that."

"Not much to talk about. Leukemia sucks. There's no two ways about it. I was just a kid, and they told me I was going to die unless I had treatment. Well, I did everything they said and I was dying anyway. It took away most of my last year of high school. And then this happened," she said and held out her hand as if to display herself. "But I'm not really sad about cancer. I was ready to die. It was all this that I wasn't ready for."

"I may be selfish, but I'm not sad about any of this," he said. "If it hadn't happened this way, I would never have met you. That demon would still have its hooks in me. So for that, I'm glad all this happened. And I'm glad we've been in that cabin. I'm glad that you would come here tonight, although, I have to admit, I didn't think I would actually be able to get you out of that cabin."

Nikka smiled. "Why not?"

"You've become a cabin rat. I think you like it A LOT."

"A cabin rat? That sounds made up."

"Well, that's because it is. I just made it up right now."

The waitress stepped into the light of their table and placed two tall glasses filled with their milkshakes and topped with whipped cream before them. "Burgers will be right out."

Jason nodded to her, but kept his eyes on Nikka. He pulled out the red straw and licked the pink ice cream from the end.

"So, is this really a date?" Nikka asked and sucked the thick shake from her straw.

"Yes. So now that the really awkward stuff is done, what do you wanna do now?" he said with a laugh. "No, but seriously. We have been roommates for a while, but I really don't know enough about you."

"Like what?"

"Well, like what's your favorite movie?" The twenty questions. He guessed that wasn't such a bad start. Better than just staring awkwardly at each other.

"Favorite movie?" She glanced up to the lamp above the table. "That's a hard one. I really like those big blockbuster comic book movies. Any comic book movie, really."

"Like *Captain America* and *Green Lantern*?"

She nodded. "Exactly."

"Okay. That's a start."

"And you? If you say some chick flick, then I'm so out of here," she said.

"Hell no," he laughed. "It would have to be anything with Adam Sandler."

"Oh, I love that guy," she said. "I loved the golf movie. The best."

He asked her another and another, and he soon saw her posture had relaxed as she leaned over the table, ready to answer his questions before he even asked them. When the food finally arrived, they placed the large plate of fries in the center of the table and talked while they ate, despite the huge size of the burgers.

The conversation had drifted to him talking about putting together a motorcycle engine and then to her favorite comic book artists. The uncomfortable air between them had dissipated, and talking with her felt as natural as breathing; as though they had been friends since childhood.

Jason devoured most of the plate of french fries—those huge steak fries that you can only find in a good grill house. Nikka definitely didn't have an issue with eating a fat burger because she finished most of it like she hadn't eaten in a month. She leaned back in her chair and watched him eat one fry after another under the light of the stained glass lamp.

Then the music from the juke box changed as the man from the couple on the dance floor stepped away from the machine and back to his wife. It was a slow song, something that had just come out in the last few years, and it was nice to listen to. Her eyes drifted to the couple, moving in sync again as they whispered to each other on the dance floor.

The flutters in his chest started when he had the idea, and he knew that if he didn't do something about it now, he may never get another chance. "Come on. Let's dance."

Her eyes grew wide as she hunched over the table and shook her head. No more hiding like a cabin rat. He took her hand, stood from the table and pulled her to her feet. She resisted a little, but didn't want to make a scene either. He walked her to the dimly lit dance floor. The couple smiled at them as Jason put his arm around Nikka and held her hand.

"I like this song," he said as he looked down at her.

"I do too," she said, "but it doesn't mean we have to be out here where everybody can see us."

"Nobody's looking," he said and glanced back to the bar. Indeed, the other patrons were either drinking and talking to each other at the bar or playing pool in the back room. The only others who were remotely interested in them was the couple across the dance floor. "See. Nobody cares except me, and you're making me look bad here."

Her eyebrow cocked and she grinned. She reluctantly leaned in closer to him and he moved against her shoulder, smelling the clean scent of soap on her skin. Her breathing stopped for a second as he whispered into her ear. "Do you see any demons in here?"

She glanced around them for a moment.

"No. Why?"

"Because," he said and his fingers grasped at the hood of her jacket. It slipped from her head, leaving her bare scalp exposed, "there's no need to hide from anyone."

She tried to pull away from him. At first, he felt a little guilty because he knew she would want to cover herself as quickly as possible, but he held her close. He wasn't going to let anything happen to her. His fingers moved along her spine and he kept his cheek close to hers.

"I love the way you look," he whispered.

Nikka pulled back enough to look into his eyes. He gazed down at her, his eyes never faltering.

"Please don't cover it up," he said.

Her eyes, at first wide and frightened, now softened as her spine relaxed and she seemed to melt into him.

The music played, and for that small space of time, they seemed to be all alone in the bar. There wasn't a single soul except them in the darkness of that place. He felt her body against his, moving in step with the music. She looked up at him, only a small glint of light in her eyes. This was his moment to do it. Maybe she would let him, or maybe she would punch him in the throat, and he wasn't exactly sure that she was beyond doing that. But there would only be one shot at the perfect time, and this was it.

He leaned down toward her. She didn't pull away, but she closed her eyes as he moved closer. When their lips touched, he remembered a time when they had kissed so many months ago. But he was only the casual observer then. Even though it was Abaddon that had instigated it, he remembered how it felt. It was so much better now, not long or breathtakingly deep. Just enough that he could taste the strawberry milkshake on her lips.

She didn't back away, and she didn't punch him in the throat. Thank heavens. Nikka just opened her eyes and smiled enough that it appeared like she was in a dream. For this moment, she didn't look at him like he was evil. He was just himself. He leaned back again and the sounds of the bar came back into their world. Jason didn't have to say anything, and neither did she.

Nikka rested her head against the curve where his neck met his shoulder and he pulled her closer to him, dancing to the music. He held her there, hoping the music would never end because he didn't know when he would be able to do this again. As they danced, they both looked toward the couple dancing near the jukebox. The woman smiled at them, the wrinkles at the corners of her eyes deep with satisfaction, for she knew that she had just witnessed something special. She, too, leaned against her husband and they danced further into the darkness of the dance floor.

Chapter 25 Nikka

Jason said very little as they drove the winding, dark road back to the cabin. Nikka could hear his steady breathing and feel his body heat through his jacket from where she sat next to him in the cab of the truck, her head resting on his shoulder. She wished that this could be their life now—the dark of the woods around them, the quiet in the truck, and feeling him beside her.

The cabin came into view, and he pulled the truck before the door and stepped into the cold air with her. She took his hand and intertwined her fingers with his. It had been too long since she had felt comfortable doing this with him. For so long she mourned the loss of him as well as Gideon. But Jason had been here the entire time, only she was too afraid to feel anything for him anymore. She now realized that the feeling had never actually disappeared. It had only been sleeping, and now it had awakened.

They stepped into the dark cabin together and he pulled away from her to light the lanterns.

As he set to prepping the little propane tank and striking the match to light the filaments, she watched him, his face appearing in brief flickers of white light until the lantern began to glow. This was something he did for them every night, for however long they had been here. He had taken care of them—of her—and she realized how much he had done since she removed the demon from him.

"Thank you," she said, forcing the words into her throat.

He shrugged. "Ah, it's nothing. We need the light."

"No. Thank you. For everything. All this." She spread her hands open to the room.

He smiled, his dimples seeming deeper in the lantern light. "You don't have to thank me."

"Yes, I do. I wouldn't have survived without you."

"Yeah, you would have. You're the strongest person I know."

He placed the lantern down on the kitchen table and turned to the small pile of chopped wood by the stove. This was his routine: to always keep the cabin lit and warm. To keep the place comfortable for her. Everything he had done was always for her.

She remembered why she had been drawn to him in the first place. He had been the mysterious guy with the motorcycle that smiled at her and spoke to her until her knees grew weak. But that was before. Now he really cared about her, so much that he would do anything to keep her safe. She finally understood that as she watched him load the split logs into the stove.

For the first time since everything had gotten so bad, she felt her knees weaken again and the bees thrumming around in her chest. She still felt the heat of their kiss on her lips and she dug her nails into her hands as she watched him. That had been the first kiss in a long time, but they had lived together for months now, with him always being so careful with her.

He would never do it, so she knew she had to.

Nikka rushed up to him as he stood to find his box of matches. Her hands eased along his jawline, and for a moment he was taken aback. When she kissed him, the bees buzzed around until she could no longer breathe. She felt his hands on her hips at first and then pulling her against him. She didn't need the fire in the stove when she could feel his heat through his shirt.

Just when she thought the bees were going to break free, Jason pulled back for a moment. His hands grasped hers and he looked at her, the shadows starkly drawn over his face from the lantern light.

"You don't have to do this to thank me," he said. He could barely meet her eyes.

Her brow furrowed. "I'm not."

He looked confused at first and his hands almost slipped from hers. "I know things are not the way you had probably imagined they would be—"

"Just shut up, you idiot," she said with a smile. "I think—no, I'm sure—I love you. There. I said it. Just don't get weird about it."

It took a moment for the worry around his eyes to soften, and he finally met her gaze. A smile slowly formed across his lips. "I have loved you since I first saw you. Even before I could actually speak to you."

"I know," she said and kissed him again. This time he didn't pull away, but held her close to him as they stumbled back against the stove.

This kiss was the breathtaking kiss she had wanted since she had first met him, so many months ago in the library, but this was truly him, raw and honest. His hands moved under her shirt, his fingers cold, and she flinched. A giggle escaped her lips and he smiled. That didn't stop him, though. Her shirt slipped away, falling somewhere in the dark of the cabin. Her cold fingers found the buttons of his top as well as he stumbled out of his jeans. Then his arms wrapped around her waist and she could no longer feel the floor under her feet as they disappeared into the shadows of the bedroom, beyond the steady white glow of the lantern in the main room.

The cabin had grown cold without the fire overnight, but Nikka tucked her arms under the thick thermal blankets. Jason slept, his body close to her with his arm draped over her bare torso and his legs intertwined with hers, and that was all the heat that she needed. She tucked her head in the space between his shoulder and his neck. He unconsciously pulled her closer and she smiled. There was no need to do anything or go anywhere, so it didn't matter that the morning sun began to creep through the single window in the small cabin bedroom. She closed her eyes and bathed in his warmth that covered her.

She let her hands rest against his bare chest, feeling each breath against her fingers. Everything was so quiet and good and right. Agent Wolfe was gone and fixing the problems that had troubled them for so long. They were secure and safe in the cabin, just the two of them. Maybe she could actually stop for a moment and take in the quiet that surrounded her. The bedroom outside her blankets was so cold, but she couldn't feel any of it now. Not anymore. She breathed in his scent and let her body relax against him as the foggy haze of sleep drifted over her.

When she opened her eyes again, the light drifting through the curtains of the bedroom was much brighter. The air she breathed had warmed significantly and she blinked her eyes clear until she could see better. The space beside her was now an empty heap of blankets. She lifted her head from the pillow and glanced around the room. She held the blankets against her bare breasts as she sat up and realized she was alone in the bedroom.

The crackling of the fire within the stove in the main room caught her attention, followed by the smell of cooking bacon and eggs. She smiled as she stepped from the bed and pulled on her jeans and T-shirt.

The fragrance of the food spilled over her as she opened the bedroom door. She moved into the main room and saw him standing over the hot stove and felt the heat that filled the room, or maybe it wasn't heat from the stove after all. Sure, the food smelled great and the warmth was awesome, but she felt her stomach do back flips when she saw him look up at her with a smile. Suddenly, she didn't really feel like having breakfast anymore.

She padded over to him and slipped an arm around his waist and he kissed her.

"Morning," he said. "Sorry. I didn't want to wake you."

"It's okay. But, I think you need to come back to bed. No. I'm quite sure of it. It's nice and toasty under the covers."

He laughed. "Oh, really. Hmm. Not a bad idea."

"I know. There's a lot more where that came from." Her fingers inched under the edge of his T-shirt and found the muscles that rippled over his abdomen tense as her cold skin touched his.

"I need to carb load first," he said with a laugh and kissed her again as he grasped her cold hand. "Oh, I almost forgot," he said and turned to the table. He handed her a steaming mug. "Some hot chocolate for the lady. It's a cold morning and those hands need some warmth."

Her hand slipped away from his torso and wrapped her fingers around the cup. "You're the best."

"I know," he said and cocked his head a little. "I also started the generator. Water heater should be about up to temperature and the TV will be working."

He had thought of everything. It had been long enough since they had monitored the local news stations. With the power of the generator, she could start the TV and at least have it in the background while they had breakfast. She turned on the television and sipped at the mug of hot chocolate as she gazed out the window at the trees.

The sky was clear and blue this morning, leaving the trees bare and without any sign of snow yet, something she hoped would never come this year. At least not while they were still hiding in the cabin. The news droned from the

TV behind her as she scanned the tree limbs for any birds, especially the little ones with the black heads and white bodies.

" . . . and we will provide more information to you as we get it. Again, breaking news this morning. We are coming to you from Saint Andrews Hospital where there seems to be a hostage situation happening . . ."

This made her turn and look at the TV, to the sliding ticker across the bottom of the screen that provided the latest details on breaking news. The camera was aimed at the front doors of the hospital, near the emergency entrance, where several police officers had gathered. The news team could only approach as far as the police would let them, but she would recognize that place any day.

"Everything okay?" Jason said as he looked at her from the kitchen.

"It's Saint Andrews," she muttered.

He stepped away from the stove and stood beside her. "Does that mean something to you?"

Her mouth seemed drier than the desert. "It's where I was dying."

" . . . as we have reported before, there is a hostage situation happening right now at Saint Andrews Hospital. Authorities have requested that everyone stay clear of Third Street down to Fifth until it has been cleared. Right now, we know that the hospital has been evacuated, but the police say that there may still be as many as eight children being held on the seventh floor by an unknown assailant at this time. . ."

The seventh floor. The children's cancer ward.

" . . . the standoff began at eight this morning when a man entered the unit and took the children hostage, threatening to take lives unless the floor was evacuated. Police and hostage negotiation units have come onto the scene, and we will bring you more information as we receive it. We have some of the initial security footage from the hospital at the moment he took the hostages . . ."

A security camera overlooking the far end of the cancer ward captured the moment someone entered the unit, a knife in his hand. Tears almost welled in her eyes as she saw the familiar hallway lined in white tiles decorated with posters and colorful art.

The man stormed into the unit and nurses and children scattered. The security footage switched to another view, one of the man coming straight at the camera. Children ran to the nurses station, but in so doing, they trapped themselves with the man between them and the exit. He rushed into the main corridor and into the light from the windows of the unit. The news station paused the footage at that point while the newscaster continued to ramble on.

The camera caught his face, his closely shaved head and his light caramel skin. The oxygen seemed to rush from the room, like it had been sucked away from the entire mountain. Her fingers grew cold despite the warmth of the mug. The cup slipped from her trembling fingers and shattered at her feet.

Everything had been so perfect this morning, but she should have known something was about to turn her world upside down.

She wanted to cry out, to scream, but the sound wouldn't escape her lips. She backed away from the television and nearly fell onto the couch as the television held on a close-up of the man's face. Now she was sure that she had not imagined it.

It was Gideon.

CHAPTER 26 NIKKA

Nikka had no doubt about what she was seeing on the television. When the cup shattered on the floor, Jason walked into the main room and followed her eyes to the TV and watched the news report unfold. Nikka felt the tremor begin in her legs first, where it threatened to drop her to the ground unless she placed a steadying hand on the back of the couch. The images on the screen were grainy, but she was sure that it was Gideon's face through that security camera.

There was no time to think or worry about it. She turned away from the couch, hurried into her shoes and grabbed the hoodie hanging by the door.

Jason grabbed her arm from behind. "Whoa. What are you doing? What did you see?"

She pulled free from him and stuffed herself into the hoodie. "I have to know if it's Gideon."

"Gideon? The guy who fell into Hell?" he said, his eyebrows raised. "There's no way that's him. He's gone."

Her eyes welled into clear tears. "I have to know for sure."

Jason sighed and watched her for a moment as she zipped the jacket and pulled the hood over her head. "Okay. Okay. Let me help you. Just give me a second and I'll go with you."

Nikka clasped her fingers together, anything to make the trembling stop. She waited for him as he put out the fire in the stove and gathered his jacket. The seconds seemed like hours as she watched the TV from the cabin door, the partially blurred image of the man at the hospital frozen in the corner of the screen while the newscasters discussed the event. Jason finally stepped out the door with her and they both climbed into the cab of the truck.

She couldn't help but bite at her nails while the vehicle lumbered down the road. The trip into the city never took this long, but it seemed to last for hours this morning. Her foot drummed against the floor as she watched out the window.

Then she felt the warmth of Jason's fingers wrap around her hand that she had left bloodied at the nail bed. In the few seconds it took for her to see the news report, she had almost forgotten about him and the way he made her skin tingle when he touched her. Her fingers curled around his and she slid across the seat to lean against him, clutching his arm as their fingers clasped together. She closed her eyes and rested her head against his shoulder while he drove down the mountain.

What if she was wrong? What if the man at the hospital was just some crazed maniac holding a bunch of kids hostage? Maybe she would see Gideon's face in every grainy image on the TV for the rest of her life. But what if she was right? What if he somehow had made his way back into this world?

She tried not to think of any possible scenario either way because she would be tied to the disappointment no matter the outcome. Just get to the hospital, and then go from there. Everything had finally become calm and clear and perfect last night. Of course, something had to disturb that perfect peace.

The truck entered the outskirts of town just as the morning rush hour had ended. Jason drove toward the hospital campus and parked at the end of the street behind a crowd that had gathered around the blocked street. Police cars cordoned off the intersection, diverting traffic away from the area around the hospital, and several news vans now lined the street around the blockade. Before the truck came to a full stop, Nikka slid across the seat and opened the door, her feet hitting the ground at a run.

She could hear Jason's voice calling after her but she couldn't stop. Her heart pounded in her ears with each step. The crowd thickened just outside the ambulance bay, where police officers held onlookers back behind a strand of yellow tape. She pushed herself through the crowd until she came to the tape. With the hood pulled over her head and her breath rushing from her lungs, she tried to duck under the barrier.

A hand grasped her shoulder and shoved her back into the crowd. Nikka looked up from under her hood to see a police officer standing before her. "Stay behind the line, please."

"I have to get in there," she said, gasping for air.

"Nobody is going in there."

"But I think I know who it is," she said.

"I said nobody is going in there. Now please step back," he said, his hand outstretched to shove her back into the crowd if needed.

The cold air seeped into her lungs with each breath as she took a step back. A hand grasped her arm and she turned to see Jason. He pulled her back from the front of the crowd and ticked his head to follow him. They moved through the thickest part of onlookers until he stopped near the service bay, away from any other onlookers.

She wanted to cry, to scream, anything to get him to listen to her. There had to be a way to find out if it was really Gideon. She could feel the tears threatening to rise again and she clenched her teeth to hold back the shout that threatened to erupt from her throat. Jason released her arm and let her pace around the front of a trailer parked at the gate.

"Nikka, chill for a second," Jason said.

She took in a shaky breath. "Chill? I have to get in there."

"I know, so let's do it right," he said, his voice even and calm, as though he had no idea how important this was to her.

She continued to pace, her fists clenched at her temples as the sight of the grainy TV image played over and over again in her memory. Jason's hands rested on her shoulders and forced her to stop. He wrapped his warm fingers around hers.

"Stop," he said. "Take a slow breath."

Nikka closed her eyes and let the air flow into her nose and out through her lips, but she still felt her knee shaking and her foot tapping at the pavement.

"You're not thinking about this clearly," he said and she felt his finger along her jaw. She opened her eyes and saw him before her, his stark blue eyes staring at her. "You can totally get in there. Easy."

Her foot stopped tapping as she looked at him.

"You can slip right in and get a good look at this guy. Even better than that, you can stop him. Just like a superhero."

The calm seemed to move from his fingertips and into her skin as he spoke. She had been too rattled to see it, but Jason could. He knew the right way from the beginning.

"Invisibility," she whispered.

"It's your super power." He smiled and let his grip slip from her hand.

Nikka pulled the hood from her head and took in another deep breath as she plotted out what she would need to do. She had to be able to hold the illusion through the crowd, into the hospital and at least up to the seventh floor. Whoever was up there holding those children would never be expecting anything like her, so she would have only a few seconds ahead of him to attack if needed. But holding the illusion that long would weaken her significantly, and she could only hope that she would have enough strength to take him down.

"You can do this," Jason said.

She hoped that he was right.

He moved close to her and she felt his hands on her waist, pulling her to him. He kissed her, his warm lips comforting against the chill. Before he drew away from her, he leaned in close to her ear. "Please come back to me."

The sounds of sirens and the blue and red flash of lights reflecting off the building seemed to fade into calm as she looked at him and felt his heat against her, even through her hoodie.

She took a step back and willed the invisibility to take over. It started as a zing in her fingertips that soon spread under her skin. Each time she did this, it came faster and easier. She felt it race up through every hair on her arm and pool over her face like water until it sealed itself. As she stepped away from him, she could see his eyes searching the empty space where she stood. The smile had drifted from his lips and she could see the worry begin to settle in the lines between his eyes.

There wasn't much time before her energy would be zapped, so she started off at a brisk run around the side of the crowd, under the tape and slipped through the front doors with a pair of police officers who had no idea she was even there. The main entry lobby was filled with officers talking back and forth on walkie-talkies to various personnel that were no doubt distributed in and around the building. She maneuvered through the men and women, careful not to bump or touch anybody while she was in this state.

Her knees began to tremble and the muscles in her thighs and back burned as though the illusion drew energy from them first. It was too early and there was still a long way to go.

She took the right hall, the same corridor she remembered to reach the elevator bank. The pictures on the wall zoomed by her and she remembered each one in sequence from her time spent here as a patient, on those few days when the nurse would allow her to come outside for some fresh air. Of course, that was before the chemo had completely depleted her immune system, and then it was goodbye outside world. Now, those pictures were dark and covered in shadows that pulled any color and vibrancy from them. They were only shuttered windows to a forgotten world.

She neared the elevator bank as two officers stepped past her. As she gazed at the green paint with gold trim, she felt the illusion shudder for just a moment. Her eyes moved to the elevator call button and she froze. If she opened that elevator, it could draw unwanted attention. Nobody else was at this elevator and the officers were stationed at the end of the hall to prevent anybody from coming down here. Getting in there and going up to the seventh floor would immediately arouse suspicion.

The illusion continued to pull at the edges of her strength and she took in another breath as she gazed at the door to the stairwell. The door remained propped open as officers in Kevlar vests moved in and out of the stairwell.

Okay. Stairs it would be. She could stay in step with the men that climbed the stairs, with their guns in hand and the radios clipped to their shoulders buzzing with chatter from the main floor.

She forced her legs forward and slipped into the stairwell without any of the officers noticing her. The footfalls of the officers echoed in time with her own.

She bounded up the steps, taking two at a time, as she felt the pressure of exhaustion begin to build under her ribs. Keep going. Keep going. Can't stop now. First floor. Second floor.

Every two steps became every step, sometimes taking a longer pause between each one. Her hand grasped at the railing to keep herself steady as she felt her ears ringing. She had to slip to the side of the staircase so that the officers behind her didn't run into an invisible object, and then her entire plan would be ruined. They all moved with ease, each of them free of the burden of invisibility that she carried up those stairs. Each breath burned in her lungs. Third floor. Fourth floor. Fifth. Sixth.

At the sixth floor entrance, the cops filed into the open door. For only a moment, she saw the army of men, guns in hand and with armored chests, ready to swarm the seventh floor above them when the call came to do so. This was growing more dangerous as she glided past the door and up the final flight of stairs.

She stumbled onto the landing of the seventh floor and the illusion shattered into unseen pieces. Her fingers clutched at her throat to pull away the stranglehold that the invisibility had created, but there was nothing there.

She gasped for a silent breath, knowing that any sound she made would alert the men on the floor just below her. At least there was something sturdy behind her in case she fainted.

As she closed her eyes, she focused on her breathing until she could get it under control. The pounding of her heart began to ease until her ribs no longer ached. The burning in her lungs faded a little bit and she opened her eyes again to see the light of a harsh fluorescent bulb just above the door. It buzzed and flickered so faintly that most people would probably not have ever noticed, but she did. And right now she needed to get away from it and onto the floor.

She pulled herself up on her weakened legs and leaned against the wall, all while she stared at that light and listened for the movement of the cops at the door on the sixth floor landing. Her fingers stretched out and felt the cold of the brick wall against her hand. Everything told her that she was here and alive and needed to keep going. She pushed away from the wall and her fingers wrapped around the silver handle of the doorway. Beyond that door lay the cancer ward, with its bright and happy posters on the walls and colorful entryway—all there to try and deter anybody from thinking about what kind of a place it truly was.

She opened the door with quiet stealth and stepped onto the main floor before the nurses station. Usually this area was noisy with the sounds of a computer keyboard clicking away and the buzzing of nurses at the station, but now it was quiet and empty. Nobody sat at the front desk to greet her as she walked in. No nurses moved about behind the desk to prepare medications or IV's. Nobody sat in the waiting area watching the televisions mounted on the wall while they waited for their child's chemotherapy to be finished.

The quiet desolation left her unnerved, like the Apocalypse had come and gone and left her here alone in the world.

She looked down the north hall for no other reason than that was the one with which she was most familiar. Months spent withering away in that hall left her with an unseen scar that still pulled and itched at her. The north hall was for the older patients. The south hall for the younger patients. They must stay separated. Heaven forbid they mingle and enjoy each other's company before they die. With cautious steps, she moved toward the north entryway, keeping in the blind spot of the cameras that spied on everything that happened here, and peered and peered around the corner.

A movement caught her eye at the end of the hall, several rooms down. Far at the end, where she used to live. Someone moved in and out of the light shining through the patient room windows. She peered again and saw the figure of a man pacing around the hallway, and a collection of eight people sitting along the wall. Children.

Nikka pulled away from the entryway and pressed herself against the wall as she felt her heart racing again. There was nobody else up here to help her if this went badly. If it was just some random crazy guy, she would have to stop him herself. She closed her eyes and felt her breathing steady, felt the quivering in her arms and legs ease until she sensed the calm flow throughout her body. It was time to do something about this.

She opened her eyes and turned toward the entryway again and watched as the man paced back and forth in the hallway, the blade of a knife flashing in his hand.

CHAPTER 27 ηικκα

ikka never heard a voice down the corridor; there was only the sound of
the man's bare feet pacing along the linoleum flooring. An occasional
sniffle or whimper from one of the kids echoed toward her, but there
were definitely no voices. Whoever he was had scared those children enough
to be quiet and stay huddled together at the end of the hall. She was too far
away to get a good glimpse at his face. There was no other alternative but to
just walk right up to him.

Despite the pounding of her heart against her ribs, she took in a shaky
breath and imagined she could feel the katana resting on her back. If he attacked her, whoever he was, she would be ready to strike if necessary. She
steadied her breathing and turned the corner while she unzipped her hoodie
and let it fall to the ground, exposing the tattoos along her arms. If this was
some unfortunate man possessed by a demon, she was ready to face him and
get the kids to safety. The jacket fell around her feet and she stepped evenly
down the north hallway.

At first, one of the children saw her, but the boy was wise enough to keep
quiet. His eyes sparkled in tears as he glanced toward her, his head bare and
cheeks puffy from the rounds of chemotherapy he had endured. He tucked his
skinny legs to his chest as he watched her.

The man continued to pace, his eyes turned to the ground and his back
toward her. As Nikka neared the group, she could hear him muttering to himself. She stepped through the shafts of sunlight pouring through the windows
into the hallway, and with each step, more of the children looked up at her.

A young girl in the corner nearly cried out to her for help, but the small noise she tried to stifle caught the man's attention. He stopped and looked at the children's pale and hopeful faces as they gazed down the corridor behind him. When he realized what was happening, he spun on his heels and held the knife out before him. The shadows drew across his face from where he stood. Nikka stopped and held her hands out before her.

The fraction of a second for him to stop and look at her seemed like hours as he held the blade toward her, his hand gripping the handle so tightly that his knuckles had gone white. His hand trembled, sending shards of light glistening from the blade. The space he occupied remained in shadow between the windows, and she still could not see his face, but she could hear his panicked and uneven breathing.

Everything became quiet in that moment, even the man before her. The tremors in his arm stopped. She didn't know if she should speak to him, so she simply held her arms before her in a display that she had nothing in her hands.

"Is it you?" his voice echoed down the hall.

Right then, she knew everything had changed.

He stepped into the shaft of light and she saw his hazel eyes and caramel skin. "Nikka?"

She couldn't speak and felt a tremor in her knees. There was no demon crawling under the skin of some human before her. This was not a mirage or a dream, either. He stood there, his clothes tattered and dirty and his bare feet leaving bloody footprints wherever he stepped.

"Gideon?" she said and nearly choked on the word, her eyes glancing over his frightened but familiar face.

The knife slipped from his fingers and clattered to the ground. His shoulders fell as tears streamed from his eyes. Before Nikka realized what was happening, he rushed toward her and collapsed to his knees as he wrapped his arms about her waist. His body shuddered in waves of sobs, his arms holding tight to her as if she would disappear into a wisp of smoke at any moment. She stood frozen for a second as he held her. Perhaps this was just another nightmare that would unveil its true meaning as soon as she acknowledged that she could feel his touch. She moved her trembling hand to his shoulder, and his flesh was as real and warm as hers.

He continued to cry at her feet and hold her as though he would never let her go. Nikka glanced up at the children and nodded her head to the side. This gave them the signal they needed to get to their feet and run for the exit. Several of them held hands as they went, rushing past her with a familiar gaze as they saw her bare head and they knew that she had once been one of them.

When the last of the kids had gone and they were all alone on the ward, Nikka pulled away from him and got down on her knees to face him in the light. She placed her hands on his face and lifted his eyes to meet hers. She could feel tears begin to well in her own eyes as she looked at him. His hands clutched hers like he needed to hold onto something to keep himself in this world.

"I looked for you—" he cried as he grabbed her hands over and over to feel that they were real. "I came here, because this is where I was supposed to find you."

"Supposed to find me?" she whispered to him. "You mean . . . before, when I was dying here—"

"I was trying to find you, but you weren't here and nobody would help me and they tried to stop me and get me to leave—"

"Shh," she said and pulled him close to calm the stream of fear that ebbed from him. His head nestled into her neck and his arms wrapped around her torso again. "I'm here now."

"I could not find you."

Her eyes rose to the space around her. She recognized the walls like she had just seen them yesterday. The same poster of a very generic sunset on the beach had once hung right outside her room. She glanced back at the room near where they now kneeled and she knew that it was the very bed where she had lay dying, the place where Gideon had first found her and gave her the offer for the life she now lived. He had come back to the place he had remembered seeing her. Even if he had no other memory, he remembered her here.

"You found me," she whispered to him. "You finally found me."

As he continued to hold her as if he would never let her go, she glanced back to the stairwell. It was only a matter of time for those kids to run down the stairs and past the sixth floor landing, for the police and SWAT team to hear their story, and for them to storm the cancer ward to take down the assailant. At best, she figured she only had a minute or two before everything went to hell.

"Gideon," she said and pulled away from him enough to look into his eyes and get his attention. "We need to get out of here before they take us away."

He seemed to understand this and nodded.

"So I need you to hold my hand. Don't let go and don't make a sound, no matter what. Okay."

She could hear a series of footsteps coming from the stairwell. The noise was loud enough to carry into the corridor. They were coming.

It was the only thing she could think of and she hoped she had enough energy left to do it. She had never used her illusion on herself and another person at the same time.

Her fingers wrapped around his, and she willed the illusion into place. It first traveled through her limbs and then she urged it through her fingertips and into his arm. It took so much more of her own capacity to seal it, but it finally covered him. She couldn't waste a moment. Nikka rose to her feet and pulled him with her down the corridor just as the stairwell door opened and the S.W.A.T. team entered the floor, guns up and ready to fire. The last of the team stormed through the door and Nikka slipped through the open door with Gideon holding fast to her hand.

The illusion pulled at her soul much heavier than ever before, but she forced herself down each step as fast as she could go. The invisibility needed to hold until they got out of the building and into a quiet location where she could hide Gideon. She nearly stumbled the last few steps, but they finally emerged onto the ground floor landing. They stepped through the door, past the collection of cops in the lobby and out the front entrance with the pair of detectives that were coming into the hospital.

As the edges of the illusion began to fray, they pushed through a barrage of reporters. Nikka didn't care anymore if someone could feel her shove past them. They had to get clear of the crowd. She led him back to the service bay where she had left Jason and collapsed to the pavement just as the illusion cracked.

Her ears were ringing and she could hear nothing else as she fell, her head hitting the ground. Everything appeared in colors of blue and white and nothing would stay in focus. Shadows moved through the light, and she felt like she was slowly sinking in a dark ocean that gradually began to pull her deeper until there would soon be no light or sound. The only thing that seemed real was the pain that had exploded in her head.

Then she felt a warm hand on her face. Somewhere in the increasing darkness, she felt an arm slip under her shoulders and then another under her legs. Somebody lifted her through the darkening water, but then everything fell silent and black.

Part Four

"I sung of Chaos and Eternal Night,
Taught by the heav'nly muse to venture down
The dark descent, and up to reascend . . ."

—John Milton, *Paradise Lost*

CHAPTER 28 NIKKA

First, Nikka heard running water in a sink. It was a quick sound, like somebody just turned on the tap to rinse a cup or something. Then came the explosive pain in the back of her head.

That was when she remembered falling to the ground and her head hitting the pavement. The pain flowed in waves around her skull and down the back of her neck. The last surge of pain forced her to open her eyes and she heard herself groan.

The heady scent of burning wood filled the dim room around her. She forced her eyelids open more to see the soft orange glow of a fire in the wood stove. Her fingers stretched out along the rough fibers of the couch cushion beneath her body. She tried to swallow, but her dry mouth felt like it was full of cotton.

"Easy," Jason's voice said from somewhere in the main room. His hand rested on her shoulder as she tried to sit up. "Just take it slow."

She pushed herself up and rested her back against the couch. Every movement hurt and her head felt heavy. A cold mug appeared in her hand and Jason encouraged her to drink. She licked her lips and then tasted the cool water.

When she had swallowed enough to moisten her mouth, she shoved the cup back toward him. "What happened?" Her voice croaked as she squinted into the darkness around the cabin. "Where's Gideon?"

"He's okay, I guess," Jason said and kneeled in front of the couch. "You got him out of there before you collapsed."

"I feel like I've been hit by a bus. No, a train." Her fingers touched the sore spot at the back of her head. Even her spine and shoulders felt bruised and road rashed. "I need to see him."

"I know," he said and glanced at the bedroom door at the back of the cabin. "But, something's wrong with that guy."

Her eyebrows knit together and the pain of it made her wince. "What? What do you mean?"

"Well, I got you back here and he was like clingy. I mean really clingy," he said and looked at her again. "I made him stay in the bedroom until you woke up. He didn't like it, but he did what I said. He's like a dog that's been beaten too much and just doesn't know what to do with himself. I'm telling you, something is off about him."

There is no way Jason would know anything about Gideon. He had only met him when he was possessed by Abaddon, so that didn't count. And he had no idea what Gideon had been through these last few months, or even where he had been. Whatever it was, Nikka knew that it had been hard. She saw it in his face when he first looked at her standing in the hospital corridor as he held the knife before him.

It didn't matter what Jason said either. Gideon was back and needed help.

"I need to see him," she said and stood up, but the action made her dizzy. Jason stood with her and caught her as she swayed. He held her arms as she found her footing, but it was something that she felt she could do herself. He didn't need to do that, and she wished he would just step back right now.

"I've got it, okay?"

Maybe she had said it a little too forcefully, but he let her go and took a step back. He set his jaw, ready to say something, but he held it and averted his gaze. "Just be careful. Something's wrong with him."

Every time he said something like that about Gideon, she felt her muscles tense and her fingers ball into fists. She had known Gideon much longer and better than he did. He really had no place to speak about him that way.

"I can handle it," she said and turned away from him.

She stepped to the bedroom door, feeling Jason's eyes on her the entire way. She reached for the door and opened it. A single lantern shone from the bedside table, casting a stark white light over the room. The bed was empty, the linens still messed from where she had left them that morning. The room wasn't that large, yet she saw no sign of him.

"Gideon?" she said, her voice shakier than she had wished.

She stepped inside and closed the door behind her; Jason didn't need to hear anything that happened in here. With the door closed against the heat of the stove, a cold chill hung in the room. She glanced along the side of the bed and to the open door to the bathroom, but she still couldn't see him.

"Gideon," she whispered this time. "It's Nikka."

She felt her fingers shaking and she bit her lip. The room was so quiet, and the lantern cast strange shadows across the walls. She took a careful step around the bed and to the dark space below the window. A knotted shadow had huddled in the corner, away from the light.

As she neared, she saw Gideon's form lying on the floor, his knees drawn to his chest, as he slept in silence. His feet were still bare and dirty, his shirt and pants frayed.

She whispered his name again and reached out a trembling hand to his bare arm. Her fingers brushed his skin, and he suddenly stirred. A cry erupted from his throat and he jumped into a crouching position. Nikka stumbled back as she tried to dodge away from him, but he grasped her wrist and then he froze as he looked at her. His eyes darted around the room in confusion, but his hand held her arm. He breathed fast and braced himself into the corner.

Nikka didn't move or speak while he held her wrist. His hazel eyes settled onto her and his face softened. His grip eased a bit, but he still held on to her and then pulled her closer to him.

"It is you," he muttered and then rushed at her just as he had at the hospital, his arms wrapping about her torso and resting his head against her abdomen. She moved to her knees with him and placed a cautious hand against his back. The breath rushed in fast bursts within his ribs, vibrating into her fingertips.

"I'm here," she whispered. His entire body seemed to press against her as if he would never let her go again. He quivered under her touch. Whether he was cold or terrified, she couldn't tell.

"You're safe now." She could feel his chilled skin through her shirt. His clothes were nearly threadbare. He needed food, a bath and some warm blankets.

When she was able to pry his hands from around her, she forced him to his feet and let him sit at the edge of the bed. His eyes followed her like he was afraid she would disappear, as she started the water in the bathtub and let the steam rise into the room. She stepped around the bed and grasped his dirty hand, encouraging him to his feet.

As she worked on getting the tattered clothes off his body, he only stood there in silence, his head hanging and his shoulders slumped, but his eyes on her the entire time. The thick silence between them started to wear against her nerves and his gaze felt uneasy. Yes, something was wrong with him, but she wasn't going to let Jason scare her away from Gideon. Whatever was wrong was exactly why he needed her help. She knew she still loved him; that had never changed.

She helped him into the bathtub where he only sat, his eyes watching her and his knees drawn up to his chest. The steam warmed the room and heated his skin, but his face never changed. Blank and afraid. She kneeled beside the tub and lathered a bar of soap onto a clean cloth. The filth wiped clean from his skin with the cloth as she moved it along his arms and shoulders. She worked until she needed to clean his face. His eyes continued to watch her, hardly blinking. The water beaded off his skin as she wiped the dirt from his cheeks. Her hand rested against his cheek as she cleaned around his eyes.

His shaky hand touched her fingers where she had placed them against his face. She stopped and looked into his hazel eyes. His skin now felt warm again where he touched her. She smiled and saw the faintest hint of a smile begin in his eyes.

"There you go," she said. "Now I recognize you again."

He broke eye contact with her and gazed down at the warm water around him. It had become a gray and cloudy mess with the dirt she had washed off of him.

"I know," she said. "It's pretty awful. We'll probably have to do it again in the morning."

The edges of a grin formed on his lips, like a little boy who had had his first bath. "Okay."

She raised her eyebrows and nodded. "Okay? So you'd be all right with me giving you a bath again tomorrow. Of course, you would, you pervert." She smiled and his eyes brightened.

Getting him out of the tub was easier than getting him into it. He had relaxed enough to let her wrap a thick towel around him and dry him off.

She walked him back to the bed where he sat down and went back to watching her again. She moved toward the door when he jumped to his feet and grasped her wrist. The edges of his eyes creased in concern.

"It's okay. I'm just going to get you some fresh clothes and some food." She touched his hand and carefully pried his fingers from around her wrist. "Just stay in here and I'll be right back."

He released her arm and took a hesitant step back. When he was in the tub, he seemed to relax and his mood lifted, but now he was back on edge and ready to run at any moment. She led him back to the bed and sat him down. As she stepped away, she could see that he wanted to reach for her again, but he restrained himself and only watched as she slipped out the door.

The door latch clicked shut, and she let out a breath that she hadn't realized she held. Her shoulders seemed to be two frozen blocks of ice and she arched her neck to relieve the tension that had built in her muscles.

"Everything okay?" Jason said.

She almost jumped when he spoke. Her fingers balled into fists again, and she bit her lip as she nodded. "Yeah. I think so. I need to get him something to eat."

"Sure," he said and turned away to busy himself in the kitchen, looking through the cupboards for something he could prepare. He palmed a can of soup and rummaged through the shelves for a pan.

The awkward silence between them thickened. Nikka wasn't so oblivious that she couldn't see what simmered just behind his stony eyes. Jason had been well aware that she loved Gideon, and for a time he had comforted her in her loss. Just this morning they were happy and content with each other. There was no concern about the past or the future until she saw the news, and everything suddenly changed.

But this was his place, his grandfather's cabin. For the first time in months, she now felt like only a guest.

"He needs some clothes," she said, but the words were so hard to speak.

Jason didn't turn around. "Sure. You can look through my bag for something that might fit."

She knelt beside the couch and found the duffle bag that usually contained his clothes. There was so many she could choose from, but she had a hard time finding something that would be appropriate. Everything in there smelled like Jason. She remembered him in this shirt or those jeans. Something about taking anything from here felt wrong. But Gideon needed clothing. Those torn scraps that he had on needed to be burned and never worn again. She finally settled on a plain gray T-shirt and black cargo pants.

When she stood, Jason was there with a mug of soup for Gideon. He reached out as far as he could, as though he didn't want to stand too close to her.

"Thanks," she said and accepted the cup. He just nodded his head and sulked back into the dark of the kitchen.

She gathered the clothes and soup and slipped back into the bedroom. The entire cabin felt frozen and empty tonight, and she wasn't sure which room was more uncomfortable: the bedroom where Gideon watched every move she made, or the main room where Jason would barely speak to her anymore.

Her eyes met Gideon's gaze from where he remained at the edge of the bed. The towel was still around his hips, but had rumpled and crept low enough that she averted her gaze and just looked up at his troubled eyes. She settled down beside him and handed him the mug.

"This should help a little," she said.

He sniffed at it and then his brow furrowed. He brought the cup to his lips and sipped at the warm broth.

"It is good," he said and sipped at it again.

"Jason prepared it for you," she said.

His eyes looked up at her from the mug. "He is good to you?"

More than he realized, she thought. Everything Jason had done had been for her since the world seemed to collapse around them. "Yes, he is."

"Then he is a good man," Gideon said in his broken speech. He took a longer sip of the broth.

Nikka searched his face as he warmed himself with the broth. "You're good, too. You know that, right?"

He finished the mug and stared into the bottom of the cup as he held it in his hands. The silence felt a little long and she couldn't tell if he was trying to remember or trying to form the words. "I do not know that."

"Gideon," she said and took the cup from him, placing it on the floor. "You are good. You need to know that." She took his hands in hers and forced him to look at her. "I thought you were dead. What happened to you? Where have you been?"

His hands trembled in hers, and she thought she saw tears glistening in his eyes. He pulled his hands away from her and curled around to lie on the bed. "I wish to sleep."

She clasped her fingers together and watched him. "Okay. We can talk when you're ready, I guess."

As she turned toward the door, she heard him bolt upright in the bed. "Please do not leave. I am afraid to be alone."

She saw his face in the lantern light, the desperate look in his eyes.

"All right."

She stepped around him and settled beside him in the bed. He rested his head on the pillow and pulled her close, like a child with a stuffed animal that would ward away the monsters at night. He closed his eyes now that he could feel her against him and he fell asleep faster than she had expected. His breathing eased, and his body went limp with sleep, but his hand clutched tight against the back of her shirt.

She extinguished the lantern and remained next to him. It took so long for her to fall asleep, but she finally rested as she relaxed next to him. But the fitful dreams came that night, the same dreams that she had fought so hard to destroy when they first arrived at the cabin. Dreams of fire and brimstone . . .

.

CHAPTER 29 JASON

The moment he saw that guy holding Nikka's hand when they emerged from the hospital, he knew things had changed for the worst.

She pulled him out of danger, from whatever he was doing in that place, and now he was here, and Jason was totally creeped out by him. There was no telling Nikka anything about it, either. She couldn't seem to see it.

But maybe he would be the same way if things had been reversed.

Something about the look in his eyes, though, bugged him. Gideon looked wild. Vacant. Like something else had come back in his place.

Not that he really knew the guy before all of this. Nikka was right about that. But he didn't act like the guy Nikka had talked about. He remembered his face through Abaddon's eyes, looking at him just before he fell into the pit of fire. He remembered Abaddon torturing him in the most awful ways. And that was it.

The moment Nikka woke up on that couch, she was all about Gideon, like a child trying to bind the wounds of a wild animal, unaware that it could turn around and bite at any second.

And things between him and Nikka had suddenly changed. In less than twenty four hours, he had gone from finally being with her to being outside the friend zone, someone less than whatever was hiding in that bedroom.

Jason stoked the fire in the stove. The chill in the cabin grew colder since they had come back from the hospital escape, and no matter how much fire he put into the stove, the place just wouldn't warm up. He sat back on the couch and pulled a jacket over his body.

Nikka had been in that bedroom for a long time now, and he tried to not look back there, but he couldn't help himself. He hoped that she was smart enough to be careful.

He was worried, yes. But he also knew that some of this was petty jealousy. As much as he tried to control it, he still loved her and didn't want Gideon in the picture anymore. But he also wanted Nikka to be happy, and that guy meant a lot to her.

Damn it. Things were going so well. Why did this have to happen?

He glanced back at the bedroom door again. It was getting really dark outside and things had grown quiet in that room. What if she decided to stay with him again? If that happened, she would leave the cabin. She would disappear somewhere into the world, and he might never see her again.

Jason closed his eyes against the thought. He couldn't just stay here and watch himself be put aside like some unneeded thing. And he didn't want to fight with Nikka. He loved her too much to do that to her.

She was tough and she could handle Gideon. He only hoped that she would see it coming if something bad happened.

CHAPTER 30 NIKKA

Smoke surrounded her, filled her lungs, and choked out any air that she tried to take in. Flashes of orange and red fire flickered through the thick, black clouds of smoke. Nikka crouched and shielded her face from the heat that burst through the flashes of light.

The smoke pulled back just long enough for her to see Gideon's face. His hazel eyes looked at her with such sadness just before Jason stepped behind him, threw his arm around his neck and pulled him into the eternal pit from where the flames and smoke billowed.

Nikka screamed, but the sound only came out as a hoarse screech, and then the fire exploded from the pit and smothered her in light and pain . . . .

She opened her eyes with a start and looked into the quiet bedroom where the first light of morning came through the window. The quaking still thrummed in her arms and legs where she had just felt the searing heat of fire burning her flesh. She raised her hand to the light and saw only perfect, untainted skin. It was only a dream. It had been so long since she had had those dreams; why had they returned now?

The arm draped over her abdomen pulled her closer and she turned to see Gideon's face, peacefully asleep and resting on her shoulder. He had finally come back to her and he was safe. So, what had spurred the onset of her nightmare again? She had tried so hard to get away from reliving that night, and now that Gideon had returned, she thought that she would never have to experience that dream again, but there it was.

She watched him sleep, each breath even and low. He looked the same, just a little worn and tired, but something had definitely affected him. He had acted almost shell-shocked, the way Jason had described his brother when he had come back from his tour in the Middle East. But he was here now, at her side where she could help him recover from whatever horrible thing had happened.

Then there was Jason. The last remnants of the nightmare still played at the edges of her memory. The orange glow in his eyes seemed to penetrate the dark around him as he stood behind Gideon and grabbed him just before pulling him into the pit. The smug look on his face told her he was more than happy to do it. But the night it had actually happened, it was Gideon that leaped into the pit and took Jason/Abaddon with him. In her nightmare, though, Jason had taken Gideon instead, and he had wanted it all along.

It was just a dream, she had to remind herself, but she couldn't seem to rid her memory of Jason's face. That wasn't him: Jason was kind and wonderful and loved her. It was Abaddon that Gideon had gone with into the pit that night, and he had done something to Gideon before he came back for her. Jason was not responsible for that.

She had to move, to get her thoughts on something else. She pulled herself up and slipped from under the bedcovers as she watched Gideon sleeping. He never stirred as she stepped toward the door and exited the bedroom.

The main room was quiet but warm with a fire in the stove that Jason had started sometime that morning. The cabin didn't smell like the usual odors of breakfast, though. She glanced around the kitchen and the empty couch and saw no sign of Jason.

Then the front door opened, letting in a draft of cold air as Jason walked into the cabin. His eyes met hers, and for a moment she thought he looked surprised to see her. He averted his gaze as he moved around to the packed bug-out-bag on the ground beside the couch. She heard the sound of the rumbling diesel pickup in the driveway.

All of it, including his behavior this morning, made her stomach sink. "What are you doing?"

He moved to pick up the bag, but she placed a hand on his arm to stop him. He stood straight and finally looked at her, the edges of his blue eyes etched in concern. "I have to go."

"Go? You're leaving?"

He sighed and looked away from her again. She was not going to let him just dismiss her and stepped into his line of sight again. "Wait. You can't leave."

"Well, I can't stay," he said, frustration building in his face.

Nikka could feel the first signs of tears welling in her eyes despite her best effort to hold them back. She placed her hands on his chest to try and stop him from picking up the bag.

He licked his lips and shuffled his feet. Anything just to not look at the tears in her eyes. "You'll be just fine. There's plenty of food in the pantry. I've chopped enough wood to last the entire year and there's enough fuel for the generator to last at least a couple of months." He reached into the pocket of his jacket and produced his cell phone. He grabbed her hand and placed the phone into it. "If you need anything, you can just call me. My number is in the speed dial."

"I don't care about any of those things," she said and tried to give him his phone, but he refused to accept it. "You can't leave me."

She saw tears glistening in his eyes as he tried to look away from her. "I can't stay here, not the way you look at me with him here. I'm not stupid. I know you love him, and you still look at me like I was the one who did this to him. I just can't do this right now, so it's best that I go. I'll check up on you, but I can't be here."

He stooped, picked up the duffel back and stepped from the room. The cabin door shut behind him and sounded like a slam, but she wasn't sure if that's what he intended. She watched him through the window as he climbed into the truck and drove away without looking back at the cabin.

There was no use fighting the tears. They flowed freely now as she clutched the phone to her chest and watched the truck disappear into the trees. Now, the cabin felt cold and empty and dark, more so than it ever had before. He had finally left her to fend for herself and she hadn't realized until now how much she had needed him, not just to keep her warm, but to keep her company. Of course, Gideon was now with her, but Jason was absolutely right about him: there was something wrong with him, and she wasn't sure she knew how to keep them both safe.

She wiped the back of her hand across her cheeks and blinked her eyes clear. There was nothing she could do about this situation now. Jason never gave her the choice. He was gone now, and she had to take care of Gideon on her own. She couldn't let him see her this way; it would make him worry so much more than he already did.

Nikka took in a deep breath until she felt that her body no longer trembled and she stepped back into the bedroom. As soon as she opened the door, she saw him sitting on the edge of the bed, staring out the window to the oncoming dawn. He didn't turn to look at her as she stopped at the threshold.

"He has left us," he said.

Nikka cleared her throat, which seemed to have gone dry again. "Yes."

"And that makes you sad?" he said, his voice emotionless and even.

"Yes."

"Why?"

She looked down at her bare feet. That was a difficult question to discuss with him, but then she heard him speak again. "Is it because you love him?"

She bit her lip and nodded. "I think so."

"Did you love me once?"

The breath caught in her throat and she stepped around the bed. Why doesn't he remember this? She saw his unwavering hazel eyes looking into the orange light, but he didn't look at her in return. "I still do."

"I—" he started, but his brow furrowed as though he searched his memories for something. "I remember."

She touched his hand that rested on his knee. "Why did you forget? What happened to you?"

His eyes finally drifted to her as though he was searching through fog and finally found a light. He opened his mouth to say something, but he hesitated, and she saw that he held back. Instead, he forced a faint smile.

"I will bathe again today, but I can do it myself. I remember how to do that now."

He stood and walked around her toward the bathroom. He shut the door behind him, leaving her alone in the bedroom, standing at the bedside where he had sat. She closed her eyes, trying not to allow the tears to flow again, even though they threatened to erupt at the edges of her eyelids. Maybe it would take some time for him to talk to her, but he was holding something back. He knew what had happened to him and was refusing to tell her.

She stood and left the bedroom to walk into the kitchen. At least she knew she could make a quick breakfast and get him something to eat. This was one thing that she could control. He had to be hungry and she needed something to get her mind off of everything this morning. She worked at heating a pan of water on the stove and started preparing oatmeal and eggs. As the meal cooked and began to fill the cabin with the fragrance of breakfast, she heard the bedroom door open. She waited for a moment and stepped into the main room to see if Gideon had come out yet.

He stood at the doorway as though he was afraid to come out of the room. A towel was tied around his hips and droplets of water dripped from his bare torso and legs, leaving small puddles around his feet.

"Oh," she said and stepped toward him. "You should dry off completely before coming out." She stepped up to him and placed a hand against his torso to encourage him back into the bathroom as the water continued to drip from his body.

He glanced down at her hand pressed against his bare skin and stepped back with her. "I am sorry." His voice trembled with confusion.

"It's okay," she said and smiled at him. She led him back onto the bathmat and fumbled around the cabinet for another towel. She produced a white towel and worked at drying the rest of him off before the remainder of the water dampened the mat.

He watched her as she worked. "I forgot something again."

"And what was that?" she said and stood with the towel in her hands.

He pointed to the stubble on his face. "Shaving. I remember shaving, but I cannot seem to do it."

Nikka laughed a little, which made him smile. "That's okay. I think we can figure it out between the two of us."

Once she found a hand razor and some cream in the cabinet, she helped him get started until his fingers seemed to remember the action of shaving. At first, his fingers wobbled like he hadn't held anything with such precision for some time.

"Good," she said, encouraging him as he seemed to get the hang of it.

When he was done, she found a damp wash cloth and cleaned off the rest of the remaining cream on his face. He extended his neck and allowed her to finish before he stepped back and looked at himself in the mirror. His eyes searched the glass as if he looked at a stranger, but his eyes soon softened when he appeared to recognize the face.

"There," she said. "Good as new." She stepped out of the bathroom and to the bedroom door. "I left some clothes for you. Get dressed and come out here for some breakfast, okay?"

He glanced at the shirt and pants on the bed, then he looked at her with renewed confusion. "Breakfast?"

"Food."

He nodded just as she stepped from the room and closed the door behind her. She leaned back against it and took in a breath, hoping to steady her nerves. She knew it was Gideon, but he had changed so much, like he was a newborn that was just experiencing the world for the first time. Did he even remember that she was a seraph? He could barely recall anything about himself; how could he remember that she had loved him or even what she meant to him?

Chapter 31   Nikka

Gideon finally emerged from the bedroom, having dressed in the clothes that Nikka had taken from Jason's bag. They were a little big for him, but otherwise fit him well. He walked into the main room, his shoulders hunched a little and his eyes darting to every corner in the room.

Nikka placed his bowl of oatmeal and a plate of eggs on the table and waved him toward the kitchen. "It's okay. There's nobody else here. You're totally safe."

When his eyes found her, he quickened his pace until he approached the table, where Nikka signaled for him to sit. He settled into the chair and glanced about the room as he squinted against the bright morning light in the windows. She placed her own meal at the table and sat next to him.

He gazed down at the food and sniffed at the steam that came off the bowl of oatmeal.

"It's just hot cereal," she said.

He glanced at her, and she nodded at him in approval. Then he moved to reach his fingers into the oatmeal and begin scooping. She quickly stopped him. "Oh, no. Not like that."

His eyes glanced at her and his brow creased. She gently squeezed his hand and placed the spoon that sat next to the bowl between his fingers. "Use this. It's a lot cleaner."

He held the spoon in his hand and looked at it as though he had seen one before but couldn't remember where. She picked up her own spoon and placed it in the bowl, scooping a bit of oatmeal onto it. She placed it to her lips.

"See. Like this." She ate from the spoon and chewed, exaggerating the motion as an example.

Gideon nodded and tried to mimic her, even though the spoon wobbled in his hands just like the razor had done. He moved the spoon to his lips, the utensil wobbling in his grip, and watched her for approval as he ate, the oatmeal half dripping across his lips and down his chin.

"Okay," she said with a smile. "That's close enough. Just keep trying and you'll remember how to do it."

He smiled as he tasted the warm cereal. "I do remember this. It is good." The spoon went into the bowl again, faster and faster until he had eaten everything and made a mess of his face. He then went at the eggs the same way.

"You were hungry," she said as she watched him.

He swallowed the last of the eggs and looked up at her. "Is there more?"

She smiled. "Sure. I can make as much as you want."

After Nikka had made a triple amount of oatmeal and eggs than she had before, he finally rested back against his chair and appeared full. She handed him a paper towel and demonstrated to him how to clean his face. He performed the action while he watched her.

"There," she said. "I think you're getting the hang of things."

"I like this food—this . . . cereal."

"I believe you do," she said and started eating hers as well.

He sat next to her, watching her as she ate her breakfast. Bite after bite, he said nothing and just watched. It was hard to look at him while he did this and made her a little nervous. She finally glanced up at him and saw him almost smile.

"What?" she said and swallowed the last bite of oatmeal.

"This is familiar," he said. "I remember eating food with you before, at a table very much like this one. But we were not here, in this place."

"No, we weren't," she said, feeling her heart replaced by butterflies. "Do you remember where we were?"

"It was much bigger," he said and looked up at the ceiling as if he could see the large rafters of the church where they had once lived together. "The windows were different. And there were long hallways and many doors."

He described the upper floors, where her bedroom once was. "Yes. It was an old monastery up on the mountain."

"A monastery. Yes," he said with a nod. "A place of God." He drew his eyes back to the table but the smile had gone.

"It was a place of God," she said.

"I want to go back there."

"I do too," she said and placed a hand over his where it rested on his knee. "But it's gone. It collapsed. There's nothing left."

"But that is where I lived with you," he said and it looked like he was ready to cry.

"I know," she said. "It was just a building, though. We're here now, in this place."

He looked down at his feet. "Will you be happy here? With me?"

Her eyebrows knit together. "Of course. Gideon, you asked me if I loved you once. You know I still do, right?"

He stood from the table, letting her hand fall from his knee. "I am tired. I wish to sleep." Before she could say anything, he stepped away from the table and stepped into the bedroom again.

Nikka could only sit and watch him slip into the room and the door shut behind him. She hoped that he would soon be able to come out of this stupor, or whatever it was. It was beginning to scare her, and now she was alone to deal with this.

Maybe not completely alone, though. Jason might have left her all alone with Gideon, but she had another resource out there. She found the cell phone in her pocket and opened the main screen. She thumbed through the contact list and found the number she had been looking for: Agent Wolfe. She hadn't heard from him since he left to take care of their EMP problem. He had never said when he would call again, but something big had really happened here and he deserved to know about the change in her circumstances. It may not be important from his end, but he needed to know.

She dialed his number and listened until the voicemail picked up.

"Andy, hey, it's Nikka. I don't know where you are or what you have discovered yet, but I really need to talk to you. Things have changed a little here and I need to know that you are okay and what's going on there. Please call me."

That was all she could do for now. Normally, Jason could have helped her out in dealing with the strangeness of Gideon and try to contact Wolfe, but he was no longer there with her.

She turned off the phone and tucked it back into her pocket before she began picking at her nails. Hopefully, Wolfe would call her back soon. She had to talk to somebody about all this.

But the hours went on that day and the phone never rang. She busied herself cleaning the dishes and then the cabin, anything to keep her mind off of what was bugging her about Gideon. She swept the floor and glanced down at the space where the bug-out-bag had once been, the pack that Jason had insisted they filled with everything they would need should they have to leave in a hurry. Now it was gone. He had taken it with him, as though it were an emergency to leave her. She looked away from the space and swept the dust out the door.

The day had begun to crawl into dusk, where the clear blue sky melted into shades of indigo and pink. Gideon had stayed in the bedroom all day, and she never heard a sound from that room, nor did she want to disturb him. Perhaps it was best to leave him in peace for now to sort out this confusing new situation for himself. But he had not come out for anything since he went in there after breakfast. At this point, she was obligated to check on him, and a little curious.

She stepped to the door and knocked on it. "Gideon. I'm just checking to see if you need anything."

Nothing. The room remained quiet. She turned the knob and pushed the door open. As her eyes adjusted to the colors of twilight entering the window, she saw his silhouette standing against the window. Gideon stood there gazing into the fading light through the trees, his back toward the door.

"Gideon?" she said and walked toward the window until she stood beside him. "Are you okay?"

His eyes searched through the shadows of the trees and the sunset, but he didn't look at her. The butterflies started in her chest again and she bit her lip as she reached out to touch his hand. As she felt his skin, he didn't start as she had half-expected him to do. Instead, he wrapped his fingers around her hand.

"There are some things I have never forgotten," he said as he stared out the window. "I did not remember such beautiful light in the sky or the sounds of the birds. But I never forgot you."

He looked at her from the corner of his eye, but didn't turn toward her. "I was lost for a thousand years down there."

"A thousand years?" she said. "But it was only a few months—"

"Time is different in Hell."

"Hell?" she said and his fingers tightened on hers.

"Abaddon put me back in there and then came up here for you again. All I knew was that I was trapped there and could not come and help you. I was tortured there for a thousand years, and the only thing I promised to myself was that I would never forget you."

He turned toward her, his eyes intense and gazing into her spirit. She realized she was wrong to think of him as a newborn. He was a returned prisoner of war, a tormented soul.

"Many things I have forgotten, but I remembered only you. Where I found you. Where we lived. What we . . . did . . . together. I thought about you everyday down there. And then I woke up on this world, in a cold alleyway, and I knew only that I had to find you. I saw you, and you were with him, Abaddon's vessel. I thought you had forgotten me."

"I would never forget you," she said, and stepped between him and the window. "I didn't know where you were or how to find you. I thought you were dead."

His trembling hand moved to touch her face and he ran a finger along the tattoos on her neck and behind her ear. "I do not think I died, but I am not sure."

The touch of his fingers sent zings of shivers across her skin. He pulled her hand against his chest and placed her fingers over his heart, just as she had done when she stopped him from stepping out into the main room and dripping water.

"I remember every time I touched you before I was gone," he said. "I have lived a thousand lifetimes, but only with you was I truly happy. I thought you were only my imagination when I saw you."

"I'm not imaginary," she said and stepped closer to him, feeling his heat through her shirt. "I'm very real."

She never thought she would see him again, let alone feel his touch. He pulled her close and kissed her just as he had before the world had collapsed around them. He had definitely not forgotten how to kiss. His hand moved to her hip and slipped under her thin shirt like he explored places that he had once known in a dream. The cold of his fingers chilled against her skin, sending goosebumps up her spine.

His fingers crept upward, pressing against her ribs, and that was the moment she thought about Jason. This felt wrong, like she betrayed everything that they had been through since Abaddon's defeat. She had thought about Gideon so many times since she had lost him, longing to feel his touch, but now was not the right time for all of this. She still had things to work out with Jason, and this was too soon.

Her fingers touched his hand, stopping their progress to more forbidden territory. "We can't—"

His hands froze for a moment, then his fingers clutched around her hands like the snap of a bear trap. The suddenness of it made her gasp just as he shoved her back against the wall. The back of her head smacked the wall, causing sparkles of light to erupt in her vision. He was on her again in a blur of shadows, his hands forcing her T-shirt over her head. The fading twilight fell over his face and she saw his eyes darken and he drew in against her, kissing her with such force that it hurt, and she couldn't breathe. His hands had moved to her upper arms, digging into her skin. She pressed her hands to his chest, trying to pull away until she could get enough space between them to turn her head.

"Gideon, wait—," she said after she gasped for a breath.

For only a second, he released her and pulled his own shirt over his head. Nikka tried to slide along the wall and step away from him, but his grasp found her arm again. He pulled her close to him and leaned in for another kiss.

She pulled her elbow up enough to press against his bare chest before he could do it. "Stop. Not like this—."

The dark in his eyes turned almost black and the grip on her arms tightened. The soft, frightened innocence that she had seen when he had first come back had melted away to the hard visage that looked at her now as though he was a predator and she was something to devour. Before she knew what he was doing, he shoved her down against the bed, making the air rush from her lungs. It took only a second for the disorientation to leave her head, but that was all the time he needed for him to pounce on her, his hands tearing desperately at the waist of her pants.

No. No. This can't be happening. Gideon wouldn't do this, but she hadn't seen the red light deep in his eyes that could be his inner demon wanting to destroy her.

She twisted her hips, trying to throw him off balance, and it worked. He fell to the side as she shoved herself up to her hands and knees and scrambled for the edge of the bed. She was nearly over the side, when his arm wrapped around her waist, his limbs all thick muscle and bone that pulled her back toward him. Her fingers reached out for anything else to grab, but she only found the edge of the sheets that gave way under her grasp.

Then he leaned over her, the weight of his torso hot against her back as he pressed her into the mattress. His breath danced over her ear as he whispered into her ear. "It is okay. I love you, Nikka."

She was sure that she had never experienced true panic in her life until that moment, when he pinned her against the mattress and succeeded in pulling away the last bit of clothing that had clung to her slender form. The shadows in the room began to creep in around her.

Stop.

Did she actually say it?

Please stop.

She tried again, but the sound was mute in her throat.

Just survive.

This wasn't right. It wasn't what she wanted from him. Gideon would never do this to her.

A terrible, cry and a scream filled the room. Maybe the scream came from her throat, but maybe she couldn't speak at all.

Chapter 32 Jason

Jason sat up from the twisted sheets of his twin bed and looked into the darkness of his small apartment. He knew it had been risky to come back here, but this was where he called home, at least the only home he knew where Nikka wouldn't be.

It was the middle of the night, and he had been sleeping heavily with the cocktails of vodka and gin that he had been able to find in the cabinet. He couldn't quite figure out what had awoken him, but his eyes darted through the dark of his room and he listened for any sounds. There was nothing.

He swung his legs over the side of the bed and put his head in his hands to stop the nausea that now ebbed in his stomach. He hadn't intended to drink enough to get hungover, but that's how it happened anyway.

The city lights shone into his room and were almost too bright with his throbbing headache. He stood and padded into the bathroom. The light flickered on, and he squinted into the mirror at the red streaks in his eyes: a product of too much drinking all day after leaving the cabin.

The nausea came again, and he scrambled to his knees and retched into the toilet. After the third time, he leaned against the cold tile wall and felt his head begin to clear despite the sour taste in his mouth. It had been so long since he had had anything to drink. Nikka's presence had eliminated the need to have a single drink, but since he left the cabin he couldn't help himself. Maybe this was what it was like to live like an alcoholic, and it wasn't all that pleasant.

He stood on wobbly legs and leaned over the sink, rinsing the foul taste from his mouth. As he stood straighter and looked in the mirror, the light in the bathroom flickered and then went out in a single pop, plunging him into darkness. He held his breath for a moment and reached back to the light switch, turning it up and down without effect.

"Damn it," he muttered and gripped the sink to steady himself.

Before he turned to the door, a ringing sound filled his ears. At first, he thought it was just a reaction from too much alcohol, but the sound continued to build until it was deafening. He clutched his hands to his ears, but the noise permeated through them until his head felt like it would split open. A trickle of blood spilled from his nose as the pain ripped into his skull. The sound vibrated into his bones and he fell to his knees.

Then it stopped as suddenly as it had begun. He still pressed his hands to his ears and gazed across the bathroom floor where he saw a shimmer of light coming from his bedroom, like sunlight reflecting off a pool of water. He didn't move or speak as he watched the light intensify and come near the door until a figure stepped into his view. The Being emitted the light as it stood in the doorway.

He felt like he couldn't hear its footsteps, or it never made a sound. He wasn't sure as he looked up at the figure that stood there.

The blood from his nose dripped to the white tile of the bathroom. Jason wiped the back of his hand across his face and sat up to face the figure.

The faceless Being stood there and looked at him for a moment, and then he heard its voice. "Help her."

Jason bolted upright in bed as he gasped. The room was dark, except for the lights of the city shining through his window. His eyes moved to every corner of the room, but everything was dark, including the bathroom. His fingers moved to his face and his nose was dry. No blood. No pain. There was nobody in his room, especially not some creature made of light and noise.

But its voice continued to echo in his brain as if he had just heard it and the sound still carried within the room.

Help her.

The last remnants of the bright light fogged his vision, but he rushed from the bed and gathered the clothes on the floor. His brain still fought with him in a dizzy swirl of images, but the effects of the alcohol had remarkably disappeared with the coming of the entity that had invaded his room. He pulled on his jeans and stumbled out the door while he tried to fit into his boots.

He knew exactly what the warning meant. He had told Nikka he would always be with her, no matter what, and he had left her the first time that his resolve was challenged. This was no dream; he knew that as soon as he had awakened. Nikka was in trouble and he had to help her now. But he hoped it wasn't too late.

Chapter 33 Nikka

Feral.

Desperate.

The last few minutes had felt like hours, but she survived it, just like she had promised herself.

The room had grown quiet and still as he kissed her, like everything was normal and what he had just done was okay. He treated her like she was his beloved now, just like before. He lay back against the pillow beside her in the dark, his ribs moving up and down with his rapid breathing.

For a moment she had thought he had become someone—or something—else. That was the only way she could just justify what had just happened. He lay there and she could feel his breath on her ear and his hand rest on her abdomen. She couldn't move at first, and every bit of her energy was gone; it was the same feeling she had when she had gone too long with the power of invisibility. She turned to face the wall, trying to find something to focus on in the dark, something besides Gideon.

"Did I hurt you?" he whispered.

Her hands still trembled, but she moved them to touch his hand on her abdomen. The way he talked to her now, the way he touched her, was so contrary to what he just did. But maybe it was her fault. Maybe she never should have gone in there. Maybe she had said something. He had been traumatized by what he had gone through, and perhaps he just couldn't stop himself. That had to be the explanation for what just happened. Gideon would never have harmed her intentionally.

She forced herself to sit upright and felt the dizzy rush in her head.

Regardless, she had to separate herself from him right now.

"Nikka?" he spoke again as she stepped into the bathroom and flipped the light switch on.

"I'm okay," she lied and closed the door.

Her knees trembled under her frail weight, but she gazed at her face in the mirror. Something was very different. Everything he had just done was frightening. Gideon had never scared her like that before, but it bothered her like an itch in her brain that just wouldn't go away. She ran cold water on her wrists and splashed her face in hopes that it would drive out the shaking she felt throughout her body.

She looked at herself again in the mirror: there was nothing wrong with her. There was nothing wrong with Gideon, she told herself. He was gone for so long, and when one holds that much longing for that amount of time, it's bound to be a little intense. That's all. Everything was going to be fine.

Except she hurt everywhere, and she winced as she saw bruises forming along her arms, around her neck, on her hips and between her legs. When she closed her eyes, she could still feel his hand at her throat or his fingers digging into her hips as he continued to hurt her without remorse.

And then she noticed the trickle of blood running down her leg.

Everything's fine. A few bruises were nothing. She had healed from far worse after she had faced a demon. She cleaned herself up with a few splashes of water and a towel and it was all as good as new. There was nothing wrong. Nothing at all.

She could have fought back harder. No. If she had, she might have hurt him. Even killed him.

Just stop thinking about it. Move on. He didn't know what he was doing. I love him, and he loves me. He just told me so, she thought.

Trying to shake the stone of worry that had settled around her, she dried her face and hands and stepped out of the bathroom into the dark of the bedroom once again.

In the moonlight that came through the window, she could see his form lying under the blankets. She searched for her shirt and pulled it over her head. Her fingers fumbled around in the dark until she found her cargo pants and she slipped into them.

The shaking wouldn't leave her hands, though. Her hands brushed against the pocket where she felt the cell phone. She pulled it from the pocket, anything to not look back at Gideon. She opened the start screen and saw that she had missed a call from Wolfe.

"Are you okay?" Gideon's voice said, breaking through the dark.

"Yeah," she said as his fingers touched her forearm. The sensation created a volley of tingles across her skin that sent painful jabs into her arm. She turned off the phone and slipped it into her pocket again.

"I have frightened you." He leaned up on his elbow and looked at her. The fingers touching her arm wrapped about her wrist and slowly pulled her down to the bed. She didn't resist because she knew he would probably force her there anyway and she didn't want him to know that she was ready to fall into a thousand pieces. That, and the ache that had settled into every muscle in her body, cried out not to fight him. She eased herself down to the bed next to him.

"I told you, everything's fine," she said, forcing her voice to stay even and not the mess that she felt inside.

He pulled her close to him, leaving her no choice but to rest her head on his shoulder. The way he held her now, so gentle and loving, it felt like the Gideon she used to know. Maybe she was wrong about what had just happened.

With trembling and cold fingers, she touched the skin of his bare chest, as though that was the thing she was supposed to do. He didn't flinch when she touched him. His fingers played along the tattoo lines on her arms, and when he touched her with such gentleness, her doubts began to thin. Her shoulders relaxed as she settled into his body again.

"Tell me if I do something wrong," he whispered. "I do not want to hurt you. I am still so confused by everything, and I need you with me."

"Nothing's wrong," she said and closed her eyes as he held her.

Nothing is wrong, she told herself again. *See. He didn't mean to do anything awful to her. It was all a mistake.*

Maybe if she thought it enough, it would be true. With him coming back out of the blue like he did and Jason leaving, her nerves were a bit on edge. That's all. Nothing more.

With his warmth against her and his breath on her neck, she fell asleep tucked into the edge of his torso, despite the ache that began to well in her pelvis.

She wasn't sure how long she had slept, but she awoke with a jolt. In the dark, she could feel Gideon convulse next to her. His body jerked into a violent seizure and she heard his breath choke in his throat.

"Gideon," she cried and placed a hand on his chest. In the moonlight she saw his eyes wide open and his face twisted in a pained grimace.

He grunted as another convulsion hit. Another cry escaped his lips as though he had been torn apart from the inside. His eyes then turned toward her, his lips peeled back from his teeth in pain.

"Run," he called to her with a choke.

"Gideon," Nikka cried. "What's wrong?"

"Run! Go now," he said before another seizure came. His hands rose to his head where his nails clawed at his scalp. "It is coming. I cannot stop it."

Nikka jumped away from him and fell to the floor as she watched his body rise above the bed. The blankets fell from his body, his limbs rigid but shaking. Then, as though he was being handled by an unseen hand, he turned and slammed into the wall at the head of the bed. His arms and legs writhed as his body rolled up toward the ceiling as though gravity had lost all meaning in that bedroom.

Nikka scrambled back to the far corner and cried as she watched him scream in agony. His eyes opened and found her once more. He reached a hand out to her, his eyes pleading for help before they flashed to bright red. His scream turned into an unholy wail just before his body fell from the upper corner of the room and behind the bed where she could no longer see him.

The ground below her feet began to rumble and shake. The walls of the cabin creaked and shuddered with the quaking in the earth. A growl, like a hungry Hell-beast rose from the other side of the bed, below the moonlight that came from the window.

Whatever lay in shadows was no longer Gideon. Nikka swallowed hard against her dry throat, reached for the door and ran from the room as the earthquake suddenly stopped. She almost fell again in the main room, but found her footing and stumbled back against the door.

The growling grew louder, permeating through the walls of the bedroom and shaking the foundation of the cabin. The rafters shook, the pictures on the walls falling to the ground in broken frames and the bookshelves toppled over onto the hardwood floor.

She stared wide-eyed through the darkness of the cabin at the closed bedroom door that now bulged back and forth as if a great beast breathed heavily on the other side.

"Seraph," a deep and vile voice spoke on the other side of the wall. "Why so scared, my love? I have come back for you."

"Gideon," she said, trying to keep the shaking out of her voice. "You have to try and fight this. It isn't you."

"Gideon? An abomination," the voice said.

The ground quaked again, but this time it threw her off balance. She fell to the floor as the lamp on the table crashed at her feet. The water line must have broken and the fountain of pressurized water sprayed at the kitchen sink. Another quake shattered the windows around her.

"There is no Gideon, for I am Pazuzu," the voice said and the quaking grew more violent.

Nikka forced her head to clear. She scrambled to her feet, running over the shards of glass from the broken windows on the floor and rushed through the front door. Just as she stumbled out onto the gravel driveway, headlights illuminated the cabin from the down the road.

The familiar old pickup truck sped into the driveway and stopped mere feet from where she fell.

Jason jumped from the driver's side and rushed to her as another quake shook the earth. Trees around them quivered, and she heard something crashing in the woods behind them. The north half of the cabin collapsed in on itself.

"There is no hope," Pazuzu said from somewhere in the cabin. His voice permeated through the forest, deep and horrible. "You will not defeat us, for we are legion."

Jason pulled her to her feet and rushed her into the cab of the truck. He climbed in after her and stepped on the gas. The tires peeled through the gravel, and the truck plunged down the dark road. The headlights barely shone the way through the forest as the ground continued to shake and rumble below them.

Nikka turned back and watched the cabin disappear from view through the back window of the truck. The vehicle seemed to bounce and leap across the road with each tremor. A tree collapsed behind them, just missing the bed of the truck.

A loud boom sounded throughout the side of the mountain and Nikka watched as a plume of fire and black smoke rose above the tree line, coming from where the cabin had once stood. But this wasn't just an explosion of fire and gas from the propane tank at the back of the cabin. This plume was much larger, and the pressure wave hit the truck from behind, almost sending the wheels in a spin.

"What was that?" Jason said, his eyes darting back to the rearview mirror.

The plume rose higher, growing bright orange and red. Another explosion sounded, and she saw a cloud of debris and smoke rise in the light of the first fire. The forest behind turned into a wall of orange and red as a wall of fire descended down the mountain.

"Hurry," she said, her throat tight.

"I'm going as fast as I can," he said.

"Hurry, I mean it." The wall of orange light tore through layers of the forest, moving faster to their space on the road.

Jason glanced at the rearview mirror again as the mountain began to glow behind them. "Put on your seatbelt."

Nikka turned away from the back window and slid the seatbelt around her torso. Jason then turned the wheel hard, and the truck bounced off the road and down the side of the open hill, through the spaces between the trees.

The headlights hardly helped as the trees zoomed by, just missing the front of the truck. Nikka closed her eyes, feeling each violent bump in the ground and tremor in the earth that threatened to overturn the truck.

The fire came close enough that she could feel it through the windows around her. The vehicle then hit a large bump, turned and spun around on a smoother surface, where the truck began to accelerate quickly.

She opened her eyes to see they were finally on a paved road and heading toward the freeway.

Other vehicles on the road had now pulled over and people stepped out of their cars to stare at the spectacle on the mountain. Nikka sat up and looked out the window to see the destruction behind them. Jason looked as well, and it appeared that a volcano had just erupted and filled the sky with fire and ash.

CHAPTER 34 NIKKA

The truck raced down the road, bypassing the many other cars that had stopped with people jumping out to see the eruption at the top of the mountain.

Jason pushed the engine until it was so loud that Nikka could no longer hear her heartbeat pounding in her ears. Her fingers clutched the seatbelt at her shoulders until her fingers hurt, but she was too afraid to let go. It was hard to tell with the suspension on the truck, but she was sure that the ground still quaked under the tires.

Jason turned the truck into the parking lot of a gas station lit by rows of fluorescent lights illuminating each pump station. The tires squealed as he careened into the lot and came to a rapid stop. He jumped from the cab and walked around to the passenger door, ignoring the attendant who stood in the lot and stared at the glowing mountain in the distant night. Jason opened the passenger door and helped Nikka unbuckle her seatbelt.

She saw him open the door, but could barely move. Her fingers still held tight to the seatbelt even though the truck had stopped. Her entire body had gone rigid, both with pain and terror of what she had just witnessed. The whole world seemed to be rushing past her now and the seatbelt was the only thing that made it slow down. She felt Jason's hand on hers, trying to release her grip on the belt.

"It's okay," he said. His voice still quivered as he tried to keep calm. "We're out of there. He can't get to us."

He pried her fingers free and pulled her close to him as he wrapped his arms around her shoulders. Everything around her made her ears ring, and she could still hear the sound of the explosion that had rocked the mountain.

When she felt the warmth of his chest, her fingers clutched at the lapel of his jacket. The tears flowed from her eyes freely. There was no way to stop it now.

"I've got you," he whispered in her ear.

Beyond his voice, she could hear the sound of a radio broadcast coming from inside the gas station, where the door gaped open. The gas station attendant still stood outside, oblivious to anybody else at the pumps, as he stared through the night at the plume of fire emitting from the top of the mountain.

Beyond the ringing in her ears, she heard a man's voice through the speakers: .... breaking news . . . an eruption on Mount Carmen . . . earthquake damages still to be determined . . .

Earthquake. Eruption. Gideon had caused all that.

Jason drew back from her and cupped her face in his hands. "Are you okay?"

Through all the sounds of the news alert and the roaring in her head, she tried to focus on her own body. With everything that had just happened, she hadn't had enough time to assess if she had been injured, and she was still so sore from everything that Gideon had done to her before the demon had arrived.

Then she felt a warm stinging at her feet and she glanced down her legs. Jason followed her gaze and noticed the drops of blood pooling at the floor of the truck. She remembered the windows shattering around her and then running out of the cabin. There had been broken glass everywhere.

She felt the pain next as Jason crouched to examine her feet. He winced as he lifted her foot up into the light.

"Um, okay," he said, not keeping a very good poker face as he placed her foot back down. "Just stay here for a second."

He ran around the side of the truck and came back with a first aid kit.

"Lay down. I'm gonna need to do a little bit of work here."

Nikka rested back into the long truck seat and stared up at the metal roof of the cab. His hand, still shaking from the quick drive down the mountain, grasped her left heel first and she waited.

"Okay, I'm real sorry about this," he said.

"About what?"

A quick, sharp pain lanced through the bottom of her foot and up her leg as he pulled a shard of glass from the sole of her foot. Her hand flailed out and she grasped the steering wheel as she tried to hold back the scream.

"About that," he said. "And this one."

He pulled another shard and another one, which felt smaller than the others. Nikka bit her lip with each pull and felt hot tears of pain flowing down her face.

He continued to the other foot, which seemed to have an indefinite number of glass shards embedded in her flesh.

"We could just call you John McClane," he said as he pulled out another one.

She grunted as the pain rushed into her legs. "What?"

"You know. John McClane. *Die Hard*. He did that bad ass move where he walked on all that broken glass to get away from the terrorists."

The pain had subsided for a moment as he held her feet before him. "Oh my gosh, I don't care. Are you done yet?"

"I think so." He reached into the truck, to the dashboard where a half-empty bottle of water lay on its side. He opened the bottle and held it over her toes. "This might sting a little."

She looked down at him as he poured the water down the soles of her feet. The water buzzed into each little laceration scattered across her skin. She held her breath to fight back another scream. But all of this distracted her from the growing ache in her abdomen that had started before the quake, hours before she saw Gideon change.

Then there was silence and she opened her eyes and looked down at him again. He produced a roll of white gauze and began to wrap her feet. For just those few seconds, she caught her breath and felt his warm hands against her cold skin. He taped the edges of the gauze and reached for her hand, helping her to sit up.

"Got 'em," he said and wiped away the tears that had flowed down the sides of her face. "Are you really okay? Did he hurt you?"

For that brief time with Jason plucking glass from her feet, she was able to forget about everything that had just happened and focus on her pain. As awful as that was, it might have been better than remembering that Gideon had just turned into some horrific monster right in front of her.

She didn't know how to answer the question Jason had just asked her. She wasn't sure if she was going to be all right. Even before Gideon had changed, something had gone terribly wrong, and she was ready to admit that to herself now. She hadn't felt well from the moment he had kissed her, and then there was everything that happened after that. It was more than just being sore: there was a deep, gnawing pain in her pelvis that had begun to build since Gideon did what he did. She would never tell Jason about what had happened with Gideon before the mountain had exploded. That would only worry Jason even more.

She nodded her head as he held her hands longer than she would have expected.

"I'm so sorry," he said. "I shouldn't have left you there with him. I promised that I wouldn't leave you and I did and I'm sorry."

"It's okay. I understand."

"No. It's not okay. I made a promise to you and I broke it. I won't ever do that again—"

She leaned down to him and kissed him. He seemed so frantic and worried that it felt like the right thing to do. He instantly quieted and kissed her in return.

Nikka held back. "But you came back."

As she looked into his blue eyes that gazed into hers with worry, flecks of pale gray debris began to fall around them like snow. She looked away from him and to the fluorescent lights around the gas station. The flecks drifted to the ground, collecting on the pumps, the truck and began to cover the pavement like snow.

"Ash," Jason said as he watched the flakes of gray settle around them. "We need to get out of here." He stepped away from her, closed the passenger door and climbed in the driver's seat and started the truck. The diesel engine rumbled to life, and he turned on the wipers, sweeping off the layer of ash that had accumulated on the windshield.

"Where are we going?" she asked and buckled her seatbelt.

"South. We need to find Andy, tell him what's going on."

"I think they know about him," she said, hearing Gideon's last words to her before they left the cabin. "He's not safe."

"Exactly."

The tires spun away the coating of ash along the pavement as Jason started away from the gas station and onto the darkened road toward the free-way.

Chapter 35 Nikka

Nikka awoke as the truck struck a bump in the road, and blinked her eyes open to the glow of a rising sun in the east.

Somewhere in the dark last night she had managed to fall asleep, although she felt the kink in her neck where she had rested against the side window. Her eyes adjusted to the gentle light as it began to settle over wide open fields of brown soil awaiting the end of winter. As the sun rose higher, the blood red hue of sunrise changed to an orange-yellow light as it moved away from the haze cast over the land by the falling ash. The bare trees that passed by them hung in dead slumber, like harbingers that watched for them along the road.

She felt Jason's hand on hers as she sat up and rested back against the seat. She glanced at him and saw the fatigue in his eyes.

"You doing okay?" she said.

He forced a tired smile toward her. "Sure. Just need a little caffeine. We need to stop soon and get some gas anyway. Next station."

"Okay," she said and rubbed her fingers against her eyes. "Any idea where we need to go?"

He shook his head. "Not really. I tried to call Andy; still no answer. He had said he was going somewhere in Nevada, so we should just aim the truck that way and drive."

Nikka nodded, but she couldn't help but feel the pressure of that distance. Nevada was a pretty big state. Wolfe could be anywhere there, or may not be there at all. He had tried to call her back, so there was the hope that he would call them again. They had nowhere else to go right now. If that was Jason's plan, it was as good as any.

The truck continued onward until Jason saw another gas station. He stopped, filled the tank, bought a large cup of coffee and they continued on, despite Nikka urging him to let her drive.

The hours went by, and the further south they drove, the less ash they saw. In the moments where they were within radio range, the news they could hear didn't sound very optimistic. The mountain had indeed erupted; it had been a silent volcano, according to one expert interviewed on the station, and was part of the same chain of volcanoes as Mount St. Helen's. It was just it's time, he said, although it hadn't shown any signs of seismic activity since the early 1980's. The earthquake that preceded it was also not unusual, given that the eruption occurred right after it. Again, that was according to all those experts. The quake had measured at a 5.6 and caused some damage in the city, but the epicenter was "somewhere around the mountain."

If they only knew what she knew. There was nothing geological or meteorological happening. This was caused by the appearance of Pazuzu, and she had a feeling that the seismic display she saw last night was just the beginning.

The landscape around them changed as the temperatures warmed. Though they were still a long way from Nevada, the tree-covered hills changed to low shrubs and Joshua trees. The sun heated the day enough to roll down her window and take in the fresh air, now that it was no longer tainted with ash.

She rested her head against the door frame and watched the world zoom by and the sun begin to descend into the west.

The hours had droned on all day without a single call from Andy. Jason had tried to reach him several more times, but there was no answer. With the oncoming dusk, she could feel the pull of despair. They were no closer to finding out where Andy was or if he was even okay.

She ran away from Hell's second-in-command back on that mountain, and now she ran toward some unknown future. Jason remained with her, and despite the comfort of his company, he had bound himself to that unpredictable fate that now hung over her head.

The truck slowed as he approached another gas station. He pulled into the pump bays and stopped, letting out a long, deep breath. He rubbed the back of his hands against his eyes.

"We need to stop," she said as she watched him.

"Can't stop. I just need more coffee."

"No," she said and leaned over the seat, grabbing the keys from the ignition. "We need to stop. I need to get out of here, and you need to sleep. We can't go on this way forever." She clutched the keys in her palm, well away from his grasp.

He scanned her face, the dark circles under his eyes growing deeper as the sun set. "Okay, fine. I'll check with the guy inside, see if there's somewhere close to stay."

He stepped out of the truck and walked into the gas station.

Nikka gazed out the window to the coming sunset. A gentle breeze blew across the road, sending a swirl of dust over the pavement and into the desert. The golden light fell over the buildings that sat across the street, like worn-out dominoes. They appeared abandoned, with weeds and dust gathering around the doors. Everything here was empty and alone, just left along the roadside of this forsaken desert town.

A collection of four crows cawed from the top of the central building, the once-white walls of which were now chipped and faded. At first she thought the nearing sunset cast shimmers of light over the building's dusty windows, but then she realized that it was light that shone from inside the panes of stained glass. It was probably the only one of the abandoned places here that actually still had life. Her eyes moved up to the doorway and she saw a faded wooden cross above the threshold. A church.

Her fingers slipped around the door handle and she opened the truck door. She stepped out, her knees a little wobbly from sitting in the vehicle for so long. Her feet moved across the warm pavement, and for a few minutes she was able to forget that each step hurt through the wraps of gauze.

The cross above the door was the only thing she focused upon as if it lured her to the threshold of that church. She stepped up to the narrow porch and opened the door of the small chapel.

The rusty hinges squeaked as she entered the building. At first she smelled dust and old wood, but then she could smell warm candle wax as she faced the wooden pews that sat in rows toward the pulpit. The place was small enough that she could see there was nobody else in the main chapel.

She stepped over the creaky floorboards of the building, a place that must have been over a hundred years old. Each step she took began to remind her of every shard of glass that had been piercing her feet, but she continued forward until she settled into the front pew and looked at the colors of the sunset through the arching stained glass window behind the pulpit.

The light glowed like a dozen colored crystals in the facets of the glass. A table covered with tea light candles sat below the window and cast a dancing light against the wall.

Her eyes moved around the window and to the inset shelves that framed it. Within these spaces she could see a statue of the Virgin Mary and another of Jesus on the cross. As she shifted in the pew, the creaking wood echoed throughout the empty chapel. Everything else about this place was so quiet and peaceful, except her and her fidgeting.

Why had she come here? There was nothing for her here, so what had prompted her to leave the truck and walk to this old chapel? There was more life in the collapsing monastery that she had lived in for several months, where Gideon had kept her safe and taught her so many things. But even that had fallen into nothing, just like the cabin. Everywhere she once thought of as home had collapsed and been taken into the earth. Dust to dust.

Her eyes moved to the small statues again, their ceramic faces chipped and dusty. Just things for people to put their faith in and then have it crushed.

"Why don't you do anything to help me?" she said, her voice echoing in the chapel. She wasn't sure who she spoke to. The statue, maybe. God. Nature. She didn't know, but it needed to be said. "Everything is dying, and you don't lift a finger."

"How do you know He isn't helping you already?" a man's voice spoke.

Her stomach about leapt through her throat when she heard his voice. She turned around and saw a man—a priest—sitting a few pews behind her. He wasn't a very big person, but maybe the uniform made him look slight. His pepper gray hair had receded many years ago along with his eyesight. His voice had a hint of a Mexican accent as he spoke.

When she didn't respond to him right away, the priest stood on unsteady knees and walked around to the pew where she sat. He nestled in beside her and reached a hand out to her. She shook his arthritic hand and she could smell peppermint and furniture polish surrounding him.

"Father Garcia," he said and gave her a look as if he expected a name from her as well.

"Nikka."

He smiled at her. "Short for Nikola."

She nodded. "Yeah."

The priest turned his gaze forward, but she continued to watch him with suspicion. How did he arrive in the chapel without her hearing him? Every board and rafter creaked in that place. A ninja couldn't get in here without making a sound.

"Well, Nikola. My question is still relevant."

"I'm sorry. I forgot the question."

"How do you know He hasn't helped you?"

Nikka followed his gaze back to the statues. "I just know."

The old man smiled and let out a little laugh. "If he has not helped you, then you would not be here right now, speaking to me."

This priest knew nothing of her situation, and how could he? He was an aging man who ran a church that probably didn't see any more than five people a month enter through its crumbling doors.

"Yeah, well, I need to get going," she said and stood.

The priest just smiled at her as she walked around the pew and into the aisle.

"It's Enochian," he said as she was ready to place a hand on the door.

She turned around to see him still staring forward to the statues. "What?"

"Those symbols on your arms and neck. Enochian. The language of angels."

Her hands trembled just as her fingers found the door. "How do you know that?"

"They told me you would be here. That is how I know that God has helped you this far. They told me you would be sitting right here when I found you."

Nikka walked back up the aisle and sat beside the priest. "Who told you that?"

His old eyes turned toward her as he continued to smile. "The angels, of course."

The adrenaline began to thread through her muscles and under her skin. The priest reached a shaking finger to her forearm and followed the curving lines of the symbols over her skin.

"Enochian. That's what it's called. And when these words are put together like this," he said as he flicked his finger to indicate the tracings all up and down her body, "then it creates a spell. A very powerful one."

Nikka leaned away from him a little for fear that he may do something else that she didn't expect, like so many things seemed to be doing lately.

"And do you know about me? Do you know what I am?"

"They didn't tell me. I just know that when I found you here, that it would mean the End of Days is near."

His eyes drifted to the window, to the fading light of sunset. The candle-light danced across his face and made the shadows darken across his eyes. The butterflies that had filled her stomach now grew still, deathly still.

"What do you mean by that?"

"You know what I mean." He turned to her, the smile still on his face as he pointed to the mark in the center of her chest. "You have the mark of the Master over Devils. They gave that to you because you were the only one that could carry the burden of it."

"Burden?"

"The one that carries that mark will be present when the Seals are broken."

"Like, *Book of Revelation* seals? Those seals?"

The priest nodded, his voice low and even. "'And I beheld when he had opened the sixth seal, and lo, there was a great earthquake; and the sun became black as sackcloth of hair, and the moon became as blood.'"

Her fingers became cold and she felt her ears ringing again.

"'And the name of the star is called Wormwood,'" he quoted again. "You know of what I speak."

She could only nod and she turned her eyes to the fading light outside the window. "What do I do to stop this?"

"There is nothing you can do," he said. "Apocalypse is inevitable. Great change will happen."

"If there is nothing I can do," she said and turned to him, "then why are you telling me all of this?"

"You must be prepared. You are an instrument of angels. You are the weapon that will ensure that the change is a good one, and that the Devil will not reign in the end."

"They're angels, though. They are so much more powerful than I am. Why can't they just take care of it themselves?"

"Archangels," he said with a little laugh. "They are very powerful, indeed. They created you. But remember one thing: The Devil was an archangel too. He knows everything that they know. He almost ruled all of Heaven once. That's why the archangels needed you and your kind, to balance the struggle between Heaven and Hell."

"How do you know all of this?" she asked.

"God works in mysterious ways," he said.

The door to the chapel opened, sending in a dry, warm wind that made the candles flicker. Nikka stood and saw Jason standing at the threshold, his breathing quick like he had been running. At first he looked worried, and he had every right to be. She had left the truck without telling him and he appeared as if he had been searching frantically for her.

"Are you okay?" he said.

She nodded. "I was just talking to this priest—" She looked down to the pew where the priest had been sitting, but the space was empty as though nobody had ever been there. She glanced at every corner of the small chapel, but it was otherwise empty. There was no way he could have moved so fast that she missed him leaving the church.

"That's impossible," she muttered to herself and continued to move down the aisle, checking each pew.

"You sure you're okay?" Jason said and took her hand, leading her toward the door.

"I don't know anymore," she said and glanced back one more time before she stepped through the old church doors.

Chapter 36 Jason

Jason had insisted on carrying her piggyback into the hotel room after he saw her limping from the church and to the truck. But when he first tried to lift her, she winced a little and he could tell she tried to brush it off.

It wasn't just her feet. There was something else going on; she was hurting just about everywhere he touched her. He carried her to the truck and climbed inside, hoping she would eventually tell him he was wrong and to mind his own business.

The convenience store clerk had provided him with directions to a place to stay. When he pulled the truck into the parking lot, the place looked pretty desolate except for the motel office lit by a single lamp. He stepped out of the truck and through the office door, but not before glancing back to Nikka. She now rested her head back against the truck seat, her eyes drifting to the neon sign above the motel. In the blue glow of the buzzing lights, he could see the melancholy in her face.

What was she not telling him?

He sighed and stepped into the office where he found the clerk, paid cash for a room and left with an old key on a big ring. Not the little magnetic card that you could just slip into the doorknob and "click," you're in. This was old-school.

Nikka lifted her head as she saw him return to the truck and open her door. Despite her protests, he insisted that he carry her inside, and she didn't put up much of a fight after that. He scooped her up as she wrapped an arm around his neck, but she held her breath with each step across the pavement as though the movement hurt. He unlocked the door and placed her back on her feet inside the room.

As soon as the door opened, he scrunched his nose at the smell of mildew in the air. The door creaked open on a rusty hinge and caught across the green shag carpet.

"Ugh," she said as she got her balance. "This place looks like the Bates Motel."

Nikka flicked on the light switch and two lamps on both sides of the bed turned on with a faint hum. Once the room was illuminated, Jason could see the coin-operated device at the head of the bed that made the mattress vibrate.

Nikka let out a weak laugh as she limped to the bed and stretched out over the thread-worn blanket.

"It's a bed that vibrates," she said with a laugh.

"Yeah," Jason said. "The guy didn't specify what room we were getting." He placed the key on the small side table by the door.

He watched her ease her head down on the pillow. She was so tired. Hell, they were both tired, but after everything that had happened, he didn't feel like bringing up any more terrible feelings tonight. He couldn't forgive himself for leaving her to suffer whatever things had happened in that cabin.

"You can have the vibrating bed and I'll sleep in the truck."

Nikka sat up on her elbows and looked at him. "Are you kidding me? Get over here." She crawled across the bed and grasped the edge of his T-shirt, pulling him toward her.

"You've been driving for almost 36 hours. You're exhausted and you're not sleeping in the truck. And you can't leave me alone in the Bates Motel. It's too creepy in here."

Her pleading gaze could melt stone. He felt her hands pull him closer, and he placed a hand on hers, releasing her fingers from his shirt.

"Are you sure?" he said.

She got up to her knees and placed her hands against his face. "Of course I am." She kissed him. He placed his hands on her hips, but she winced again and caught her breath at his touch.

Jason pulled back a little. "What's wrong?"

She averted her gaze and sat back on her heels. "Nothing. It's okay."

"No, it's not." With his hand still at her hip, he lifted her shirt to see a line of bruises and scratches that looked like fingerprints along her hip that extended down under her waistband. There were more that wrapped around her back and up her ribs. And then he finally noticed the darkening bruises around her neck.

He felt heat rising around his neck and he clenched his jaw. Nikka pulled the edge of her shirt down and looked at him again, but this time he could see the shame in her eyes.

"He did this, didn't he?" Jason fumed and watched the expression on her face. He could see the light seem to vanish from her eyes. As his gut began to turn and twist as the realization hit him.

"Did he rape you?" Jason said, but he already knew the answer before he asked it. He knew exactly what had happened after he left her alone with that bastard. He backed away and tightened his fists against his temples as he watched her shoulders fold in and she dropped her head as he said it.

The urge to hit something grew in his chest. Just throw a chair against the wall. Break a window. Crush Gideon's skull with a baseball bat.

His eyelids pinched closed when the pit in his stomach grew. "How bad did he hurt you? I—I can take you to a hospital or something."

"Hey," she said and propped up onto her knees again. "I'm okay."

He couldn't look at her, at what he had allowed to happen. Jason turned away and placed his hands on the table, hunching over to catch his breath.

Her hand settled on his shoulder. He hadn't heard her step from the bed, but maybe his ears were ringing too loudly or something. Then her hand slipped around his face and he looked at her.

"I can handle myself," she said. "You're not responsible for anything that happens to me."

"I should have been there," he said and opened his eyes. How could she even want to touch him after he let this happen to her? None of this had to happen, and even if she said it wasn't his fault, he would always know that it was.

Her hands remained on his face no matter how he tried to turn away from her. "Stop it. What's done is done. I'm alive and we're here now. What matters is stopping what's coming. That's all."

She slipped her hand in his and pulled him away from the table. "Now, no more driving. No more worrying. The only thing you need to be concerned about is making me stand here after you pulled glass out of my feet."

Nikka moved over the bed and pulled him down with her. He crawled beside her and lay against the pillow, looking at her as she rested next to him. With his fingers still entwined with hers, he felt his rigid spine soften as he wrapped his arm over her torso and pulled her as close to him as possible. Her breathing stayed in rhythm and he matched hers, his face resting against the back of her head, close enough that he smelled the faint scent of soap against her skin.

He wouldn't let her go, not even when he slept. Not again.

CHAPTER 37 NIKKA

The worried lines in his forehead smoothed as Jason's breathing began to slow. The anger still rippled off his shoulders until he fell asleep. This was exactly why she didn't want to tell him anything, about how much she hurt.

Now, he knew what had happened between her and Gideon before things began to fall apart. A demon had attacked her, had done something unspeakable to her, something that she never thought she would face in her lifetime. A demon in the guise of someone she trusted. The thought of it left a sour taste in her mouth and made her queasy.

But there was nothing to do about it now. It was in the past, a terrible past, and there was so much more to concern her now. That demon, Pazuzu, was now free, and she knew he was worse than Abaddon. He was the devil's right hand.

She closed her eyes and felt Jason's arm around her, an embrace that felt desperate and sad. These were all things that needed to wait until tomorrow. Things that she and Jason would have to work through and face after they both had a good rest, away from the road and the evil things that crept through the night.

Just when she could feel the blanket of sleep begin to settle over her, her thoughts drifted to the darkness of the cabin. She saw a pair of ember-orange eyes in the shadows watching her, the beast breathing in and out through clenched teeth. His hands touched her flesh and moved down to her hips like two hot paws laced with sharp nails. Then he was on her, pressing against her back and holding her down until she couldn't move or scream. The demon wrapped a clawed hand around her throat and then she felt the sharp pain between her legs . . . .

She stirred back to consciousness with a start and looked down at the silver slip of moonlight on the floor again. Jason breathed slower behind her, and she eased herself against him enough to feel his body heat against her. Even if she couldn't sleep, at least she would know that he was right beside her, and the vision of the demon was just a nightmare.

At some point during the night, the visions cleared and she had fallen asleep until she awoke to bright morning light shining through the window. She sat upright and glanced at the space beside her on the bed, but it was empty and cold.

Her head cleared and she jumped to her feet, but the pain of the glass lacerations and the ache in her pelvis reminded her that she couldn't move too fast. She limped to the bathroom, and there was no sign of Jason. The ground felt like it dropped from under her as her stomach quivered and rose into her chest. None of his clothes were on the ground or even a used towel on the bathroom floor.

Was he so angry with her that he left? Just left her there in the motel room to face his anger on his own? With his guilt of leaving her in the cabin, she never thought he would do this, but maybe she underestimated him. What if he just couldn't look at her anymore, after what had happened? What if he had decided he couldn't love her knowing what Gideon had done?

The main door opened and sunlight poured into the threshold beyond his silhouette. She felt the release of anxiety slip from her stomach as she staggered against the wall and closed her eyes.

"Nikka," he said and rushed to her side. "What's wrong?"

Her fingers clutched at his shirt and she steadied herself. "Nothing."

"Something's wrong." He helped her to the edge of the bed. "Wait. Did you think I was gone?"

"It doesn't matter," she said as her eyes fell on the paper sack he had placed on the small table across the room.

"It does matter," he said and knelt down on the carpet and forced her to look at him. "I won't leave you. I just went to grab some breakfast. You seemed so tired, I just didn't want to wake you. Okay? I'm here."

She forced a smile as he pulled her in close and their foreheads touched. "Okay."

His finger touched her chin. "And I just wanted to see if Norman Bates would show." A smile broke across his lips.

"Shut up," she said and shoved him away with a laugh.

The familiar smile had returned to his face, even if his eyes looked at her with sadness and concern. At least he had come back and tried to lighten her mood.

"I got some breakfast. It's not the best, but it's what I could find." He turned around and began to unpack the greasy breakfast sandwiches from the paper bag.

For the rest of the morning, they lay back in the bed and ate breakfast while trying to watch anything on the black and white television. It received only three channels, one of them in Spanish, and none of her high school Spanish lessons helped with that. He made jokes and laughed, but she still felt a little rattled by his earlier absence. Not only did it concern her, but the fact that she remained unnerved by it made her worry. Of course, there was no way she would tell him. Then he would feel like he could never leave her side, and that was a ridiculous concept.

The phone call came, as hoped, from Wolfe. But the information was not what she had expected. The reception was distant and broken at best, indicating he was driving while he talked to them.

"I'm in Nevada right now and I've located the device," he said. "But I need you guys to wait. There is something happening right now that I can't get into, but you need to stay out of Nevada. Just hang low and off the radar."

"No, Andy. If you found it, we need to disable it," Nikka interrupted.

"It's not that easy, but there is a window of time opening up and it will allow us access to it, but only for a short time. When that happens, I will call you in. In the meantime, I can't have you two getting caught. The FBI here is all over your pictures. They know you're coming. They know what we're doing."

"So what do we do until then?" Jason asked.

"Keep moving. Don't stay anywhere for too long. I'll be in touch." His voice crackled as the signal wavered.

"Be careful," Nikka said, but the call dropped and she wasn't sure that he had even heard it.

Jason didn't wait once the call was over. He gathered their things, tossed them loosely into the truck, and they left the motel.

After that, the road became long, and days wandered on as they rode in the truck like two gypsies, never lingering for more than a day anywhere.

Chapter 38 Nikka

The phone remained silent, and days went by as they drove through every little town on the outskirts of the desert. She was sure Jason could feel it, but she needed to get out of the truck and have her feet on solid ground for more than a day.

They had been doing this for a few weeks, and the vagabond lifestyle was just a little more than she could stand right now. She wasn't sure if it was all the driving or just poor sleep, but she had no energy anymore. If she found a good bed, she was ready to sleep all day if she could.

Either Jason felt the same way, or he sensed it in her. He pulled the truck into an oasis of trees and discovered an abandoned farmhouse with several outbuildings and a barn. A perfect place to find some shelter for more than one night. It wasn't visible from the main road, and there was a functioning well with a pump behind the barn. Fresh water. A quiet place. They could place the foam mattress Jason had purchased in the back of the truck and just rest for a few days.

The truck drove over several ruts in the dirt road as Jason maneuvered it toward the back of the barn. The motion of the vehicle began to make her dizzy, and that, coupled with the fatigue, began to turn her stomach. He finally stopped the truck and he glanced over at her.

"You okay?" he asked.

She must have looked as bad as she felt. "I just need to walk around a bit."

He stepped out of the truck. Nikka opened her door and stepped down onto the ground covered in dried weeds. The dizziness still swirled around her head, but she leaned back against the truck and closed her eyes.

She felt the trembling start in her knees first, like a wave of weakness growing from her feet. Nausea began to burn in her chest and tickled at the back of her throat. She leaned forward, her hands on her knees.

"Whoa," Jason said as he stepped around the truck. "Maybe you should sit down."

"I'm fine."

"Yeah, well, you don't look fine," he said and pulled her arm around his shoulders as he walked her into the shade of the barn. "Just sit down here. I'll get you some water. I think there are some crackers or something in the pack."

She eased down to the ground and leaned back against the wall of the barn. Maybe it was the heat or she had developed a case of motion sickness. Whatever was going on, it reminded her of being back on chemotherapy.

Her eyes opened suddenly and she glanced down to her fingers. She flipped her palms around until she could see the backs of her hands. The skin had grown so pale. Were they looking a little thin? Her fingers worked up to her face and around her eyes. Maybe it was her imagination, but did her cheeks seem hollow and sunken?

No. It had to be just her nerves working extra hard on her.

She glanced up at Jason as he rummaged through the pack in the truck, looking for anything that might help her. He hadn't noticed her worry. Not yet.

Nikka closed her eyes. It's nothing. Just a little car sickness.

The cancer can't come back. That would be impossible. She was cured. Right?

"Here you go," Jason said as he crouched beside her with a bottle of water in his hand.

She opened her eyes and accepted it, forcing a smile and hoping that he didn't notice her worry. "Thanks."

The water was cool against her throat and helped to push the nausea away. See. There was nothing to worry about. She was still healthy and everything was going to be just fine.

It had to be.

Chapter 39 Jason

They lay together under the stars in the absolute quiet of the desert, hearing only the distant cries of a coyote. The nights here were warm enough, unlike the mountains way up north, and they could comfortably sleep outside.

It was a lot like camping when he was a kid, when his grandfather took him hunting and they slept outside in sleeping bags and listened to the forest.

She had curled next to him, her small hand resting on his chest as he gazed upward to the moonless sky. The day's drive had been long and hot, but they had found a desolate spot off the main road and into the dunes where nobody would happen upon them. The perfect place to spend the night.

"You're quiet tonight," she said. The pressure of her hand changed when she shifted closer to him.

"Just tired, I guess."

"Then why aren't you asleep?"

She had a way of knowing what was in his brain. He rolled to his side and gazed at her through the dark. "Too tired to sleep."

"You mean too worried," she said and moved her hand away from his chest, but he caught it and pressed her hand against him again.

"Yeah. Are you feeling okay? You just don't look like you're doing too well with all of this."

The sound of her breath catching in her throat worried him. "I'm okay, just exhausted."

"Do your feet still hurt? Maybe I could get some medication at a drug store—"

"I'm fine," she said with a smile and leaned in closer. Her lips touched his before he could say any more. At first, it was a gentle kiss, one of reassurance. But she didn't pull away from him after that.

He released her hand as she reached her fingers around the back of his neck, the pressure of her kiss sending waves of shivers down his chest. It had been too long since they had a moment to share, just the two of them alone without the fears of the pressing world falling around them. He only had one night with her, one memorable night, and he had missed the taste of her ever since then.

Her body shifted against him as she arched her neck back, inviting him closer. His lips moved down to the curve of her jaw and to the space below her earlobe, a place that made her gasp. The clutch of her fingers on his shirt pulled him down toward her. His hand moved from her arm to her side, against the angled curve of her hip until he found the edge of her shirt. The warmth of her skin at his fingertips made a knot of heat spark along his spine. He didn't feel the tension at first, but then moved his hand further up her abdomen, tracing close along the edge of her ribs.

The moment he touched the flesh below her breast, she gasped and her entire core tightened.

"Stop," she said, her voice weak and quivering. Her hand flew to his wrist, her fingers frozen around his wrist. Her body had gone rigid under him, and he pulled away from her, gazing at her face through the dark.

She had turned away from him, but he knew she cried as she held his wrist with an iron grip.

"I'm sorry," he said, the heat in his spine now ice cold. "I didn't mean to hurt you."

When he pulled his hand away from her, she finally released her grip, but her body shuddered with the silent cries that she tried to hide from him.

"Where did I hurt you?" he said, afraid to touch her again.

"You didn't," she said, her face still turned away and with eyes closed to the dark.

Even through shadows around her from where they lay in the bed of the truck, he could see her knees locked together and her arms wrapped around her torso. That was the moment he knew what had happened. He would recognize the memory of trauma anywhere.

They hadn't been intimate since the day that Gideon had returned. And after what the demon had done to her, Jason had given her space and time to heal, but not all wounds were on her skin. That was evident as he watched her hands shake against her abdomen.

"Hey," he whispered and touched her face. His fingers moved along her jaw and he turned her head to face him. The sparkles of tears glistened against her skin in the faint starlight. "It's okay. You don't have to be ashamed."

"I'm sorry," she said, wiping away the tears at the edges of her eyes. "You didn't do anything wrong."

"Don't be sorry. You have nothing to apologize for."

A weak smile formed on her lips and she sniffed. He smiled back at her, even though his thoughts tended to drift back to Gideon and how much he wished he could beat him with a tire iron. That bastard had done this, had instilled this seed of fear in the woman that had been a fearsome warrior.

His fingers intertwined with hers as he lay back against his elbow, his heart rate slowing down again. "When you're ready, okay?"

She nodded and curled back against him, her head tucked into his shoulder. "Okay."

Even though her body trembled for several minutes next to him, she fell asleep shortly after she had gone silent. The steady rhythm of her breathing lulled him, but he couldn't fall asleep, and Nikka had been right. He was too worried to sleep.

Worried about getting a call from Wolfe. It had been weeks since they had heard from him.

Worried about Nikka. Something was wrong with her, and not just the anxiety and trauma of what she had endured at Gideon's hands. Although she tried to hide it, she wasn't feeling well, and the bruises on her body and lacerations on her feet had already healed. He was not quite ready to address this with her, but if it continued he was going to make her talk about it. And with her feeling this way, what happened when Wolfe finally decides to meet up and finish this thing? She was in no shape to deal with that.

But other days came and went, and she seemed fine. She was full of energy, and he watched her practice with her sword in the light of dawn.

He hoped that when the call came, she was having one of her good days.

CHAPTER 40 NIKKA

Nikka was sure that Jason was aware that something was wrong with her. Until she knew what the problem was, she didn't want to bring it up. Most likely, it was just a factor of all the stress she had been under. If she talked about how fatigued she felt, as well as the nausea, then he would probably insist that he take her to a doctor or something. They couldn't risk being discovered by the police. There was probably nothing really wrong with her anyway. Suck it up.

And then there were the memories that showed up at the wrong time. She loved Jason and she hoped that he knew that, but when he touched her in just the right way, those memories came flooding back. When that happened, she could no longer hear or feel him. It was only darkness, red eyes, and a lot of pain and fear. After she had come apart at the edges, Jason didn't touch her like that again, and that was the most depressing thing of all. She longed for that closeness with him, but feared it at the same time.

She only hoped that he would wait for her to be ready.

The days drifted by like this, but Nikka knew that each passing day grew closer to the time the phone would ring again and Andy would be ready for them.

And then that day arrived.

Wolfe and Cavanaugh were prepared. It was time to travel to Nevada, and Agent Wolfe arranged to have them meet at a motel along the freeway on I-15. As soon as Jason had started the truck, Nikka could feel the butterflies swarming in her stomach, to the point that they stirred up nausea that seemed to stick in her throat. She leaned against the window and watched the world pass by in the evening hours as the sunset melted over the desert.

The truck turned through the dusty roads to a series of main paved streets and then to the freeway. Nikka saw the increase in traffic that surrounded them, each car that passed seeming to make her stomach turn. As her head rested against the window, she saw the faces of the drivers that moved past them. So many people, and nearly every one of them was a mask for something else just under the skin. Demons moved in herds down the freeway, toward the destination on the signs that she knew was the light to the moths: Las Vegas. Each car that zoomed next to them just made her sick. There were so many of them at this point that she was sure Jason would have to pull the truck over for her to retch.

Nikka turned away from the window and Jason glanced at her. "Are you okay? You're totally white."

She swallowed the lump that began to form in her throat as her stomach threatened to betray her. "They're everywhere. So many of them."

"Demons?"

She nodded. "It's like they know something big is about to happen."

"They don't usually make you sick," he said, and flashed a concerned look her way.

But perhaps this is why she hadn't felt right since they escaped the mountain. The demon hoard had multiplied. Pazuzu was loosed onto the world. She had sensed this battle coming for a long time now, and her body was fighting against it.

"I've never seen so many of them at once." Nikka closed her eyes and tried to concentrate on the sound of the engine as they moved south along the freeway, the lights of Las Vegas creating a halo over the desert in the coming dusk.

The road hummed below the tires, every seam in the pavement feeling like a thump to her stomach until she couldn't take it anymore. The nausea grew until she felt the saliva build in her mouth. "Pull over."

His hands tightened over the steering wheel just as he saw an exit for a rest area. The truck rounded the turn and he pulled into the lot before a building that stretched over a landscape of curving sidewalks and desert-scape cacti. Few other cars had stopped in the lot where he parked. Before he could completely stop the truck, Nikka opened the door and rushed toward the women's restroom.

The nausea came in waves now with the sound of each passing car that raced down the freeway toward Vegas. She hurried beyond a group of young women, but she didn't stop to see if they were fully human. The sickness caught in her throat as they brushed by her and she could only assume that they weren't.

With a hand over her mouth, she pushed into the restroom and found the nearest stall where she fell to her knees and retched into the toilet bowl. Her stomach churned again until there was nothing left. She finally leaned back on her heels and rested her cheek against the cold metal wall of the bathroom stall. The cool sensation eased the nausea just enough for her to listen to the room around her. Thankfully, it sounded empty.

She wiped her trembling hand across her forehead and stood on shaking knees. As she pushed open the stall door, she chided herself silently. They had spent too long in the cabin, away from the evils of the rest of the world. Being away for so long had made her weak; it made her too sensitive to creatures that she had been created to fight. Now, there were so many of them around her, all traveling to their unspoken and sacred event in the middle of the Nevada desert, that their unnatural form was finally having an effect on her constitution.

She walked up to the bay of sinks and leaned her elbows on the cold metal rim while the water ran over her fingers. She splashed water on her face and let it drip into the basin.

The trembling began to ease as the water trickled from her lips and chin. She took in a deep breath and let it out in a slow release. As she rinsed her mouth with the cold water, the sound of the main door opening caught her attention. Just in time, she thought. She can get in and out without anybody knowing that she just lost everything in her stomach only a minute ago.

But then she felt the icy chill fill the room and her breath coalesced into a cloud of white as it escaped from her lips. The cold tickled at her fingertips and frosted against the bottom of the sink. Something had just entered the bathroom that she could not yet see, but the air around it froze in dread.

Chapter 41 Nikka

The water pouring from the tap turned to a frozen, slushy mess as the pipes groaned against the frost. Feet in thin-soled shoes with a slight heel tapped into the room, each step getting closer and closer. Nikka didn't look up; she didn't have to see it to know that it was a demon, and not just some drone. This was something bigger and much worse.

Nikka moved to stand up straight when a hand grasped her neck with such force that the muscles in her shoulders cramped. The hand then forced her head forward into the mirror, shattering it into a thousand tiny splinters across the sink bay. The demon then threw her across the room where she crashed against the white-tiled wall and fell to the floor.

The force of the crash drew the air from her lungs, and she coughed as she lay on the ground, trying to reorient her vision. She rolled onto her stomach and saw the woman's feet in sandals stepping toward her. She felt a hand on her neck again, like someone grabbing the scruff of a dog, and it pulled her to her feet.

Hot blood rolled down her face and into her eye from the initial strike of the mirror. But she could see the demon's face now: a woman with shoulder-length auburn hair and thin arms. If not fueled by the creature's strength, she would have been a simple waif of a person, all 90 pounds of her. The woman's lips curled into a snarl as she looked at Nikka.

"I thought I sensed something odd in here," she said as her brown eyes began to glow red like two coals in her eye sockets.

Nikka felt the woman's hold on her neck move around to her throat. The fingers began to crush down on her windpipe and she could no longer breathe.

"Who could have thought I would find a seraph," the woman said.

The pressure in her head nearly blinded her as Nikka clutched at the woman's wrist. The woman's mouth opened in a wide grin, exposing a row of needle-like teeth that were as clear as glass. Black oil oozed from the corner of her mouth and Nikka could smell the rot coming from her breath. With a maw like that, Nikka knew this one had to be a lieutenant.

Before the pressure on her throat closed any tighter, Nikka let go of her grip on the woman's wrist and reached behind her shoulder. She found the hilt of the sword and began to draw it from her back. Just as the sword began to appear, the demon threw her back across the room again, but Nikka found her balance and landed on her feet, sword in her hand and free.

The blue flames erupted along the blade, casting the restroom in a blue light. The demon growled at her and smiled again as the oil continued to drip down her chin. Nikka steadied herself and jumped with her front foot.

Right as she forced herself forward, another attack from behind caught her before she could leap toward the demon. Arms reached around her torso and pulled her shoulders back. The unsuspected blow disrupted her balance and the inertia rocked through her arm. The sword loosened from her grip and toppled to the ground, the flames dying as it fell from her hand. The second creature behind her pulled her back and turned her into the wall, slamming her against the tiles again.

The force cracked the mortar between the tiles and she could taste the copper hint of blood that trickled down her throat. The hands moved her into position, and she felt a powerful and distinct strike into the back of her ribs. The hit felt like a spear had been jammed into her back, and before she could catch her breath, the arms pulled her away from the wall and turned her around while they held her wrists behind her.

As Nikka turned, she caught a glimpse of the second demon, also a small thin woman but with short black hair and easily a half foot shorter than the first. Two lieutenants. The first demon walked over to her and grasped her bony fingers around her jaw, forcing Nikka to look at her.

"Not so tough without your little knife," she said. Her hot breath fell on Nikka's face.

Nikka glanced behind the demon and saw the sword lying halfway across the room in front of the bathroom stalls. Too far away to grab. She had only one other option left right now. She concentrated whatever energy she could gather into her limbs.

"You know, Pazuzu said that we were to bring you back to him if we found you," the first demon said.

The sound of his name almost broke her concentration, but she willed the energy until her tattoos began to tingle.

"I don't know why he would want you alive."

"Maybe a little sentimental," the second demon said, and Nikka could feel its rotten breath in her ear.

The tattoos shimmered into a faint blue-green light. The energy surged toward her fingertips, almost ready to fire at the demon before her.

"I've never killed myself a seraph before, and now that I have the chance, I don't really feel like passing it up. Maybe, begging for forgiveness is better than asking permission. Don't you think?" she said, glancing to the demon behind Nikka.

The power continued to build on itself until she felt the full strength of it rise in the palm of her hand.

"So I think I'm going to beg forgiveness," the demon said and grasped at Nikka's throat just as the energy came full force into her hand. Before she could heave it at the creature, the demon threw her toward the stalls. She crashed through the first and the walls toppled in sequence like so many dominoes. Her body fell against the back wall as the metal cubicles fell around her.

Nikka gasped for air and felt the power fizzle against her fingertips and disappear without her concentration.

"That's right, sweetie," the demon said as it stepped over the pile of toppled stalls and tore each one away, searching for Nikka in the rubble. "Pazuzu told us every little trick you have, including that fancy one with the ball of light. It was nice to have the high general back, and he provided us with a lot of information about you."

She tore another panel free, sending it crashing into the wall behind her. Nikka tried to crawl toward the door, in the space against the floor and the lowest layer of panels. In that small amount of light, she could see the edge of her sword lying on the ground beyond her reach. Each movement forward made her ribs ache and the joints along her spine seemed to scrape against one another. She pulled herself toward the edge of the panels again and reached for the sword, but her fingertips barely brushed against the end of the hilt.

The metal stall panel that covered her flipped from off her body, letting the cold chill fall against her skin. A frozen hand wrapped around her ankle and pulled her across the floor and away from the sword.

Nikka watched the blade getting further and further from her reach, but in those few seconds that the demon had her ankle she let all her concentration fall from the sword and to the energy in her core. She willed it into her arms as hard and as fast as she could; something she had never had to do before. The power flooded just under her skin in a quick, fluid movement and her tattoos illuminated with a rapid light. The power rushed into the palm of her hand, where she could feel it collect into a solid ball.

Nikka turned on her hip and lifted just enough to see the second demon that dragged her across the floor. The creature saw her only a moment before she threw the energy toward it. The first demon turned toward her just when Nikka released the power. The light raced into the torso of the woman at her ankle. The force of the strike threw her back as the demon screamed. Her hand released Nikka's leg as she fell back, the light moving through her body and separating the beast from the human. The body collapsed and the demon disintegrated with the light that exploded against the back wall.

The first demon stepped back and howled as she saw the light strike her partner. Nikka turned away from her and scrambled to her feet with the sword in view. Her feet slipped on the wet tiles, and as she leaped forward to grasp the sword, the demon grabbed her from behind. They fell to the ground again as Nikka reached for the blade, but her hand still couldn't reach it.

The demon screeched and wailed as it clawed at her back like a rabid animal. It turned Nikka on her back and jumped onto her, its limbs pinning her against the tiles. The creature had become so enraged that the human could no longer contain the beast. Her skin had cracked and peeled into bleeding sores along her neck and arms. Its mouth opened in an unnaturally wide scream as it howled at her, its eyes roaring into a blaze of red. The creature's fingers had extended into long needle claws that struck against Nikka's flesh. Each lash felt like fire, and Nikka tried to find the beast's weakness, but it had overtaken her.

The demon reared onto its legs now, spindly limbs that had become thin and stretched with gray-brown skin. It screamed at her, the sound shattering what was left of the mirrors and windows. The hand full of needle claws raised into the air, ready to come stabbing down through Nikka's heart. The claws flashed through the fading light of the empty windows and Nikka almost closed her eyes against the final blow.

Another glint of silver broke through the slash of claws and the creature halted, the sound caught in its throat in a thick and guttural grunt. For only a fraction of a second, the demon stood frozen, gazing down at the sword that now protruded from the center of its chest. It had all happened so fast that Nikka hadn't seen Jason standing in the shadow before them, his hands trembling on the hilt of the blade.

Chapter 42 Jason

Jason waited outside the truck, leaning against it as he eyed the people driving in and out of the rest area. There was no way he would ever want Nikka's gift of seeing what was behind their faces, but he was sure that the place swarmed with demons. He kept his head down and shot a glance toward the building as he waited for her.

The place had grown quieter. Only one other car remained in the lot now and no others had pulled in over the last several minutes. How long had Nikka been in there?

His eyes wandered down the sidewalk and up to the door of the women's restroom. Two women stepped inside, probably the two who had driven the only car in the lot. The door closed behind them and he turned his gaze away.

Las Vegas resided to the south, and he could see the light from the city hover in the sky in the distance. Nikka's words still rattled his brain. She had never seen so many demons collected together. All driving south, toward Sin City. Figures. That place would be the perfect location to collect a swarm of demons.

Wolfe hadn't said much of his plan, but he sure hoped it involved running into Gideon again. He had never wanted to beat someone down so much, and that feeling had simmered for weeks until it was the perfect stew of hate and retribution. It really didn't matter to him if he was a demon, either. That actually made it so much better. That way he had no remorse if he killed him.

A sound echoed across the lot and drew his attention back to the women's restroom. The area still seemed so empty, but nobody had exited that room in a while. Those two women were still in there, and Nikka hadn't come out yet.

A crashing sound came again and he saw the lights above the restroom door flicker.

Something was wrong.

He felt his heart stop in his chest. Before he knew what was happening, his feet pounded against the pavement in a sprint toward the building. His fingers felt cold, but his face was hot as he ran, the sounds of war coming from behind that door. The air temperature plummeted as he neared the door. His fingers found the door handle, and it felt like ice against his skin.

Another screech of metal on metal.

He pulled the door open and entered the room. Water sprayed from the line of broken faucets and fractured sinks. The mirrors along the wall shattered all at once when a horrific wail exploded from inside the restroom.

Jason rounded the corner to see the creature, its brown, leathery skin stretched across sinewy muscles and its clawed hand raised in the air, ready to strike at Nikka.

She lay against the cold, wet tile, holding back the beast. Her sword had fallen away from her at some point during the skirmish. It now lay in a puddle of water at his feet.

He reached for the sword, but it didn't glow in his hand or erupt into flames like it did when Nikka touched it. It didn't matter, though. He held the hilt firmly and rushed at the demon that was ready to kill her where she lay. The blade entered into the creature's back with little resistance.

The demon froze for a moment, and the guttural screech stopped in its throat. The beast glanced down at the sword and its limbs still hung in the air, as if it waited for the inevitable destruction of its damned soul. But then its red eyes glanced up from the sword and back to Jason with hatred and contempt.

He released the sword and stepped back as the creature's eyes tracked him. The water pooled around his feet, making him almost slip backward as he stepped to the far wall. His knees nearly collapsed under him as the demon watched him.

The beast smiled, its blackening skin cracking at the corners of its mouth with the effort. "Nice try."

It began to laugh, its attention still on him.

Then, Jason saw Nikka lift her head. She was still alive. Bleeding, but still alive.

The demon shifted as it turned back to look at him, the sword still protruding from its back. It faced him, the hilt of the sword now within Nikka's reach. Jason saw the spark of the idea begin in her eyes, and he knew what he had to do.

"Hey," he said to the demon as it almost turned back to finish Nikka. The creature kept its gaze on him. "Time to go to Hell."

The demon's lips curled over its teeth into a sneering growl.

Jason watched as Nikka's hand grasped the hilt of the sword. As soon as she touched the sword, the blade erupted into blue flames, and the creature screamed in agony. Nikka twisted enough to get the momentum and forced the sword through the side of the demon's chest, slicing cleanly through it. The blade swung again, and it cut clean through the creature's neck. The demon crumpled away from her as the head fell across the floor.

The demon exploded into a cloud of ashes and embers. Jason shielded his eyes, smelling the scent of char fill the room.

Then everything fell still except the sound of the spraying water that covered the floor. He pulled his arm away from his eyes to see that Nikka had turned away from the ashes, but now the water around her grew more crimson with each second. She didn't move, but he heard the ragged breathing as her chest rose with each shallow breath she now fought to keep.

CHAPTER 43 NIKKA

At some point after Nikka had closed her eyes, the night had descended around her, and she felt hands pulling her from the cab of Jason's truck. She could hear his voice, but there were others around her as well.

When she finally opened her eyes, she saw the harsh neon lights of a sign shining out to the darkened road that ran in front of the cheap motel.

The arms that carried her shifted her from the truck, across the lot and through the door of a room with a single bed and a kitchenette. She felt another wave of nausea rise from her gut as they placed her on the bed. The lamps at the nightstands lit up Wolfe's face.

She smiled when she saw him, but the act of it made her face hurt. "We found you."

"More like I found you," he said with a forced smile. She could see the worry etched in the lines around his eyes. "Megan's going to take a look at you, okay She was an EMT before she was my partner."

Jason sat on the bed and his hand closed over hers. Then Megan appeared at the bedside and knelt down as she scanned her face.

"How're you doing, kiddo?" Megan asked.

"Had better days," she said and felt the breath catch in her ribs. The pain stabbed into her lungs and she forced herself not to cough.

"Is she gonna be okay?" Jason said and flashed a look at Megan.

"Of course I am," Nikka said and felt the surge of nausea again. She tried to sit up, but Jason's hands moved to her shoulders.

Oh no. Not now. She would just die if she threw up on him now.

"Whoa," he said.

Nikka glared at him and sat up anyway, despite the pain that screamed from her ribs. She pressed her hand to her mouth as she felt her stomach ready to give way.

"What's wrong?" Megan asked.

"I need—" Nikka started, but the words stuck in her throat. At that moment, she didn't care if her damn leg was broken or her head was gushing blood. She wasn't going to lose it in front of everybody. She forced herself around Megan and stumbled on a painful ankle to the bathroom. Just as she shut the door behind her, she fell to her knees and retched into the toilet again. Her ribs shifted with each heave and the pain brought tears to her eyes.

When her stomach had calmed enough, she flushed the toilet and closed the lid, but she wasn't sure if she would be able to get back onto her feet. She wiped her fingers across her lips and her gaze fell upon the streaks of blood that laced up and down her arms. Bloody fingerprints dotted the edge of the toilet where she had grasped the sides. The brown-red streaks were still damp and beginning to get sticky. Her fingers moved along her face, to the wet streams that slowly trickled down her cheek from a sore laceration on her cheek and above her eye. She held her trembling fingers away from her face and saw that they had been covered in blood.

"Nikka," Megan said from outside the door. "I'm coming in, okay?"

She couldn't find her voice, but it didn't matter. The bathroom door creaked open, and Megan peered around the door. She stepped carefully, as though the floor had been covered in broken glass. She approached Nikka and crouched down as she placed her hand resting on her back.

"Did you just start feeling sick?" she asked. "How hard did you hit your head?"

Nikka closed her eyes as another wave of nausea threatened to rise again. She could tell where Cavanaugh was going with her questions: she had seen it enough on TV to know that some people with serious brain injuries will start to throw up. Megan didn't need to know everything. She didn't need to know that Nikka was beginning to worry that the cancer may be trying to come back again, or she would look at her the way Jason did, like she was some fragile little thing.

She shook her head. "It's not my head. It started a couple days ago, and it got worse when I began to feel all the demons coming this way."

"Let me help you up," Megan said and aided Nikka up to sit on the toilet lid. Her curious brown eyes scanned her face.

Jason stepped into the bathroom and pressed himself into the corner as he looked at her. The way he held his balled fist in front of his mouth bothered her. He only did that when he was too nervous to say anything. His blue eyes watched her without wavering as Megan looked over her injuries.

"Okay," Megan said and stood. "I'm going to run to the drug store. The first aid kit has some things, but I need more dressings, some butterfly strips, more gauze and tape. Why don't you guys work on getting her cleaned up. I can't tell how much of this blood is hers or the other woman's."

Without saying a word, Jason nodded and stepped up to the towel rack to remove a clean wash cloth. Megan slipped around him and out of the bathroom while he soaked the cloth with warm water and sat on the edge of the tub. He took Nikka's hand, and she could feel the trembling in his fingers. The warm cloth felt soothing against her skin as he wiped the blood free from her hand.

"Hey," she said to him. "I'm going to be okay. Looks a lot worse than it is."

"I shouldn't have let you go in there alone," he said, his voice shaking.

"Into the women's restroom? Yes, you should have."

He squeezed the blood from the cloth and rinsed it with water from the faucet in the tub. "I should have been able to protect you."

She grasped the cloth from him and forced him to stop. "It's not your job to protect me, remember? This is part of what I am. This might happen from time to time; that's why I need to stop them from hurting anybody else."

His fingers wrapped around hers. Just when she thought he was going to hold her hand, he forced the cloth from her fingers and began to clean her arm again. "It's my job if I say it is. That's how this thing with us works, you see. It's our job to protect each other."

It was pointless to argue with him. Nikka smiled as she watched him, but she had forgotten how much it hurt her jaw. "Okay."

In the time Megan had been gone, Andy had stepped into the bathroom to help Jason clean the blood from her skin. Nikka hoped that all the blood running into the drains was not all hers, because there had been so much of it on her arms and face. The laceration above her eye was still bleeding though, and Jason pressed a towel against it. The bone underneath the laceration was sore, and she distinctly remembered her face getting smashed into a mirror right in that spot.

Andy finished cleaning her left arm and lifted it to check the cuts along the underside, but the motion sent pain into her ribs. Nikka winced, and he froze. She held her breath for a moment until the muscle spasms in her chest stopped. She knew that whatever was happening in her ribs wasn't a good thing.

The bathroom door opened again and Megan appeared with two grocery bags full of supplies.

Jason stood but still held fast to Nikka's hand. Megan placed the bags along the side of the bathtub and glanced at the two men, who watched her expectantly.

"All right, guys. We need a little girl time," Megan said with a smile and hands on her hips.

Andy nodded, but Nikka held to Jason's hand.

Megan sat on the edge of the tub and looked up at him. "I need to examine her better, especially her chest. She's going to have to get undressed."

"It's nothing he hasn't seen before," Nikka said and splinted her side as the spasms in her chest began again.

Megan smiled at her. "I get that. But I just need some room, okay? I'll be quick, and you two can see each other again real soon."

"It's okay," Jason said with a squeeze of his hand. "She's knows what she's doing."

He slipped his hand free and stepped from the room, shutting the bathroom door behind him.

Megan got to work, at first opening the packages of gauze and butterfly tape. She cleaned the wound above Nikka's eye and started placing the small strips of tape to close the laceration. When she had finished all the open wounds on Nikka's face she sat back.

"Now I need to take a look at those ribs," she said and motioned to Nikka's T-shirt.

Nikka worked at slipping one arm out first, but it was much more difficult to lift her other arm. Megan aided her until she had removed it. It almost looked like Megan winced when she first looked. Nikka glanced down, past her black bra and to the multitude of purple bruises along her ribs. Megan touched the area, but even the lightest sensation sent waves of pain into Nikka's chest.

"They're definitely broken," Megan said. "But there's really nothing else to do about them. Just pain relief for now."

Cavanaugh ran her fingers along Nikka's arms and she saw the criss-crossing scratches along her forearms. Too many to butterfly tape. Instead, she cleaned each one individually and started to wrap them in gauze dressings up to her elbows.

"Nikka," Megan said her name, the cadence dropping like her mother used to when she was ready to have a serious conversation. "We need to talk about something. I need you to just hear me out."

She felt her stomach sink. That didn't sound good. "Okay."

"I wanted them to leave because this needs to be private."

Megan tied the last strip of gauze into place and then fished around the grocery bags until she found what she wanted. She pulled a box from the bag and held it out to Nikka.

At first she wasn't sure what it was, but then her eyes read the packaging. Her lips went dry and a lump formed in her throat. Her trembling fingers wrapped around the box.

"A pregnancy test?" she said, the sound barely making it past her dry tongue.

Megan averted her gaze and her fingers fidgeted around the hem of her shirt. "It was just a feeling I had. I think you just need to be sure."

With everything that had been going on, her thoughts had never once happened upon this. But for some reason Cavanaugh was concerned. There was no way, though. Impossible

Nikka swallowed and absently chewed on her thumbnail as she looked at the box. The bright purple and blue packaging curled behind the picture of a smiling woman. A woman who had no other care in the world except finding out the results on a stick. Was she happy? Was she relieved? It didn't matter, because that woman wasn't real, not like the company wanted you to believe.

Nikka looked up to Megan. "What do I do?"

Cavanaugh forced a weak smile. "Oh." She took the box from her and opened it. A bundle of directions written on folded white paper fell out and she removed a white and blue stick from the box. She unfolded the directions and held out the side with the illustrations toward Nikka. "See. Just pee on the end here." Nikka held the stick between her shaking fingers. "It's pretty easy."

Megan stood up and began to wring her hands together. "I'll step out; give you some privacy." She stepped from the bathroom, leaving Nikka holding the stick between her fingers.

She looked at the small display window on the stick, the place where the answer she hadn't searched for would appear. The directions slipped from her fingers and fell to the floor. Every ache and pain throbbed deeper now that she looked at that blank display window.

It had to be done. If Megan was concerned about this, then she should be too. At least, that is what she tried to tell herself. There was really no way. Not after having cancer and so much chemotherapy. The doctors had told her and her parents before she had even started chemotherapy that she would likely never be able to . . . well, to have the ability to get pregnant. All those toxins not only try to kill cancer, but do their best to kill the body too. Anything that survives is a miracle, and a woman's eggs are usually the first casualties in a war against cancer.

There was just no way.

She shook the thoughts from her head and picked up the directions from the floor. Everything that the illustrations demonstrated, she followed perfectly. After she had finished, she stood, buttoned her jeans and placed the stick on the edge of the tub as she sat on the toilet lid again, watching the stick as though it were a time bomb. Somehow, that vigilant waiting made the pain in her ribs ease up a bit.

Megan knocked on the door and Nikka let her in.

"Everything going okay? Need any help?" she asked.

Nikka could barely speak and felt cold as she watched the stick from where it rested on the porcelain. Megan neared her and placed a hand on her shoulder.

"How long does it usually take?" Nikka asked.

"About five minutes," she said.

Nikka began to tap her foot, but felt the impact of it in her ribs. One minute. Another tickle of nausea began to rise into the back of her throat. She swallowed it back as Megan grasped her hand. The sound of water dripping in the sink grew louder and louder.

Three minutes.

Her teeth scratched against the edge of her thumbnail again before she knew she was even doing it. The spasms in her ribs subsided a little now as she took in only shallow breaths.

Megan looked at her watch. "It's time."

Nikka still looked at the stick sitting on the edge of the tub. The little window was too far away for her to see what it said, and she was too shaky to move from her little perch on the toilet lid.

"Nikka—" Megan said.

"I know," she said and reached out a trembling hand to the stick. As she drew it closer, she could see the blue streaks within the window, and she didn't need to pull it any closer to see what it said.

Positive.

The stick nearly fell from her grasp. The blue lines dispersed into waves as tears filled her eyes.

"Is this a good test?" Nikka stammered. "I mean, is it reliable?"

Megan squeezed her shoulder and gazed down to the stick in Nikka's hand. "It's very accurate."

"Okay." She blinked her eyes clear.

All the pain that she felt in her body drifted away as her mind swam in confusion and questions. In a way, she was happy. There was still some part of her that remained human, despite all that had happened to her. The power that had been given to her had cured her cancer, but it obviously had healed her body in so many ways. Whatever had taken away her cancer had given her a new life, and now it was ready to fulfill yet another life.

But in the brightness of all that vitality, something nagged at the corners of it all. She had spent her time with Jason, a mortal who loved her and cared about her and would be so happy about this. This would normally be good news for somebody like him, but with the threat of the demon army and what the future held could change all that. He was already overly protective of her. This would make it so much worse. If she told him anything, it would have to wait until after they had stopped the EMP threat.

And then there was Gideon. She hadn't felt well since the night he had . . . well, raped her. The word was awful and so was the truth of it. What if the aftershock of that horrible night still germinated inside of her?

"Are you okay?" Megan said.

"Yeah. Just a little overwhelmed." Nikka wiped the tears from her eyes. She placed the stick into the back pocket of her jeans as she stood. "Please don't tell them anything."

"It's not my secret to tell," Megan said and hugged her.

CHAPTER 44 NIKKA

Nikka limped from the bathroom with Megan at her side. The guys had stepped outside and waited at an empty picnic table at the end of the parking lot. As soon as Jason saw them, he jumped from his perch atop the table and rushed to her side.

His hands cupped around her jaw and he examined the lacerations on her face. "Are you sure you're gonna be okay?"

"I heal fast," she said with a tired smile.

His blue eyes turned to Megan. "Thank you." Then he glanced at Andy. "Thank you both."

"It's really nothing," Megan said and sidled next to Andy. Their fingers intertwined as she leaned against him. "She saved my life. I would do anything for you guys."

"Okay," Wolfe said and cleared his throat. "We aren't going to get anything done tonight. I got a room at the end for you two. We'll be in this room. Tomorrow, we regroup and go over the plan. As for tonight, just get some rest."

"We don't have time for that," Nikka said.

He eyed her with his flinty stare. "Rest. We need you in the game. You won't be any good to us if you aren't one-hundred percent." He stepped close to her and left a gentle punch against her shoulder. "I'm not asking."

"Whatever, Dad," she said with an exaggerated roll of her eyes as she turned away from him. Jason took her arm and did what he could to help her toward the room.

As soon as Jason opened the door, the musty smell of a closed-up room drifted through the door. Another cheap motel. Another questionable room. At this point, she didn't care. Wolfe was right about everything; she needed rest so badly right now that it didn't matter if the lamps near the bed were probably purchased in some garage sale twenty years ago. She settled on one side of the bed and rested her head back against the pillow. The pain in her ribs continued to throb and she couldn't find a position where they wouldn't hurt.

Jason pulled off his jacket and sat across the bed from her. "Something else is wrong."

"What do you mean?"

"I mean, something else is wrong with you. I know you well enough now to see when you're not telling me everything. What did you and Cavanaugh talk about in there?"

She turned her gaze to the corner of the room where she noticed the peeling of the yellowed wallpaper. If she looked at him now, he might start to realize that he was right.

"Nothing. She just wanted to look at all the other bruises."

"You're sure. She didn't say anything else."

"She's just worried about everything that we're doing out here. That's all."

He watched her, waiting for more, but she could see that he wasn't going to press her, at least not tonight. But he wasn't stupid. He knew her better than anybody else in the world, and it was getting harder to keep anything from him. For her own sake, though, she needed to keep this secret for now.

His fingers touched the top of her bare head. He leaned down and kissed her cheek between the bruises.

Her body ached at every joint, and she wanted to sleep, but she knew that it would be difficult tonight. Every worry rushed through her brain, bouncing and careening and crashing into one another. When she wished that everything could go back to being simple, she remembered "simple" included her lying in a hospital bed in the cancer unit. That was the easiest life had ever been. There were no decisions to make. No secrets. No life and death struggle for the fate of the world. There was only her and her IV's and her oxygen mask. There was only the battle to take each breath.

With the lamp lights off, the room plunged into darkness. She could feel him slide into the bed next to her. He was so careful as he moved and placed his arm along her side. She let him pull her closer until she rested her head on his bare chest, feeling each breath move in and out. Nikka closed her eyes, but sleep still would not come. It didn't matter, though. She just wanted to feel him next to her and hear him breathe as he held her.

Wolfe had wanted them here now because he must have known something was ready to happen. His plans to regroup tomorrow would probably involve the organization of their attempt to get the EMP device. Andy knew exactly where it was, and whatever the demons had planned for it, he must have suspected when it would happen. With the number of demons flocking down the freeway, it was going to be big. She had taken on a hoard of them before, but nothing like the numbers she saw moving toward Las Vegas. Jason and Wolfe had to know that they were outnumbered despite her powers as the seraph.

And that was when she realized that Wolfe had known this all along. That was why he wanted to do as much of it on his own as possible. He had been looking for some way to keep her and Jason out of the fray. For Wolfe to call them back to join him meant that he had failed. He had no way of doing it on his own. Either he knew they would be outnumbered or it was too dangerous. Maybe so dangerous, that it could get him killed.

Or get them all killed.

Jason's breathing had slowed into an even cadence, indicating to her that he had fallen asleep. Although it hurt, she wrapped her gauzed arm around his torso and opened her eyes to the darkness around them.

Perhaps they would survive all of this. She could defeat the horde and Wolfe could disable the EMP. Then, she and Jason would just disappear into the world, away from all of this and never see another demon again. And then she would tell him her secret when it was all over.

But what if, after the battle had been won, the secret was truly for Gideon? He was still a demon to his core, the worst kind second only to the Devil himself. What if the thing growing inside of her was a demon as well?

Nausea rose into her throat again as the thought raced into her brain. She sat up, careful not to stir Jason beside her, and padded into the bathroom. This time, the sickness didn't come as fast as usual. She turned on the faucet and ran cold water over her wrists as she leaned over the sink, just in case the nausea returned. Beads of sweat collected on her forehead. She splashed the cold water on her face and let it run across her dry lips.

What if this baby was truly a demon?

Her hands and knees shook every time the question entered her mind. The air around hergrew thin and stale. She shoved open the bathroom door and rushed through the room to the main door. When she opened it, the warm Nevada air hit her with a breath of fresh oxygen. She stepped out into the night under the flashing neon lights of the motel sign next to the road.

Wolfe had truly found the most out-of-the-way place for them to stay. The road was so quiet, almost post-apocalyptic quiet. In the far distance to the south, a halo of orange light hung in the sky over a city, what she assumed to be Vegas. She felt the dry, desert air against her skin and filling her lungs. At least it wasn't the musty, dank feel of the room anymore. She took in a deep breath and tried to clear her thoughts of the disturbing images that continued to plague her. At the peak of her breath, her ribs reminded her that they were still damaged.

She stepped down the sidewalk toward the motel office, with its darkened windows and bars locked over the main door. At least the ice machine at the end of the walk provided some illumination from its fluorescent lights at the top of the dispenser. The sidewalk felt warm against her bare feet with each step toward the machine.

She placed her hands under the dispenser and several chunks of ice fell into her palms. The cubes slipped around her fingers until she held them against her ribs and felt the cooling relief at the swelling along her side. It had to help, at least a little. She leaned back against the machine and looked out again to the halo of lights over the city in the distance.

The buzzing of the neon sign above the parking lot came in spurts as the vacancy sign sputtered with surges of light. The bulbs were nearing the end of their lives, but it didn't seem to stop the sign from trying so hard to prove that it worked. With each buzz, Nikka felt a little sting of anxiety. That puzzled her at first, until she realized that it was the only sound she could hear. The palm trees and shrubs in the desert around the motel never made a noise. There was no breeze drifting through that small parking lot. The chirring and clicking of insects remained lost in the darkness of the desert.

The day had been warm enough, but now a chill descended upon the surface of the parking lot. At first it had been merely a shiver that ran up and down her arms, but now her breath slipped out in quick white puffs. A silvery fog collected around the base of the palm trees at the edge of the parking lot and stretched out in cotton tendrils across the black pavement until it tickled around her bare feet. She stepped back from the cold fog and pressed against the side of the ice machine, but the mist stretched toward her like a living being reaching for a life force to drain.

Nikka held her breath, and a movement caught her eye. Something shifted in the inky blackness just beyond the light of the motel neon. It writhed and pulsated, black within black. More motion drifted around the perimeter of the lot, like unseen creatures darting around the property, but stayed away from the flickering lights of the sign. They moved silently, the way a group of bats swarm just outside of the light, collecting the insects that strayed from the untrue safety of a lamp. More motion raced in the darkness as the deep chill settled around the motel.

Something moved just within the reach of the neon light and she saw its face for only a moment. Black, oily skin stretched tight over bones and sinew. Curling horns cork-screwing out of a skull. She had seen beasts like this before. They had once crawled from a gaping and burning hole in the basement of the collapsed building. Abaddon had released such creatures and they had roamed free. Now, they swarmed just outside the light of the motel as though something had summoned them here and kept them at bay until the right moment.

Her hands had clutched into white-knuckle fists. The fog stretched toward her feet and now tried to crawl up her legs and freeze her joints. She felt beads of sweat form on her brow and her palms grow moist. She knew she had to move or the mist threatened to consume her, and perhaps when it had her frozen and helpless, the beasts would come and tear her apart.

She shot a glance down the row of closed doors along the motel. Each room was quiet, any occupants unaware of the fury that now stalked them just outside the light. Then her eyes fell on the still and silent frame of the pickup truck, the rusted and old vehicle that had driven them to safety so many times.

Jason was at the end of the motel, asleep and vulnerable. She nearly choked as she saw the mist curl around the base of the tires and creep toward the door to the room where he slept.

She dug her nails into the palms of her hands. This was enough to urge her legs to move. She pushed away from the ice machine and sprinted across the ocean of silver-white fog, keeping the room door in her line of sight. Maybe the beasts saw her move. Maybe they bounded for her now on cloven hooves that sprang over the mist. Her feet pounded against the pavement and the fog seemed to pierce open wherever she stepped. Her ribs ached as the cold slipped down her throat with each breath.

The door knob met her hand, and she forced the room open. Tendrils of mist curled around the base of the door and seeped into the room, over the loops of the carpet and under the table.

She leaped into the room, ready to escape the claws of anything that might be trying to grab at her in the dark.

But everything was so still and quiet now. The pungent copper smell hit her first, something cloying and very different from the stagnant air of a shut-up room. Wisps of fog slipped from her lips with each breath as she stepped into the icy room that now felt like a deep freezer. It was so much colder in here than it was outside.

Blue and violet light shone through the window from the neon sign, casting a glow that fell over the bed. At first she thought it was only a trick of the flickering light, but the glistening shimmer in the center of the bed never changed when she stepped closer.

She saw Jason's face, his head resting against the pillow, and his eyes gazed toward the ceiling in an unblinking stare. His mouth gaped open, but his ribs never flexed to move air. The glistening rose from the center of his chest.

Jason's silent stillness forced a lightning pain into her chest. If she watched him long enough, he would breathe . . . he would blink. She stepped closer to the bed and that was when she saw the gaping hole in his chest and the sharp fragments of bone that lined the wound. The blood pooled at the edges, likely dragged there when something had pulled his heart from his rib cage.

"No, no," she cried and nearly collapsed as she ran to the edge of the bed. Her fingers reached for his face and felt the fading warmth on his cheeks. The smell of the blood that soaked the sheets made nausea fill her gut again. Anywhere she tried to touch him felt sticky with fresh blood. Tears poured down her cheeks, falling across his still body. Her legs trembled and threatened to collapse under her as she watched his blank, empty stare.

"Did you weep like that for me," a voice said from the threshold of the doorway, "when I had died?"

Nikka turned and almost lost her balance against the bed. A figure filled the doorway, the edges of the neon lights framed around his close-shaved head. He stepped into the room and the light shining through the window cast across his face.

Gideon smiled at her, the same smile he used to give her when he watched her practice in the old church. But she knew there was no caring under that grin.

"What did you do?" she said, but choked against the tears that now flowed.

He stopped and cocked his head to the side. "What I had to do. I will stop anybody that comes between us."

Gideon shifted to the side and Nikka could see something in his hand. His arm swung back and he heaved the object across the floor toward her. The mass split in two and rolled toward her like bowling balls into the light and then came to a stop. The final roll revealed two heads, the hair matted in blood, but she knew she looked at Wolfe and Cavanaugh. Their eyelids hung half closed and lips curled open against their teeth. Nikka fell back against the bed and felt Jason's limp arm against her. The blood that filled the sheets flooded across her hand and dripped down to the floor around her feet.

As she felt his hand and gazed down at the severed heads, her body shuddered in cries that she could not stop. Gideon watched her and leaned casually against the wall. Each sob wracked pain into her chest from the fractured ribs.

He smiled at her and his hazel eyes turned dark. The black orbs then morphed into two ember-red flickers that watched her. "I will be there when you arrive. When you have no other choice, you will come to me every time."

Nikka awoke with a scream and darted upright. The room was no longer a deep freezer and the feeling of moist sheets around her were just the edge of her sweat-damped shirt. But the screams were real and tore at her throat. Tears fell down her cheeks and she felt her body shudder into waves of crying.

Jason bolted out of the bed and glanced around the room for a second until his eyes adjusted to the light. He clambered over the bed and placed his arms around Nikka.

"What's wrong?" he said and tried to calm the quaking in her spine, but there was nothing he could do.

Her hands grasped at his bare shoulders and pulled herself against him. She felt the heat of his torso, his untarnished chest and the heartbeat that still resided within. He still moved around her and spoke and breathed. There was nothing wrong with him. It had been a nightmare.

But the dream still lingered at the edges, inside the shadows of the room. The copper smell of blood hung on the sheets.

"It's okay," Jason said as she clutched onto him like he would disappear any moment. "It was just a dream."

Just a dream.

Nikka knew better. If being a seraph had taught her anything so far, it was that she never just had dreams anymore.

A seraph had visions.

CHAPTER 45 NIKKA

The others sat around the picnic table at the end of the motel parking lot as the sun rose over the deep blue mountains to the east.

They spoke in hushed tones while Nikka paced along the sidewalk, chewing at her thumbnail again. She didn't care that her ankle hurt with each step and that her ribs still ached. Her gaze darted along the roadside that seemed to swim with visions of hideous beasts in the blackness. Although it was barren of anything, even other cars, she could still feel the disembodied demons stalking them at the edge of the pavement.

She hadn't told Wolfe or Megan what she had seen last night, but Jason knew when he awoke and saw the gray color of her skin. They didn't sleep the remainder of the evening. Instead, they just held each other as she tried not to close her eyes. He had turned on every light in the room to hold back the shadows just for her sake, but she continued to smell the scent of blood all around them.

Now they huddled around the table together, shooting concerned glances her way, as Wolfe presented the plan to them. Despite trying to keep their voices low, she could still hear them deciding the best way to proceed.

"My intel says that the device is located here," he said, pointing to a map of the Nevada desert that he had splayed out over the surface of the table. "It's an Air Force base about ten miles south of here. One of my sources found heat signatures that suggest it's located at the south end of the base. It's not terribly specific, but there are two towers at that end, just north of several hangars."

"An Air Force base?" Jason said. "Are you kidding me? There's no way we'll get in there."

"We can get in through the side gate by the runway. It's dark and there's very little coverage back there. Once we get in, I need a distraction while I head to the tower. Once I find the device, I can disable it. But I need a good five minutes to do it."

"How do you propose we do that?" Jason asked.

"A diversion through a series of explosions," Megan said, standing at the end of the table with her arms folded across her chest. "We can set up a suppression along the barracks. It'll be dark and most of them should be settling down."

Jason took a step back from the table. "Wait. You're talking about attacking an Air Force base. These guys are trained military personnel. We'll be no match for them. We're gonna get arrested on sight and sent to prison for a very long time if they don't kill us first."

"They are in possession of the EMP," Andy said, his voice calm and even. "And I guarantee that almost every one of them is a demon."

"Andy's right," Nikka said and faced them. The trio went quiet and watched as she approached them. "They will be possessed, and the few that aren't will be so convinced that what they are doing is right that they won't bat an eye to do it. But Jason's right, too. They are all highly trained just for scenarios like this. I imagine that's why the device was put there to begin with."

Megan looked at her and Nikka could only see a vision of her hair matted in blood, her brown eyes rolled up into her skull as her head rested on the floor. She turned her gaze away from Cavanaugh long enough to clear her thoughts.

"It's too dangerous for all of you to go in there," Nikka said.

Andy stood. "We can't give up. The device is right there. We know where it is now and we can stop it."

Nikka nodded and placed her hands on her hips. "I know. That's why I will go in and disable it. Alone."

The three of them began to move and speak at once, their energy dispersing like a whirlwind over the table.

"That is not an option," Andy said.

Jason stepped up to her and placed his hand on her shoulder. "Nikka, you can't do this alone."

"You said it yourself," she said and shook his hand from her shoulder. "It's too dangerous. I can get in there undetected, invisible. I can find that thing and destroy it. Myself."

Jason stood straighter and looked at her. His eyes seemed to have darkened from their usual bright blue. "I know you can, but the base is enormous. You'll be drained before you can make it out."

She averted her eyes and looked at her shoes.

He sighed. "But you know that already. Don't you."

"I can do this," she muttered.

"Not without me," he said and stepped closer to her. She felt his hand on her face, lifting up her chin to look at him. "Remember. We protect each other."

She tried to hold back her tears as she looked at him. "Not this time."

"You don't know how to disable the device," Wolfe said.

Nikka still watched Jason, seeing the sadness in his eyes. "You can show me."

"Why are you doing this?" Jason whispered to her.

She pulled away from him and felt his fingers slip from her chin. "Because if you all go in there, you will die."

"How do you know that?" Megan asked.

"They know we are coming. Gideon will be there, and he's expecting us."

Jason just watched her and she knew that he realized what her dream had told her last night.

"How can he know?" Wolfe said.

"I'm not sure," Nikka said. "Maybe he can see everything that I'm doing. It doesn't matter. He just knows."

Jason shifted his stance and crossed his arms over his chest. "Then it won't matter if you go in alone or with the rest of us."

"It will matter," she said, a little more forcefully than she had intended. "If you go in there, you will die."

"And so it's okay if you die?" he said, pointing his finger at her. "In what world is it okay for you to just leave me like that and not allow me to help?"

He was shouting now. She had never seen him bristle like this at her, his eyes narrowed to slits and his voice was loud and directed at her.

Megan stepped between them, and Nikka saw the glance toward her, that knowing look that held the secret between them.

"Calm down," Megan said, her palm held out against Jason's chest. She looked at Nikka. "He's right. We're all here because this is the most important thing we will ever do. We need this, and it's not right for you to take this away from us. We all know the risks involved here, and yet we have chosen to stay this far."

Wolfe stepped around the table. "We're going to see this through."

They all stood together now, looking at her as a united collective against her desperate idea. There was nothing she could do to change their minds. They were right, of course. She didn't have time to learn how to disable an EMP device, but she had just planned on winging it and hoping that it worked out. That was reckless and she knew it. But so was an assault on an Air Force base with an army of four.

"If this was just a collection of normal people, I would say that you were right," Megan said. "But we are far from normal. We have you."

Nikka looked up at her, her brow furrowed.

Megan smiled. "You're a tank, Nikka. You can get us in there."

"She's not a tank," Jason said and she saw him grin as well. His eyes softened again as he looked at her. "She's a seraph."

CHAPTER 46 NIKKA

As the sun began to set, the heat of the day seemed to penetrate every corner of the motel room. The coming night felt ominous, like a predator just waiting on the horizon. The fading light created shadows of the Joshua trees, leaving elongated monsters that reached over the uneven desert floor. Just above the mountain line, a blanket of black clouds collected and crawled across the sky.

Nikka had slipped away from the others and into the silence of the motel room. She sat on the edge of the bed, feeling the room getting darker every minute that ticked onward. The hours had faded fast today. Too fast. And they could all feel the tension building around them. With the night would come the assault on the base, and perhaps the end of them all. The anxiety began to simmer in her gut, flittering around like bees.

She knew that everyone was gathered in Wolfe's room, sifting through bags of supplies, guns, ammo and other weapons that the agents had gathered in their travels to end up here. But she couldn't look at any of that now. The clicking of gun metal made her too nervous. Instead, she sat at the edge of the bed and gazed down at her duffel bag, to the folded leather coat that she had placed in there so many months ago.

The stitching along the edge of the collar still held even after all that it had been through. She pulled the coat from the bag and unfolded it over the bed as she examined it. This coat had gotten her through the most dangerous thing she had ever done. She had worn it when she brought down Abaddon. It had done what it was promised to do: it protected her and let her attack unimpeded. Just as Gideon said it would.

Gideon had made it for her, stitched together with his own hands because he had believed that every superhero needed a costume. She remembered the smile on his face when she first buttoned it up and stood before the mirror. That was when he cared about her mission. When he worked hard for his penance and still sought redemption. When she had loved him more than anything.

As she ran her fingers along the hemline, she recalled sitting with him before a warm fire in the comfort of the old church. At a time when the church was their only refuge. She knew something bad was about to happen even then. She begged him not to go anywhere, and he told her that he wouldn't.

"I promise," he had said.

But he had left the next day on what should have been a simple task, and Abaddon had taken him away from her. That was the spiral downward toward the Hell that had changed everything. Gideon sacrificed himself to get her out of that basement where the portal had opened. He had fallen to some unknown realm that had destroyed him.

She knew that something was off about him when he had come back to her. Jason had tried to warn her, but she wouldn't listen.

The darkness of the room deepened around her. She slipped her shirt and jeans off of her pained body and pulled the coat over her shoulders, closing the silver buttons over her black bra.

She remembered Gideon lying beside her in the bed at the cabin. What he had done to her was terrible whether it had been him or the demon, but now she recalled the look on his face just before the quake had come. He was a man suffering from post-traumatic stress disorder, just like any soldier coming home from war. And like one who had been tortured, he had also been conditioned to respond appropriately. He hadn't come back as a damned soul. At least not at first. Something had triggered it, just like a conditioned animal. When it hears the ring of the bell, it knows how to respond because that is how it was trained.

Something had conditioned Gideon. She knew exactly when the trigger had fired. She remembered how his face twisted. And for so long she had forgotten what he said just before she had run from the room. He told her to run. To get away fast.

He had warned her that something was coming. Gideon knew that he would have no control over what was about to happen. And just like Jason had been with Abaddon, he was being controlled from behind the curtain.

And maybe, just maybe, that meant that she could still save him. If he was going to be there tonight, then perhaps there was still a chance that she could bring him back from the brink of Hell. He had saved her from death. Now it was her turn to save him.

She pulled on the dark cargo pants and laced up the black boots. Everything that Gideon had put together for her—his Superhero. But she could only stand there. Her limbs didn't want to move.

What if she failed him? What if she failed them all?

She flexed her fingers and folded her discarded clothes, placing them in the duffel bag. Anything to get her mind off of the weight of what was coming tonight. She gazed down the length of the coat: a sleeveless duster that opened just below her diaphragm and drifted down around the back of her legs. Designed to expose as much of her tattoos as possible and amplified her power when she needed it. Her eye caught the space below her navel and the spiral tattoo that surrounded it. Her hand touched her exposed abdomen just above her waistband.

Somewhere in there a life gestated just below her fingers. This being would be a miracle in so many ways, but she felt the pangs of sadness flood into her eyes and cloud her vision. When the dust of tonight settled, would it just be another secret taken to the grave?

She lifted her eyes and pulled her hands away from her abdomen. The last hues of light had now disappeared and left the desert in shades of violet and dark green. She straightened her spine and flexed her arms, feeling the power surge just under her skin and erupt in little sparkles of light along her tattoos. She flexed her neck from side to side, loosening her joints and driving away any of the lingering pains that still hung around her ribs.

Nothing could matter except the fight right now. Everything had to wait until it was over. She would stop the EMP and then she would save them. She had to.

Even if she didn't believe it.

She turned away from the bed, collected her duffel bag, and strode out of the motel room. The others had gathered behind the back end of Wolfe's SUV. She tossed her bag into the back of Jason's truck and met them at the SUV. Jason turned as she neared, his fingers buckling a strap of the bullet-proof vest he wore.

A wide smile appeared on his face as he scanned her coat. "Badass. I love it."

Chapter 47 Jason

Megan and Andy, both with Kevlar vests on, loaded rounds of bullets into clip chambers. Jason's Kevlar vest felt a little snug, but he actually liked having it against his chest. The sound of the bullet rounds clicking against the gun metal gave him a rush of adrenaline that pumped into every vessel in his body. He hadn't handled a gun in a while, but it was something he never forgot.

Nikka stepped beside him and gazed into the back of the SUV, at the collection of weapons spread across the floor mat. Andy glanced up at her and held out another bullet-proof vest.

Nikka shook her head. "No thanks."

"Come on," he said and shoved it toward her. "You'll need this."

"I can't move freely with it on," she said and tossed it back into the SUV. "And I need all the flexibility I can get."

"You're sure?" Megan said with a heavy stare.

Jason noticed the long and loaded gaze between Megan and Nikka. Those two shared a secret. Without a doubt.

"Positive."

Jason hosted two handguns at his belt and then touched Nikka's arm. "Can I talk to you for a second?"

She nodded and walked with him along the parking lot. Now was as good a time as any to do this. With the way the sky was darkening and the trembling that began in his hands, this day already didn't feel right. Missing this moment could cause a lifetime of regret, if there even was a lifetime remaining.

"I need to ask you something," he said and glanced back to the others at the SUV, to Megan who stood behind the vehicle. He couldn't have them listening to what he wanted to say.

"What's wrong?" The worry began to settle within the storm of her blue eyes.

"I need to say this before we go, because I may not get another chance and I don't think that I can live with myself if I don't say it now."

"What's this about?"

He swallowed dryly and his blue eyes met hers. "When all this is over, we need to get out of here. Just the two of us."

She smiled, her eyes brightening. "Sounds good to me."

"And Vegas is right there," he said, his hand opening out to the halo of light on the horizon. "What do you say we just get married and run away?"

She stepped back for a moment, her hands on her hips and a crooked smile on her lips. "Are you proposing right now?"

He crossed his hands over his chest and cocked an eyebrow. "Yes?" he said, although it sounded more like a question.

The smile faded from her lips and she stepped closer to him. "Are you only asking because you know we're going to die?"

What kind of a question was that?

"No. Hell no." He placed his hands on her shoulders and closed the space between them. "No. I'm asking because we need to plan for the future. Right?"

She cupped his jaw in her hands, kissing him quickly and pulled back. "Then I'll give you my answer when this is all over and we are standing right here again."

He watched her step away from him, but as she turned away he saw the hint of anxiety fall across her face. The bottom of the duster flapped against her boots with each step she took, getting further from him and to an uncertain future. The dust picked up from the breeze across the desert, carried from the oncoming storm.

Part Five

"The fear of death follows from the fear of life.
A man who lives fully is prepared to die at any time."

— Mark Twain

CHAPTER 48 NIKKA

A moonless sky covered the open desert, with only stars glittering in a blanket of black. The deep night hid any sign of the ominous storm clouds that coalesced around the valley. Only the sodium lamps set at intervals along the perimeter of the base provided enough light from a distance to see the wall of a chain-link fence.

Andy had been correct: there were no armed guards, as Nikka had expected. Just an open air strip leading straight to the main base, which appeared to be a collection of various buildings lit in the same artificial light.

After Andy had cut through the fence, he guided them along the perimeter toward the central part of the base. The space was large, though, something that didn't translate well from a map. There were many more buildings and hangars than Nikka had originally thought. So many places for demons to hide.

As they neared the edge of the fence that entered onto the main street, Andy stopped and crouched behind a nearby brick structure. The exterior lights couldn't reach into this corner and provided enough shadow to conceal them. He held his assault rifle against his shoulder and peered around the corner.

It took him only a second to glance and then turn back to them.

"There are five men outside the first barrack to the north. Three hangars to the south. The towers are beyond that."

"And we don't know which tower is holding the device," Nikka whispered. She wanted to curse, but held her tongue. They probably had only one chance to choose the correct tower. As soon as the base became aware of their presence, a literal army would descend on them. She sighed and pulled back the hood that had covered her bare head. "Well, we won't find it hiding here."

Andy pulled the camouflage bag from his back and unzipped the top. Megan reached inside and produced two packages bound in duct tape, each with a single fuse protruding from the end. She kept one and handed the other to Jason. Everything was ready to change in a hurry, just like they had planned. Two explosions, timed in sync, at the far end of the barracks. The diversion that would give them just enough time to get to one of the towers and find the EMP.

Jason nodded as she handed the bomb to him. He knew what to do. They had gone over it so many times during the day, enough that it made Nikka's head hurt and she had to hide in the motel room for just a little while. And it wasn't the plan that made her sick. It was that Jason and Megan had to plant those devices undetected and make it back to the shadows before they exploded.

Nikka looked at the ground as Megan and Jason stood, ready to run back to the end of the barracks. She could feel her heart pounding against her ribs and she tried to focus on the pain that still resided there. Her stomach turned somersaults and made her nauseous. Just one more thing to add to the anxiety.

Andy peered around the corner and watched the men down the street. Megan and Jason waited for his signal, ready to run at the moment his hand went up. Nikka couldn't watch them, though. She stayed crouched in the shadows, her head hung and her elbows resting on her knees. Nobody breathed, keeping everything around them in dreaded silence.

Then Wolfe's hand went up. Megan darted first, and Jason followed after her as they stayed in the dark line of the building. The disappearing sound of their footsteps made Nikka's stomach heave, but she inhaled and pushed away the nausea for just a little longer.

Time in the shadows crept slower and slower as they were pressed up against a cold brick building. With each second that passed, Nikka was sure that they should have been back by now. Andy continued to watch the patrolling soldiers around the corner, as still as a statue.

"Something's happening," Andy whispered.

The rhythm of her heart ticked faster. "What's going on?"

"They all left. Heading back through the side alley."

The soldiers had moved from their position?

"What does that mean?" she asked, trying to keep her voice steady.

He said nothing else but just watched for a few seconds longer. Then, he turned back and pressed himself against the wall, holding his gun ready.

Just as she was prepared to stand and run, the sound of crunching gravel echoed along the wall from behind them. She held her stance, ready to call her power into her hands when she saw Jason's face. Megan ran behind him and they stopped beside Nikka.

Megan held out her wrist and kept her eye on the digital watch that counted down. Andy stood and pointed his rifle out with the stock resting against his forearm. Cavanaugh watched the numbers tick down as she pulled a hand gun from her belt.

5 . . . 4 . . . 3 . . . 2 . . . 1

A deafening blast erupted from somewhere at the edge of the compound. The ground trembled and the brick wall behind them shuddered. As the sound still rang in her ears, Andy touched her forearm and then moved out around the corner, his gun held out and ready within his sight line. Nikka ran beside him, beyond the front entrances to the barracks.

In the distance, nearly to the other end of the base, she saw the first tower. It rose about five or six stories above the ground, but not much above the other buildings surrounding it. The second tower behind it was even shorter.

Shouts of several men echoed among the buildings and a siren began to wail in the distance. The wasps were stirring.

The main door into the first tower was just beyond the third hangar. Her ribs ached with each breath, but she knew it would just be for a short time. She pushed her legs harder and sprinted ahead of Andy toward the tower.

The street suddenly glowed into beams of bright light as spotlights flooded their path. Nikka stopped as shouting came from the tops of the surrounding buildings. Soldiers began to pour from around the sides of the hangars, but many of them looked as surprised to see them as Nikka did. Some had guns at their sides, hands clambering to unclip them from their belts. Andy nearly stumbled into Nikka, but he stopped, the barrel of his rifle moving to each new face that appeared in their way.

They were going to be surrounded if she didn't think of something quick. They needed something swift and strong, something big enough to clear their path. In a flash of memory she remembered what that had happened to her back in the monastery. The moment that Gideon had first revealed his true nature to her, the seraph power had grown so strong and came from out of nowhere without her control. She had to run outside and let it erupt so that it wouldn't hurt Gideon. Something that powerful had enough energy to force its way through the onslaught of soldiers.

Focusing on each new face that looked her way, she saw the slithering demon behind each mask. Dozens of drones hiding behind human faces. They all came at her now with a singular purpose.

She pulled the energy from deep inside her body and felt it rush into her core. It needed to build, like a volcano, in order to have the power that she had produced back in the church. More demon soldiers came, guns in hand, and ran at them. The power built upon itself, churning like so much lava under a fault line. It trembled at the edges of her will, ripping at its restraints. It tore free and rushed into her arms. The tattoos glowed bright white as she leaned into the power, opening her arms wide.

A circle of blue-white light raced from her body in a concentric ring of power. Like a sonic wave, it mowed through the oncoming horde of soldiers. Each man within its attack field felt the full power of it tearing through his torso and shredding the drone from the inside. The men collapsed to the ground as the ring rushed out and dissipated into the dark.

The enormity of the power left her frozen for a second, until Jason took her hand and she stirred from her stupor. Sounds of more men coming from all over the base ricocheted along the road where they stood. Andy continued onward and Nikka pushed her legs into a sprint as well, the four of them nearing the tower.

Wolfe was the first to the door. He shoved it open and they raced inside the dark room, barricading the door behind them. The space echoed with each step they took. Nikka moved away from the door to face the engulfing darkness of an automotive shop that stretched deep into the base floor of the building. Motor pits dotted the floor. Chains hung from the ceiling, suspending engines and other bulky auto parts. The tart odor of oil and diesel fuel filled the room.

Andy ran around the first bay of pits and to the stairwell along the far wall. The others followed as the sounds of fists pounding on the door came close behind them.

Nikka pushed up the stairs, although the power wave she had just produced drained her deeper than they could know. The stairwell remained dark, with only the single windows at each landing letting the glow from the outside lamps to light their way.

Andy pushed through the door on the top level and they emerged onto the roof. He had his rifle up, ready to fire if needed, as he stepped across the roof.

The building was so quiet, even from the ground floor. As they had ascended the stairs, Nikka had felt the nagging concern that the device wouldn't be left so unprotected. The building was empty for a reason. There was nothing for anybody to protect here. The roof was barren and there was no EMP here.

Andy let the barrel of his gun drop as he glanced around the rooftop. "Shit," he said.

Nikka ran to the edge of the rooftop and gazed across the expanse of the compound. Soldiers now ran down the streets, away from a smoking blaze that consumed the barracks. Instead, the soldiers approached the base of the first tower. They didn't care that the other buildings were on fire. Hundreds of men swarmed the streets, so many more than she thought would be here this late at night. It would only be a matter of minutes for them to rush the main door and find them at the top of the building.

But another motion caught her eye. She saw a group of three men standing out of the fray. They were each soldiers, identified by their camouflage pants and gray T-shirts. Two of them carried a wooden crate out of the back of a Humvee and placed it on the ground. They were frantic as they unlocked the crate.

"Andy," she shouted, keeping her eyes on the men.

Wolfe ran to the roof's edge. As soon as he arrived, she pointed to the third man, who now crouched and removed a flat silver object from the crate. It appeared to be a laptop that lit up when he opened the main screen. The man pressed his thumb to the finger-pad plate and the screen came to life.

"What is that?" she asked, afraid of his answer.

She felt him grow stiff next to her. "That's a detonator."

The man carried the laptop at a swift run away from the horde of men trying to access the first tower. He moved through another swarm that rushed past him as he darted into the main access door to the second tower.

Nikka looked down to the base of the tower, to the horde that had collected. She could feel the cold ascending up the side of the building and settle at her feet. So much evil in one place would freeze the air, even in the Nevada heat.

Banging at the rooftop access door caught her attention. The demons had them surrounded already.

"What do we do?" she asked and looked at him.

His eyes scanned the rooftop, the power lines, the phone cables. Everything that touched this place, his mind now worked over any possible escape route.

"Have you ever zip-lined?" he said and forced a grin that created a crooked dimple in his cheek.

"I take it that I'm about to." She swallowed as she followed his gaze to the phone cable that draped from a pole at the top of the roof and dipped down to the base of the second tower. "Damn it," she muttered as she began to figure out his logic.

He stepped back from the edge and pulled the rifle strap over his shoulder. Megan and Jason approached and watched as Andy detailed his escape plan. He began to unstrap his Kevlar vest as he spoke.

"The cables will take us low enough to drop," he said. "Use your vest. Jason, we'll hold the straps, and ladies . . ." He flashed a worried smile to Megan. "If you could please hold on for dear life."

Nikka felt her stomach begin to churn again.

"We'll only have a second or two once we hit the ground," he continued. "Nikka, that's when you take over. You need to create a path for us."

She nodded her head. "Now, *that* I can do."

Andy stepped up to the cement edging of the rooftop as though he had no fear of heights. He swung the vest over the cable that started at the pole in the corner of the building. He glanced down at Nikka and held out his hand to her. Her fingers went cold and she had to force her legs to move. She climbed up onto his back as he guided her hands around his shoulders.

"Hold on tight," he said. "And jump when I say."

"You've gotta be kidding me," she mumbled.

"What?" he said and glanced back to her.

"Nothing. Jump when you say jump. Got it." She clenched her fingers so tight that she almost lost feeling in her hands.

"Okay," he said, and without a moment wasted, he jumped off the edge of the building. Nikka felt the sudden surge of movement as they slid down the length of the cable. She closed her eyes and held tight, afraid that her hands would slip if she saw the dizzying height under them. Cold air rushed past her ears as she tried not to scream. Dropping. Dropping. Her stomach felt like it would rise into her ears. Their momentum increased with each beat of her heart.

"Jump!"

She barely heard his voice against the rush of air in her ears. She opened her eyes and let go without thinking about it. The ground had to be another ten or so feet under her, but she saw it coming. She willed the power into her limbs even before she felt the ground under her feet. Everything around her was a rush of dark and light now, and just like Andy had said, they would only have a couple of seconds.

Her feet touched the ground and she landed in a crouch just as she reached behind her shoulder and withdrew the katana. The sword blazed to life, the blue flames lighting the shadows around her. The crowd of surprised soldiers around her spread out as the blue fire flickered in their dark eyes. She heard another zip, a thud, and then knew that her team had landed with her, ready to enter the second tower.

Chapter 49   Nikka

lack, oily eyes in the faces of every soldier that surrounded them gazed back at Nikka. The gleam of the blue flame reflected back at her like obsidian sitting in their skulls. Under the skin, she saw the writhing and slithering demon that inhabited each body, making a mockery of their service and turning each man into a puppet. They continued to swarm around them after they heard the land of her footfall and there were just too many to save.

Hands reached for her from all directions. She braced her legs, swung the sword in a swift arc around her body, driving the soldiers out of her way. But some of them attacked anyway. The katana blazed through the dark of the shadow cast between the two towers. Each strike hit something, blood, like tar, splattering over the pavement. She didn't have time to check behind her, but she felt Andy step beside her and saw the flash of the rifle's muzzle.

The horde continued to rush at amher, and then she saw the barrel of a gun in the hand of a soldier who stood at the edge of the circle. The soldier raised his hand and stepped forward, almost too quickly. The gun fired, the quick white-hot flash blooming at the muzzle. She raised her arm, defensively shielding her face.

A sudden surge of power burst into her arm, sending a wide arc of blue light that surrounded her and her friends for only a second. The bullet struck the light at the moment it formed. It careened off of the disk, leaving only a ripple in the thin blue veil that protected them. Then, it disappeared as fast as it formed, leaving her even weaker. But she sliced through with her sword, despite the burning ache that grew in her arms.

Their defense was enough to cut a swath through the horde. At the corner of her eye, she saw Jason step into their circle, his handgun out and firing.

Each blast of the guns in the hands of her comrades left her ears ringing, but she kept her stance and plowed through the army of demons until she reached the door. Her hand landed on the knob, and she prayed that it wasn't locked. The knob turned, and she stepped aside to fight back the horde as the other three fell into the room. Nikka rushed inside and braced herself against the door until Andy and Jason could barricade it.

She stepped back with the rest of them and listened to the barrage of sounds outside the door. Something crashed through the glass windows to her right, but stopped with a thud as it hit the iron bars that lined the windows.

"That won't stop them for long," Megan said and loaded another clip into her gun.

Nikka nodded and turned to face the dark room. She searched through the dim light until she found the stairway that would lead to the upper floors. Without thinking about it, she broke into a run, the sword in her hand and lighting each step. Andy followed behind her, taking two steps at a time, as they rushed up the staircase.

The soldier must have taken this route. The device had to be on the roof top. If he had the detonator, he was ready to arm it, and she hoped that they weren't too late.

She approached the fourth floor landing and faced an iron door that wouldn't budge. Andy forced his shoulder into it, but it never moved. He raised his gun, ready to shoot at the lock, but Nikka could see a thick bolt in the frame of the door. They weren't going to get in that way.

She stepped back and willed every bit of energy she had left into the palm of her hand. At first, a small wisp of blue-white light sparked into life, hovering just above her palm. As she forced more power into it, the wisp grew into an orb, swirling with hues of blue and violet. Her tattoos glowed brighter with each surge of energy, leaving the landing lit as bright as a magnesium flare. Andy shielded his eyes from the intensity of the light as she pulled the orb to her chest, feeding it even more power from the tattoos along her limbs and torso. The light throbbed and pulsated, ready to break free like a hungry animal. She braced her foot back and thrust the light toward the door. The energy crashed into the iron, twisting it free and forcing the door open in a screech of metal-on-metal.

Once the door was open, she rushed through onto the open rooftop with Andy following behind her.

At the center of the roof, she saw a structure braced with steel beams and rising about five feet over the surface of the building. It was angled sixty degrees toward the east, and as she approached, she realized that it was a rocket. The soldier she had seen on the ground now stood at the base, his face lit by the glow of a computer screen. He seemed not to notice them as they approached, despite the deafening sound of the door crashing inward.

Andy rushed up to him, his rifle muzzle aimed toward the soldier's head. She could see the FBI agent in him as he almost glided over the surface of the roof, his hand on the trigger.

"Stop what you're doing," Andy shouted at him. "Stop. Right now, or I will kill you."

The soldier froze and glanced at him. In the light from the street she could see the drone underneath his skin. Possessed. Just like the rest of them.

"You can't stop this," the soldier said and then laughed as though he were ready to be handcuffed and taken to a psych ward. "It's destiny."

"Step away from the computer," Andy said, his hand and his gun steady.

The soldier raised his hands and faced Wolfe. "This is my one job, and you damn well know I'm gonna do it."

Nikka could see the screen that faced toward her. A single window in the center of the screen said Press Enter for Ignition. All he had left was one click of a button and the rocket would power up, undoubtedly taking the EMP with it into the atmosphere, somewhere over the center of the United States. The soldier stood within arm's reach of the computer and he would likely press that button before Andy could shoot him.

"Soldier," Nikka said as she sheathed her sword. She held her hand up to him, signaling him to wait. "I know you can hear me in there."

"What are you doing?" the demon said, his oily black eyes turning toward her. "Trying to appeal to the human? Well, guess what? He's long gone."

"I know you're in there," she said and read the name on his T-shirt over the left breast. "Carlson, is it? Private Carlson?"

The soldier's eye twitched and his smile faltered for a moment.

"You're still in there," she continued. "There is a way out. You can take control again. You can get rid of him."

She stepped closer as his head ticked to the side as if something fought back inside his body. Andy kept his gun trained on him, though, as she took another step. Nikka held her hand steady before her, watching the black gaze twitch again. Maybe she could get him distracted enough to step back from the console before he pushed the button, then Andy could rush him and take him out.

Then, the soldier's eyes stopped twitching, the blackness in his eyes seeping in around his eyelids. He smiled, his teeth yellowed and broken. And that was when she knew she had lost him.

His hand suddenly dropped to the keyboard. At that second, Andy's rifle fired. Just as the bullet struck his head, the soldier's hand hit the Enter key. He collapsed to the ground with a coin-sized hole in his forehead as the circuitry on the rocket came to life. An alarm sounded from somewhere behind the computer.

Nikka rushed to the console and her fingers found the keyboard. The alarm pounded in her ears as she hit every key she could think of to delete the order, but the keyboard was terminally locked.

"No," she screamed at it.

The alarm came quicker and louder.

The frame of the rocket rumbled just as Andy grabbed her shoulders and pulled her away from the launch frame, both of them falling to the ground as the initial flare started.

A white blast erupted from the base of the slender projectile and the sound grew deafening. A secondary blast broke the rocket free from the base and it launched, driving into the atmosphere with a trail of smoke and light behind it.

Everything collapsed into thick silence as her ears rang from the roar of the blast. The sound of Andy's voice calling out to her came in muffled tones. She knew he was asking her if she was all right, but she could only see his lips moving and the hushed sounds of his voice.

The flare of the rocket still left a blinding residual in her vision as she rolled away from Andy and watched the trail of light ascend into the sky. It rose further until it disappeared among the stars.

She pushed herself to her feet and stumbled across the roof to the edging as she watched the sky. The rocket had disappeared into the black and there had been nothing. Was that all there was to it? Maybe it was bound to fail after all. Cold air drifted from the horde that began to gather at the base of the tower. It tickled over her fingers where she clutched the cement siding. Her eyes tried to focus into the bed of stars where she saw the rocket disappear.

The ringing in her ears began to fade, and she heard Jason's voice in the distance. His hands touched her shoulders, trying to pull her from the edge.

A sudden burst of light filled the sky from a central locus among the stars. It was a quick flash, and if she hadn't already known what it was, she would have assumed it was lightning. There was no sound, no shockwave. Nothing that she had expected. Just the brief burst and then it was gone. Nikka held her breath and felt Jason's hands grow still as he saw the light.

1 . . . 2 seconds. Nothing.

5 seconds.

12 seconds. The light on the horizon flickered for a moment. She turned her gaze to the orange halo that hovered over Las Vegas. From this vantage point, she could even see the outline of buildings, the eternal spotlight at the top of a pyramid, and a structure that resembled the Eiffel Tower.

The halo of light throbbed for a moment and then gradually began to dim until the entire city had gone black. Then the lights around the compound flickered. One by one, each of the sodium lamps dimmed. A transformer at the north end of the base exploded in a shower of sparks and the entire compound plunged into darkness.

It had happened. The EMP had done its job, and she couldn't stop it.

Jason's hands pulled at her again and turned her around to face him. She could see the desperation in the lines at the edge of his eyes, and then the sound of his voice was clear again.

"We need to get out of here."

The iron door crashed again as Megan and Andy worked at barricading it. More banging and shouting came from behind the door.

"We're cut off this way," Andy shouted and backed away with his rifle at the ready.

Jason stepped away from her and ran to the edge of the roof. He gazed down at the army that now rushed into the building from the ground level doors.

"Jason," Nikka said as he continued to look down at the ground. She repeated his name until he turned around.

He rushed to her when he must have seen the fear in her eyes.

"I want to give you my answer."

He placed his hand on her face. "No. Not now. Remember, you said you would tell me when we got back to the motel. You can tell me then when we make it back safely."

She knew what he was doing; he was trying to give her hope. But there was nothing left to do. They were surrounded by hundreds of soldiers-turned-demon. There wasn't a second zip-line that could miraculously give them their escape. This was the ending she had anticipated all along.

He leaned in to kiss her and she placed her hand at the back of his neck. His lips against hers. The smell of his jacket against his chest. These were things she never wanted to forget.

The door crashed open, and she first heard the volley of gunfire from Andy's rifle and Megan's hand gun. Jason pulled away from her and looked at her one more time before he turned to face the horde and drew his gun toward them. Nikka reached behind her back and found the hilt of the katana. She unsheathed her weapon and faced the horde as the fire licked along the silver blade.

Chapter 50 Nikka

The horde descended on them like a flood. Andy's rifle mowed down several of them on the front line, but they soon overpowered him.

None of the demons fired at them, but just rushed at them with pure numbers until they had taken Andy, Megan and finally Jason. Then they grew quiet and surrounded Nikka, each of their faces lit by the blue flame. They had dragged her friends to the front of the line, disarmed and collared by the soldiers behind them.

She held her sword out before her, ready to take down any of them that came for her. She willed enough of her remaining energy into another sphere of power in the palm of her hand. As soon as she had collected enough, she could purge it through the crowd and take down as many as it could clear. Maybe it wouldn't be all of them, but it would be impressive.

She held her hand out to the side as the ball pulsed and vibrated. She gazed at her friends' faces and then looked at Jason, his eyes never wavering from her.

"Let them go," she shouted, "or I'll kill all of you with one blow."

The front edge of the horde glanced at one another, unsure of what to do. But a voice spoke from the rear of the crowd and it made them all stop and lower their heads.

"I do not believe you have enough left to do such a thing."

The horde began to part down the middle, creating a path as a figure approached from behind them. He stepped closer until the light of her sword illuminated his face, but she didn't need to see him to know that it was Gideon.

His fingers stroked the faint stubble at his chin as he walked into her circle. The tailored suit that covered his frame looked like he had spent plenty of money in Vegas recently. He straightened the dark gray tie against his white shirt and his hazel eyes fell upon her.

"I do believe you are all spent."

Of course he would know that the power drained her. He was just waiting for the right time to appear, just when he knew that she had very little damage left to deal.

"Let them go, Gideon," she said and brought the sphere of light up to her chest.

"Can we just talk? It will only be a minute or two." He cocked his head to the side and gave her a second. Nikka didn't move, though. He flicked his fingers toward the crowd and they dispersed, taking her companions with them. They filed away from the rooftop through the single door until there was nobody left but the two of them.

"You are disappointed," he said as he stepped around her. "I can see it in your eyes. You actually believed that you could stop it."

Her hand tightened around the katana and she forced more power into the sphere. He stepped beside her until he appeared in the light of the blade again. She readied the ball to throw it at him.

But he placed a hand in his pocket and smiled at her. "You do know that will do nothing to me." He pointed to the sphere in her hand. "You see, this is all me. In the flesh, so to speak. This is no longer a vessel that I inhabit. This is my true form now. A little gift from my father. He gave me any form that I desired and I chose this one. I cannot be removed. Or exorcised, if you will."

She felt her strength falter and the sphere collapsed into threads of light until it melted back into her skin. The smile that spread over his lips when he saw this sickened her. He seemed to be playing with her like a cat plays with a mouse. He waited for something, but she wasn't sure what it was.

"This isn't you, Gideon," she said, keeping her sword before her.

The wicked smile disappeared from his face and he glared at her. "Stop calling me that. My name is Pazuzu. It has been since the beginning of time. Gideon was just a construct, the name my vessel had carried before I took it . . . before I lost my way."

"Okay, Pazuzu. You wanted salvation once. Why will you give it up now? You were so close—"

"I was never close," he said, his face suddenly twisting in anger. "And that is the torture of it. Over two thousand years I paid my penance, serving under the rule of the angels. And for what? To be thrown back like unwanted refuse?"

His voice rose, and she felt her hands shake. The violence in his eyes simmered with red, like two hot coals that began to settle in his sockets. The air around her began to freeze against her skin. Gideon inhaled and closed his eyes. The chill faded, and his face softened into a smile again.

"Sorry about that," he said and stepped closer to her, close enough that she could smell the expensive cologne on his neck. "Where are my manners?" He motioned for her to sit with him along the siding of the rooftop.

"No thanks," she said, her suspicion rising. "Why are you doing this?"

"Okay. Right to the point, I see." He moved closer to her again. "My father—my real father—gave me an opportunity to have anything that I wanted. Of course, in exchange I would have my legions returned to me as they were in the old days. My troops of soldiers who are just as loyal to me today as they were then. Win/win, I think."

"And what did you ask for?"

His smile slipped just a little and he looked at her with a strange flicker in his dark eyes. "I asked for only you."

Nikka felt her strength failing her again. She stepped away from him, but she knew that he could probably overpower her at this point. The sword could do some damage, but she wasn't sure how much.

"Why?" she asked.

"Why?" he repeated and seemed to be a little hurt by her question. "Nikka, this is still me. I am the same one who fell in love with you. I have not changed, and I know that you still love me." He stepped to her side and leaned into her.

She knew that he wouldn't touch her. Not yet. But she could feel his breath in her ear.

"Otherwise, you would not have opened your legs to me."

This made her wince and she turned, swinging her sword in the air and landing it just under his chin.

"I loved Gideon," she said, but felt her voice crack a little. "He was a good man and you're not him."

"No. I am Pazuzu, the ruling Prince of Demons. I am so much more than he ever was."

"What makes you think that I would ever go anywhere with you?"

A sardonic laugh slipped from his throat. "I am so glad you asked. You asked me to let them go. I could do that, for certain favors from you."

She saw the lie in his face. Gideon was never good at lying and neither was Pazuzu. He waved away her gaze like it was a bothersome pest. "Stop looking at me like that."

"Like what?"

"Like you know me so well. Let me show you what you do not know about me," he said and turned away from her. He strode to the open doorway and glanced back to her. "Are you coming? You will not want to miss this."

She didn't like the tone in his voice: cocky, arrogant and vicious. But she followed anyway, staying well behind him and her sword up and ready. He had moved fast and glided down the stairway before she had even taken her first step.

The blue light from the sword shone the way until Nikka made it to the first floor. Everything was so dark now that the lights had gone out, but she could see a crowd of soldiers around the main floor, their faces lit only by torchlights set around the pillars. And then she saw her friends, each of them on their knees in the center of the room, hands bound behind their backs.

Gideon stepped around the crowd of his soldiers and faced her. Torchlight illuminated the room in a medieval golden glow.

"Here they are," he said and held his hand out to them as if they were on display. "They are all yours."

She eyed him and stepped toward the center of the room. "For what price?"

"Give me the sword."

The breath stuck in her throat and she nearly choked. "What?"

"The sword for their lives."

"Don't do it, Nikka," Andy said, his voice forced and desperate.

Gideon exhaled, annoyed, and stepped up to the nearest soldier. He reached for the holster at the man's side, pulled the handgun out and stepped back into the center of the room. He aimed the gun at Andy's head.

"I said give me the sword." His voice remained even but tense.

It was only a second. Time enough for her to take in a breath to say something to him. But Pazuzu was not patient. He had no intention of trading with her. His finger squeezed the trigger. The blast of the gun filled the room before she even knew what happened. The bullet pierced Wolfe's temple at the same moment and he collapsed to the ground. Nikka gasped, and in the time it took for her to make another sound, Pazuzu pointed the gun at Megan and immediately fired without hesitation. Her head kicked back as the red blossom appeared in her forehead and she fell back.

Nikka felt her knees weaken. *This can't be happening. This can't be happening.*

She cried out as the sound of the gun still echoed along the stairwell.

Gideon took another step into the center of the room and placed the hot muzzle of the gun to Jason's temple. The demon then looked at her with a cold stare. Jason held his breath and his eyes met hers. Her chest almost seized as she cried out to him. "No, Gideon. Stop, please don't hurt him."

Tears flowed freely down her cheeks and the sword trembled in her shaking hand. Jason's blue eyes watched her, his face angry and tragic at the same time. "Nikka, don't do this. He won't let us go, no matter what you do."

Gideon's even stare followed her as she watched Jason.

"Please, Gideon, please don't."

"The sword."

She watched Jason, hoping that this was not the last thing he would ever see. Her trembling hand held out the blade toward Gideon. "Take it, please. Just let him go. I'll do anything you want."

Gideon took a single step away from Jason and pulled the gun back. "Very well. Drop it and kick it away."

She continued to watch Jason, at the tears that now flooded his eyes. They both knew how this would inevitably end.

Her fingers opened and the sword clattered to the ground, its fire extinguishing as soon as it left her touch. She brushed it across the floor with her foot. Gideon smiled as she stepped toward her.

"I know you do not believe me," he said. "I promised I would not kill him, and I will keep that promise."

She felt a sudden blow to the back of her head. The fire light began to spin and she fell to the floor as her world faded away into a sea of darkness.

Chapter 51 Jason

The tart smell of the muzzle flash still hung in the air like a ghost as Jason watched Nikka fall to the ground. The soldier standing behind her just looked down at her, his eyes black and cold.

Gideon stepped around him while he signaled the men to carry her away. Jason felt like his head was about to burst. The blood pounded in his brain and he tried to stand, but the soldiers behind him held him down on his knees. He clenched his fingers into tight fists and felt the knots build in his shoulders and neck.

"I'm gonna kill you," he said through clenched teeth.

Gideon let out a laugh. "That will never happen."

"Yes, it will."

He crouched down and leaned his elbow on one knee as he looked at Jason. "And how do you think that would ever be possible? You are no match for me."

"Before I die, know that I will kill you for everything you did to her."

Gideon's eyebrows rose. "What *I* did to her? You mean, what she wanted me to do. She may not have asked me, but I know she wanted it."

Jason tried to lunge at him again, but an arm reached around him and collared him until he could barely breathe. Gideon smiled as he watched this, reveling in his anger. The orange glow welled within his pupils.

"She moaned for me that night. And there's more to come. I am not finished with her yet."

Jason felt his head get dizzy and his lungs fighting for air.

Gideon nodded to the soldier, who then released his grip. Jason fell forward, coughing and gasping for oxygen.

"I will keep my promise to her. I will not kill you, not Abaddon's former vessel. No. There is so much more for you to see, and that would be far more painful than death, I assure you." Gideon leaned in closer to him. "I am so much stronger than you will ever be. You cannot defeat me, try as you might. I was an archangel once."

His voice rose and his eyes widened like a mad man. "I am practically a god, the son of the Devil. You have no power here, for this is now my realm and Nikka is my slave. I will not kill you. I will leave you alive to witness everything that will unfold, because I and my legion have won."

Gideon stood and looked at the soldier behind Jason. "Get him ready. I would not want him to miss a thing."

He stepped away, leaving Jason on the ground coughing and gasping.

Chapter 52 Nikka

A cold splash of water first stirred Nikka's senses. She opened her eyes as the water dripped from her eyelashes and trickled across her mouth. Then she felt the pain in the back of her head like a bomb had exploded in her skull. She blinked her eyes clear until she could focus on the dim torchlight that surrounded her.

Her wrists and shoulders screamed in pain as she tried to turn, and she realized that her hands were bound in chains above her head. She found the ground under her feet and tried to stand to take the pressure off of her shoulders, but her toes could barely touch the floor. The cold of the room prickled against her flesh. She glanced down between her arms to see that her clothes had been removed, all except her bra and panties. Now she hung, suspended from the ceiling, freezing and dripping with water.

"Wake up," Gideon's voice said from the edge of the torchlight.

She tried to focus beyond the light, but the pain still throbbed through her head. She could see the faces of other soldiers in the room that surrounded her, but she couldn't find Gideon. She searched along the edge of the men until she saw Jason. He knelt, hands behind him, and a soldier holding him down by his shoulders. She could still see the tears in his eyes as he watched her, helpless to do anything. Then Gideon stepped into the light and smiled at her.

"You are my property now," he said to her as he stepped up to her. He placed a finger along the tattoos that decorated her arms. "You know, back when Rome ruled most of the European continent, slaves would be marked with brands to denote that they belonged to someone."

She tried to lean away from him, but she had nowhere else to go. She shivered at his touch and closed her eyes as he ran his finger along her rib cage, tracing the tattoos down to her hip.

"For you, there is now a change of ownership. These will need to be removed. The angels will no longer lay claim on you after tonight." He nodded to a soldier that stood behind her.

She felt firm hands grasp her arm at the elbow and hold her tight. She tried to pull free and then she saw the blade of a Bowie knife. He brought it to her skin and then the first cut entered her skin. The searing pain intensified and she screamed as he began to flay the tattooed skin from her arm.

Blood trickled down her arms, her ribs and to her legs with each slice of the knife under her flesh. She tried to hold back her tears, but it was useless. Each slice and tug of her skin brought them to the surface of her eyes.

Jason shouted out to Gideon to stop, but she couldn't look at him. There was nothing he could do.

"Shut him up," Gideon said, pointing to Jason.

The soldier behind him produced a roll of duct tape, probably the same one that he used to bind his wrists, and placed a strip over his mouth. Gideon stepped toward him and looked down at Jason.

"You are here as a spectator only," he said. "Any more outbursts will result in your dismissal."

He turned away and stepped back toward Nikka. The soldier's hand moved from her elbow and grasped her shoulder to hold her still as he started another cut down her upper arm. She screamed again until she could taste the blood in her throat. The warm moisture ran down her back and dripped in the crimson pool forming at her feet. He continued to cut and pull and tug the skin in wet strips from her body.

The knife began its descent along her ribs when she finally lost consciousness. But the relief was short-lived when Gideon placed a vial of smelling salts under her nose. This brought her back into her body where the pain now swelled in her leg at the edge of the knife.

Gideon stepped around her, now aware of the forming pool of blood on the floor. The soldier moved around to face her and glanced over to Gideon as he did so.

"Sir," he said and motioned to his white collar.

Gideon glanced down to his shirt to see a spot of blood that must have spurted during one of the soldier's more aggressive cuts. At least the cutting stopped for this brief moment and Nikka could breathe as she watched Gideon slide his jacket and shirt off his torso.

"You seem to be making a mess," he said to the soldier.

"Sorry, sir."

"No sorry. Just finish this up," he said, waving an impatient hand toward Nikka.

The soldier turned back to Nikka and brought the knife toward the mark in the center of her chest when Gideon grabbed his wrist. The blade hovered just over her skin.

"Not that one," Gideon said. "Leave it for last." The creases between his brows deepened as he looked at the mark and held the blade at bay.

The soldier nodded and moved down to the spiral tattoo around her navel. She cried as the knife slid under her skin. As painful as it was, she tried not to move in case the knife slipped. She had to protect so much more than just herself now and the soldier was so close to her pelvis. The tattooed skin peeled off with another welling of blood that dripped down her legs.

Each cut and tug felt like hours, and her strength had now vanished. She couldn't loosen her wrists. She couldn't stand. She could barely breathe. But the cutting continued down her legs despite the depths of agony she now endured.

Then, everything went quiet. She couldn't stop the trembling in her body, and she could no longer tell if it was from the cold or the blood loss. Her heart raced now just to keep her conscious. Her head hung between her arms, her face soaked in tears and cold sweat.

"Get her down," Gideon said.

She opened her eyes enough to see two soldiers unlock the manacles at her wrists. As soon as the clasp opened, she collapsed to the floor. Her legs could no longer hold her upright. There was so much blood on the floor, and more continued to flow from the open wounds up and down her body. She lifted her hand from the wetness on the floor and looked at the blood dripping from her fingers.

Gideon stepped around her and crouched down to gaze into her eyes. "You no longer belong to the angels, my dear." He snapped his fingers to a soldier behind him, who produced her sword. He placed the katana in Gideon's hand. "I just want to try something."

He held out the blade to her, its lifeless steel now nothing more than a novelty without the touch of the seraph. "Take it. It is yours, after all."

She looked up at him, blood dripping from the open wounds along her bare scalp. Whatever cruelty he was about to unleash couldn't be more than what he had already done. Her trembling, blood-soaked hands reached out to the hilt. She waited for him to strike her or laugh at her and take it away again, but he didn't. He held it out for her to grasp at any moment.

Her trembling fingers touched the hilt and wrapped around it. She felt the tears flow down her cheeks again when the blade did nothing. No fire. No light. Just any old sword in a woman's hand.

Gideon clapped his hands. "Just what I thought. The power is in the tattoos. The angels have abandoned you."

She cried as she let her hand fall with the weight of the sword, but Gideon grasped her arm and forced her to hold the dead sword. He smiled at her like a spoiled child playing with an injured animal as he positioned himself at the end of the sword and made her hold it in her shaking hand.

"Now is your chance. Strike me down with it. Put that blade right in my heart," he said and held his hands out, demonstrating that he wouldn't stop her.

The blade quaked in her hand and then clattered to the floor when it slipped from her wet fingers. Her shoulders slumped as she cried. Even if she had the strength to do it, she didn't have the will. She knew that he would never let her kill him. It was just another show of his power over her. He had to prove to himself and the others around him that he had just broken the seraph. She was no longer a threat.

"Why can you not kill me?" he said and leaned in closer to her, taunting her. He grabbed her hand and forced it against his bare chest. "Is it because you still love me so much? You could not bear the thought of killing me?"

"Gideon," she said, weeping. "Please don't do this."

His eyes flashed to a glow of orange-red hate again. "My name is Pazuzu." He grabbed her chin and forced her to look at him. The veins in his neck throbbed as he gazed down on her.

"If you love me so much, show me," Gideon said.

He grasped her arm and pulled her toward him. The force made her scream in pain, but he groped at her anyway. Her last vestige of strength surged in her muscles as she kicked at him and tried to crawl away. The blood slicked against the floor made her foot slip out from under her. She fell on her abdomen as she reached out to grasp the edge of the dangling chain.

His hand clamped onto her ankle as her wet fingers fumbled for the chain. He dragged her back toward him, her outstretched fingers leaving long streaks of blood along the floor.

He pulled her toward him and forced her on her back as he straddled over her. His hands pinned her wrists above her head.

"Show me how much you love me," he said with a guttural, animal growl that erupted from within his voice.

She cried out as he forced her knees open and he worked at the zipper on his pants. The soldiers in the room just stood in the circle around them, blank dark eyes, and watched Gideon grab at the edge of her underwear. And then she saw Jason, who fought against the binds on his wrists until his face was red.

Nikka screamed as Gideon held her down and tore at her underclothes. Not again. Not this time. The sound came louder from her throat than she could have ever hoped. It rose from deep inside her chest where it broke free with a rush of sudden painful light. The one remaining mark on her chest erupted into a bright violet illumination and the rush of energy hummed in sync with her scream that could have awakened the angels.

Gideon froze for a moment and released her hands for only a second to shield his eyes from the intense light that had burst from her chest. The power coursed up her arms and then seized control of her body. Her back arched with the surge of the light. It blasted outward from her chest in a sudden wave of energy and power. It forced Gideon backward, and he fell far across the room.

The shockwave hit the soldiers that stood around them, sending each one crashing into the walls. Gideon collided into a pillar that crumpled around him as he fell.

The light vanished as rapidly as it had erupted, and now the room had gone quiet and dark, with only a single remaining torch on the ground to illuminate the space.

CHAPTER 53 GIDEON

The world around him had grown dead quiet except for the tearing pain in his head. Images of light and dark flashed behind his closed eyes: thousands of years-worth of memories flooded his senses. Every seraph that Gideon had mentored and trained looked at him now and showed him his own history. Their hands lifted him up through the black, foul hole that had swallowed him and taken his salvation.

All is not lost.

He felt the pain move from his head and into his eyes, like the spark of a fuse burning to the eventual end. The shade that had blinded him now began to lift, and he saw his body rise out of the pit, their hands guiding him further toward the soft glow that surrounded them. He looked to each face of the men that carried him and he recognized them all.

The whispering voice was gone, that awful voice that told him to do things and made him hurt the woman he loved. It made him do such terrible things to her, from the moment it had released him from the darkness. The voice told him to find her. It told him that he must force himself onto her, and then it snapped its fingers and he responded like a rabid dog. It told him to come to this place and wait, that she would come to him. She would be his reward for his obedience.

How could the lost seraphs help him after what he had done?

The spark gained momentum and traveled down into his chest where it buried itself deep inside of him, burning and rising into a fire that threatened to consume every cell in his body. He wanted to scream and beg for death as it built into an inferno that pulsed through each tortuous vein.

Redemption is not easy.

He closed his eyes, but the light burned through his eyelids. The pain was nothing like he had ever felt. Nothing like this since The Fall. In the Beginning, Creation had been difficult and sometimes painful, with the building of worlds and stars. All things that he had not pondered in his two thousand years of living above Hell, trying to find a way home.

A soul is a bright thing, wonderful and awful at the same time.

Gideon screamed as the light forced itself into every muscle.

His eyes opened just as the pain consumed his body, but now he found himself in near-darkness. The smell of blood entered his nostrils, sweet and terrible. He remembered that it had pooled at his feet. The light was gone, but at the same time it was still there, just under his skin. He could feel it like a living thing sitting somewhere in his chest. The cold cement floor pressed against his back and he remembered falling back against it. Falling hard. Something had thrown him there, just before he entered the realm in Between. The place where he saw everything that he had once tried to forget.

He vaguely remembered the dark space where he now lay with the smell of the blood. What had happened?

He turned to his side and felt his ribs spasm. A cough erupted from his throat, dry and rough like sandpaper. A chunk of cement rolled off his abdomen as he turned. His spine ached with every movement.

What happened to the light? Where were the seraphs that had lifted him from darkness?

A single, small firelight danced in the center of the dark room. It cast his shadow across the floor as he sat up and dusted the bits of fallen cement and rubble from his bare skin.

Fire. Torchlight. Cold darkness and blood.

A shot of pain ripped through his head, and for only a second he remembered a face. The woman. Beautiful and sad and crying. Blood dripped from her head and her arms. Blood pooled at her feet like a stigmata. He felt tears burning his eyes as he saw her blue eyes look at him with such despair. Who was she?

The pain stabbed at his heart and he couldn't breathe. He gasped and clutched at his chest, trying to ease the suffering.

She is Nikka.

I did this to her.

Tears flooded his eyes as the images came back to him. Everything in reverse: he had fallen hard. Why? She had done this to him, because he had made her suffer. He did this all to her. It was her blood that he smelled when he awoke. He remembered the sound of her cries as he watched a blade move across her skin. All on his orders. He had tried to take her against her will. But he loved her: why would he do such a thing?

Because he was evil to his very core. The voice only manipulated it, molded it to its liking, used it against the woman he loved.

He blinked tears from his eyes as he looked toward the torchlight. As his vision cleared, he saw a form beside the light, lying still in the shadows. He felt the sick drop of his stomach because he knew it was her.

Gideon stumbled to his feet and rushed across the fragments of the broken pillar. Her body laid there, blood still seeping from the wounds that coursed up and down her body. That sweet and coppery smell of her blood still hung in the air. He collapsed at her side, his trembling hand reaching for her face. Her beautiful and innocent face.

Her eyes flickered open, and he felt the tears coursing down his cheeks. "What have I done to you?"

She didn't move, but only looked at him for a moment. Then a smile crept across her lips—faint, but it was there. "Gideon?"

His hand moved to grasp her hand, wet and sticky with blood. "I am here."

"I can see light around you," she muttered, her breath weak and shallow, as her gaze hovered just over his head. "It's all over you."

He wiped back a tear from his cheek. What was she talking about? What light?

Then a large chunk of cement fell from the ceiling and crashed in the space where he had once been lying. A crack formed along the ceiling and inched its way across the room. The building could come down on them at any time.

"I need to get you out of here," he said and leaned down. His arms worked under her body, but then she screamed as he touched her wounds. The bleeding wounds were everywhere, and she cried out any time he tried to move her.

The sound of her weeping seemed to tear at his heart and he moved his hands away from her. "I am sorry," he said, his hands shaking, afraid to touch her anymore.

The crack made a snapping sound as it raced across the ceiling. He needed more help. Gideon glanced around him and saw another familiar face. The blonde man lying at the edge of the firelight. He remembered him, especially the way he had looked at Nikka. The man stirred from unconsciousness, probably from the same thing that had made Gideon fall.

"I will be back for you," he said to Nikka and stepped across the room to where the man lay, his arms bound behind his back and a strip of tape over his mouth.

With shaking hands, he removed the strip of tape and gently slapped the man's face until his eyes opened.

His eyes blinked a few times until his gaze fell onto Gideon's face. The muscles in his shoulders tensed as he tried to move his arms. He became agitated, his lips curling back over his teeth.

"I'm gonna kill you, bastard," he growled at him, fighting against his restraints.

"Stop," Gideon said, trying to keep his voice even. "I will loosen your bands. I need your help to get her out of here."

Jason eased his struggle and looked back across the floor to where Nikka lay bleeding. "You did this to her, and I'll make you pay."

Gideon nodded and worked his hands around the strips of duct tape around Jason's wrists. "I know."

He tore the strips free and Jason immediately shoved away from him and stumbled to his feet. Just as he tried to move toward her, Gideon heard the sound first. It was something that he hadn't heard in millennia. A low singing, something that Jason couldn't hear.

They were coming, and Gideon knew why: they were coming for her.

He stood and looked across the room at Nikka. There was no time left.

The sound grew as he got to his feet and sprinted toward her. Desperate and fast. He only had a few seconds. They were almost here.

But it was too late. His body hit an invisible wall, something that now surrounded Nikka. Jason rushed up to him, his hand reaching out and touching the shield as well. The sound built upon itself and as they looked through the room, they both saw a shimmering light appear in the darkness above Nikka's body, like light reflecting off of water. The light opened, a split in the seam between worlds.

The creature stepped out of the rend, its body white and lithe on two legs. Its head came through, a white wave of a mane behind its wide jaw. Beautiful and elegant and fearsome all at once. Wide, muscular shoulders and arms widened the tear between realms as it stepped through and crouched over Nikka's body. Eyes that shone with a hue of violet looked down upon her.

Gideon could see that she had opened her eyes and watched it as well.

Jason shouted beside him, fists pounding on the shield that the creature had put up to keep them out. Gideon could only watch the beast as it scooped her up into its arms and held her against its muscled chest like one of its own children. Her bare head rested against its shoulders covered in white fur.

He could fight against the wall until his hands bled, just like Jason did now. But there was no use. Gideon knew that this creature came to take her away. He had known it would happen eventually. He knew it the moment he first saw the new tattoo on her chest. She had been marked for this, and this was the creature to bring her home.

The cherub.

Light erupted from the rend behind it, filling the entire space and the singing sound turned into a deafening roar. Something else had entered this place now, something that accompanied the cherub. He covered his ears, but watched the creature carry Nikka toward the split in the world. A bright light surrounded them and filled the entire room, so bright that he thought his eyes would burn out from his skull. He wanted to scream, the sound was so loud. He could no longer hear Jason pounding on the shield, but only watched Nikka in the hands of the beast.

The creature cradled her against its chest and turned. But as it bent down, ready to enter the tear in the world, Nikka's eyes opened and she looked back at them from where they stood on the other side of the shield in the blinding light that surrounded them. Her bloodied hand, shaking and weak, reached up and stretched her fingers toward him. The cherub stepped into the rend and the folds of darkness swallowed them both.

The sound and the light instantly faded as did the shield that held him back. She was gone, taken back Home. He closed his eyes. Gideon felt tears falling down his cheeks as his knees buckled underneath him. He fell to the ground as the sound of the cracking cement echoed in the room.

Then sudden silence.

The room had become quiet again, not even the sound of Jason standing at the shield. He heard a gasp of breath behind him and he opened his eyes.

Jason was lying on the ground, naked and shivering in the dark, his hair and skin glistening in fresh moisture, his clothes burned away with the intensity of the light that had engulfed him as well. In the flickering light of the torch, he saw the intricate Enochian tattoos etched along Jason's arms, down his flanks and legs. They were raw and new, brought by the Beings that had entered the room with the cherub. The archangels had been there.

A new seraph, given to him to mentor and train just as he had with Nikka.

CHAPTER 54 JASON

Jason stepped up to the truck, parked at the lot of the motel just as he had left it. The morning sun had begun to peek over the mountains to the east. His hand clutched to the side of the pickup bed as his legs wobbled under him. The walk through the desert, wrapped in a blanket he had found on the base, watching Gideon from behind the entire time was about as bad as things could get.

That, and the memory of the tattoos being seared into his skin while trapped in the fierce light that had taken over his body.

He had glared at Gideon as he tried to keep his distance during the trek away from the Air Force Base.

That asshole had killed Nikka.

And then he had to wake up with the same tattoos all over his body, just like Nikka's. He was having a difficult enough time wrapping his head around the fact that, as soon as some monster had come through another dimension and taken her away from him, something else had grabbed him and forced these marks all over him. Is that what she had experienced when it happened to her? It had been painful and terrifying all at once.

This was all Gideon's fault.

The bastard had said nothing when he woke up. Just stood there shaking and silent and crying. And then the sword appeared at his side. Not a katana, like Nikka's. It was broader, heavier. Like a Viking sword. As soon as he stood, he touched it and the damned thing lit up in blue fire, just like when Nikka had touched her own sword. He knew what to do with it only because he had been around her long enough to learn. He had placed it over his shoulder, just as he had seen Nikka do, and there it stayed as he searched his brain for the best way to run it through Gideon's heart.

He didn't care that Gideon was supposed to train him. Whatever happened, he would use his time to make him suffer for what he did.

Jason steadied himself against the truck and pulled the duffel bag closer to him. At least he could get himself a change of clothes and maybe the keys to the truck. Ditching Gideon here for now seemed like a good plan.

Gideon shuffled across the parking lot and sat on the bench of the picnic table. He still hadn't said anything. Only stared out across the desert, his face expressionless.

Jason pulled the bag closer to him and unzipped the top, but felt a pain in his chest as he looked down. It was Nikka's clothes. Her things filled the top of the bag and his clothes were under hers. He felt the sting of tears in his eyes as he lifted out her jeans and shirt. Her scent still lingered on them. He brought them to his nose and held the bag close to his chest.

The tears flowed down his cheeks. It didn't matter if Gideon was right there to see it. This was his moment, his last good-bye to her.

As he clutched the cloth next to his chest, he felt something in the pocket of the jeans she had worn the night before. He wiped the back of his hand against his eyes and fished into the pocket. The thing was firm and elongated as he pulled it from the garment. He blinked his eyes clear as he stared at it.

He had seen enough TV commercials to know what it was that he now gazed upon. The little display window of a pregnancy test caught the light of the sun and he felt his fingers tremble.

Positive.

Nikka had been pregnant.

His stomach almost dropped, like he was stuck at the top of a roller coaster that would never hit bottom. Fresh tears filled his eyes as his fingers tightened around the stick.

Gideon was going to die for this. For Nikka and her baby.

T h e   E n d

About the Author

When she isn't delivering babies, Carrie Merrill is a prolific writer who has put pen to paper since the age of 8, when she wrote her first story about a dragon that lived in a cave across the river from her house in Idaho. A day has not gone by since that time when she didn't have a story floating around in her head. Her first book, *Angel Blade*, received great praise. She is currently a full-time OB/GYN in Montana with her six rescue cats when she isn't writing about the things that lurk in the dark.

Angel Blade

by Carrie Merrill

Angel Blade is a new adult paranormal novel that involves a strong female protagonist in a supernatural setting, but dealing with issues such as loss of home and family, the burden of being female in a male-dominated realm, and romantic entanglements that can jeopardize her future.

Nikka is dying of cancer until a stranger provides her with a cure, but it comes at a steep cost: she must become a Seraph, an angelic being with the power to exorcise and destroy demons. With Gideon, the stranger who introduced her to this life, she learns of the battle between Heaven and Hell and about the part she must play to fight the demon horde and destroy Abaddon, the Prince of Demons.

Then she meets Jason, a man with a troubled past who also brings the promise of a normal life, and his offer may be too good to let go.

Available in paperback and ebook from

Soul Fire Press

www.soulfirepress.com

And bookstores online and off